I0757546

Hard Survivor

Copyright © All rights reserved. No part of this book may be reproduced, stored in a retrieval system, or transmitted in any form or by any means — electronic, mechanical, photocopying, recording, or otherwise — without the prior written permission of the publisher, except in the case of brief quotations used in reviews or scholarly works.

Dedication

For Kate

TABLE OF CONTENTS

CHAPTER ONE
SERENDIPITY

He felt a drop of sweat running down his cheek and dripping onto his neck. It wasn't the first. Three days of stubble blocked the sweat from forming a straight line. His throat burned. Fetid hot air rushed in and out. He breathed through his mouth to make up for the huge oxygen debt from running. He carried thirty pounds of gear and a rifle. It was hot, and the sun beat down with relentless intensity between the clouds. Squatting next to a low concrete wall, he leaned out to see who was shooting at him. Aspen leaves fluttered in the light wind. The tall grass in front of the nearby building swayed as the wind passed through. Other than that – there was no movement and no sound outside his heavy, deep breathing. Caleb recalled his training. He scanned the terrain with precision, dividing it into pie-shaped sections. He searched for anything unusual. Shape, shine, silhouette, shadow. He repeated these words his NCO had drilled into him. He scanned for his adversary. Before finishing, he spotted something out of place. Smelled, not spotted. Something rank, drifting in the wind from behind a propane tank across the yard. Elevated on two low concrete footings sat a 1,000-gallon propane tank, the object of concealment for whoever had decided to interrupt his foraging.

Tracing the outline of the tank, Caleb spied the toe of a boot underneath it. Shifting his weapon to his off-hand, Caleb dug his 4X monocular out of his belt case and took a closer look. Yep, a boot. Ah, a slight movement of that boot! Caleb replaced the monocular on his belt and aimed his M1A rifle at the tank. Hmm, I wonder if there is anything inside that tank? The 7.62 x 51mm cartridge from his rifle could penetrate one side of the tank. After that, it's anyone's guess. Caleb recalled that shooting a gasoline tank wouldn't cause an explosion. But he wasn't sure if the same was true for propane. How big of an explosion would a thousand-gallon tank make?

Adrenaline surged in his bloodstream, making it hard to resist the urge to act. Sweat dripped down his face. Why is it so hot? The sun wasn't completely out, he thought to himself. A noise on the other side of the tank broke his reverie. The shooter was shifting position, and the gravel or broken glass under his boots was making noise. Shifting in his own position, Caleb dropped to a knee and assumed a firing position. Whoever was hiding behind the big tank pulled his foot back, and there was no boot toe revealing the direction of his adversary's travel. Caleb put the red dot from his optical sight to the closer end of the tank, as he would likely see movement under the tank if the shooter went that way. He could put a round right through that boot and wreck his opponent's day. Caleb waited and worked on slowing his breathing and managing his fear.

Minutes crept by. No sound, no movement. Caleb couldn't smell anything or hear anything and wondered if he had imagined the whole thing. Adrenaline levels seemed to be dropping, and fatigue grew. His muscles started cramping, and his support leg was going numb. If he had to get up and run, it was going to be a bitch. Shifting to manage his growing problem would generate noise and reveal his position. Crud! What to do? He opted to lean back and put his trigger hand on the ground and take the weight off his bent leg and scoot backwards a bit on his butt. Luckily, it went smoothly and quietly. A tactical retreat was the best option at this point, and gaining distance would give him extra reaction time when things got exciting. Reaching out with his hand for balance and support, he butt-scooted along the cement wall and gained another ten feet of distance with minimal noise. Feeling a bit safer and the blood flowing back into his legs, he got his feet underneath him and moved into a low crouch, his rifle in a low ready position. Nothing from behind the tank. Suspicious, Caleb stood and crossed the open area to his right and came alongside the building. Screw it, he thought, and advanced adjacent to the building in tight rolling steps, ready to engage the moment anything happened. The angle changed between Caleb and the propane tank; increasingly, he was able to see behind it. Seeing no one, he advanced quickly with his head on a swivel — scanning left and right for threats breaking the tunnel vision common in high-stress situations.

No one was behind the tank. Approaching closely, he could see a trail left by someone moving in a straight line away from the tank towards the jack pine trees on the far side of the grassy area. Whoever this guy was, he had sense enough to keep the tank between him and Caleb as he performed his own tactical retreat. Caleb, realizing his opponent could be putting crosshairs on him at that moment, sprinted back in the direction he had come from to get some cover. No shots rang out as he ran. Turning the corner at the far end of the building, Caleb slammed himself against the wall and froze in place; this cat-and-mouse shit was getting old, he thought. Breathing heavily, the sweat returned. What now? I have no idea where this guy went; is he flanking me? Did he just leave? Decisions, decisions.

The original point of being here was to scope out this building for a particular electrical part Caleb needed for his solar array. The AC transfer switch had burned out again, and without a replacement, his system was dead in the water. Maybe there was a way to bypass it, especially since there was no longer any municipal juice to switch over to. Caleb was just not enough of an electrician to figure out how to bypass it and thought simply replacing it would be the best and easiest option. Figuring out where this warehouse was after the internet had vanished had been much harder in a world without Google. The fact that there was even a place where he could possibly find the necessary part was amazing, but now he had to contend with some a-hole trying to ventilate him.

Not willing to give up on the mission, Caleb looked for an advantage. Mixed orange and blue pallets sat stacked against the wall of the building; Caleb counted them as his gaze ascended – 18 high, standard shipping configuration – completely useless information now he realized. It was high enough; if he climbed them and they didn't tip over, he could reach the downspout pipe on the wall of the building and shimmy his way up onto the roof. High ground gave him an advantage defensively, plus unimpeded views of the surrounding area. Getting back down might be an issue; he'd work that out later. Trotting slowly, he approached the stack of skids. He surveyed his surroundings for any threats. Seeing none, he slung his rifle across his back and began scaling the stack. Hands and feet fit easily in the spaces between the stringers of the pallets as he climbed steadily. Getting closer to the top, the pile of pallets began to sway under his weight and movement. Remaining still for a few moments, the swaying slowed and then stopped. Climbing again, he scaled the few remaining boards and pulled himself on top. The stack now swayed dangerously. Caleb held still as he waited for the swaying to stop. A half minute or so later, things had calmed down. On top of the pile, he could see the pipe he had spied from the ground without difficulty. To reach it he had to move to the edge of the stack and lean out a bit. The good news was – the pallet stack would lean towards the stationary building; the bad news was – he had no idea what would happen once he pulled his weight off. In for a penny, in for a pound he thought. Again, he surveyed his surroundings for movement. His father's lesson of look twice – move once came unbidden to his mind. Dad was teaching him about stalking animals for the house's deep freeze; the same advice held true in combat. Make haste slowly was another father favorite. Yes, you could only die once but Caleb intended that to be a faraway problem to deal with, not a today problem.

Leaning out, he got both of his leather-gloved hands on the pipe and used this attachment to the wall to stop the movement of the pallet stack. The rooftop was only a short distance away and, tugging on the pipe, it felt quite sturdily attached to the warehouse wall. The texture of the wall was some sort of stucco finish which was coarse enough to give his boots purchase. With a deep breath and a heave, he pulled himself from the pallet stack. Clinging to the pipe, he looked over his shoulder at the now swaying pile of pallets. It moved back and forth quite significantly but did not topple over. That was good news. Pressing on upwards, he ascended the pipe. Trying that rock-climbing gym, a couple of times last year gave him a rudimentary idea of what to do, but an expert climber he was not. A little hand over hand and some desperation-based clinging to the pipe were working. Getting one hand up on the edge of the rooftop was a major relief. Pulling upwards, he slapped his second hand onto the edge of the roof, felt something metallic protruding which he gripped, and began the awkward process of pulling himself up and onto the tar and gravel roof.

Breathing heavily and sweating from the exertion and some fear, Caleb lay on his back with his pack and rifle positioned beneath him. The sun bore down on him as the cloud cover thinned overhead. Birds in the nearby trees made themselves known, but what species they were or what they were up to was of no interest to him. Just birds making noise, he thought; they were completely oblivious to the collapse of the world he was living through. Rolling to his knees, Caleb got upright again. Unslinging his rifle, he assumed a high port carry position and, in a slow trot, headed toward the far edge of the building nearest the propane tank. The top of the building had various makeup air units, air conditioning units, and the like, but no sky lights. Sky lights would have made it easier to see what was inside the warehouse, but the rooftop hatch was what he was really looking for. Before that, however, he was going to have to deal with this shooter who had taken several shots at him.

Having navigated the length of the building, Caleb crouched again as he reached the far edge. Squatting down behind the cover provided by the raised part of the wall above the roof, he took a quick look over the parapet. The propane tank hadn't moved – ha-ha! he thought to himself. He didn't spy anyone or anything out of place. Time to pull out the monocular and have a good look, he thought. On the other hand – with the sunlight stronger now as the cloud cover thinned, the reflection off the lens of his monocular might be a bad idea. That flash could be seen hundreds of meters away and draw unwanted attention. Caleb lifted his head above the low wall and began his pie segment inspection of what he could see with the naked eye. The ground had various bits of windblown indiscriminate garbage strewn over it and no obvious tracks anywhere. From where he was positioned, he couldn't even see his own footprints on the ground from when he had approached the warehouse earlier.

Caleb sat back down with his back against the low wall. Fact one – there was an unknown assailant out there somewhere. Problem but a known problem. Caleb had learned that the warehouse was locked up tight and would present a problem for getting inside before someone shot at him. If Caleb was going to have to break in, the shooter would likely also have to break in to gain entry. Breaking in was rarely a quiet affair, and in doing so, would give Caleb the heads-up he needed so he could defend himself. Fact three – all warehouses had rooftop access points for tradesmen, HVAC technicians, and various inspectors to do annual checks and so on. If Caleb could get in from the top, he could scour the warehouse for what he came for and be relatively safe from his unknown attacker.

"Crash!" Something big fell over by his original entry point onto the roof. Hot-footing his way back to the entry point, Caleb had a quick look over the edge. The stack of pallets was now lying in a spread-out pile. Ducking down to avoid profiling himself on the edge, Caleb knew for certain his enemy had not taken off after all. Well, there goes my exit plan, he thought. No gunfire had rung out during his quick look, so either the shooter wasn't ready to engage yet or had decided that stranding Caleb on the roof was good enough. Walking in from the edge and limiting his exposure to being targeted, Caleb began searching for the roof hatch. After a minute or so, his eyes landed on it. Protruding two feet up from the roof, the meter-by-meter square box was in its normal closed position. Walking closer, Caleb unslung his pack and dropped it on the roof next to the hatch and laid his rifle against the pack for quick retrieval. Using both hands, he gripped the lid and pulled upwards. It lifted with little effort and angled upward until it was vertical. He pressed the hold-open device into place, so it wouldn't slam down again. Digging out his Streamlight flashlight, he directed its beam down the dark column into the warehouse below. Inside, attached to the wall, were the yellow-painted metal rungs of a ladder leading down into the warehouse and the darkness below.

Since the access point looked tighter than expected, Caleb retrieved the fifty-foot length of rope that he always carried in his pack. Tying one end to the central carrying handle of his pack, he lowered his backpack, hand over hand, to the floor below. He decided to tie the other end of his rope to the top rung of the ladder, unable to articulate the reason for his decision. He thought it might be handy to have his rope hanging down at the ready in case some unforeseen eventuality occurred. Slinging his rifle across his back again, Caleb climbed up and in and then descended but left the hatch open at the top. It didn't look like rain, and he liked the small amount of sunlight that made its way to the bottom of the ladder.

As soon as his feet hit the cement floor, Caleb unslung his rifle and snapped on the flashlight affixed to the picatinny rail on the side of his rifle. M1A's usually didn't come with side-mounted rails, but he arranged for a gunsmith to affix one for him before everything fell apart.

Scanning right and left, he could see he was inside a mechanical room of some sort. What looked like a fire suppression system, a series of pipes, ran along one side of the room with pressure gauge dials attached to each one. The room was unlit (no big surprise there) and roughly a couple of hundred square feet. The exterior wall was at one end and a man door at the other. Caleb untied the rope from his pack and put the pack back on. He considered leaving it here, but there were several useful tools inside that would likely come in handy during the exploration of this facility.

Approaching the man door, he clicked off his rifle-attached light. He did not want to send a beacon of light into the rest of the warehouse – either giving a warning to whomever might be secreted inside or sending light through a window to give away his position to someone on the outside looking in. Before opening the door, he stood silently and listened carefully. He stood with his mouth open as he had picked up that tidbit from somewhere that his hearing was slightly improved by having his mouth open. Caleb did not know if that was true or not, but he figured there was no harm in trying. Silence was all he heard, no machines whirring or even HVAC running, just dead silence.

The door opened easily from his side. He opened it just a crack and peered into the darkness. Sunlight filtered in from various exterior windows and illuminated different portions of the building. He could make out floor-to-ceiling racking as far as the eye could see under these conditions. It was too dark to see much more than that. With the abject silence and lack of any movement, he decided to click his rifle-mounted flashlight back on and begin exploring.

Almost immediately, he noticed a mustiness in the air. With the power being out, the HVAC and make-up air units hadn't been running. His flashlight revealed a lot of dust in the air as he swept it back and forth, surveying the warehouse. The floor revealed a layer of dust as well; no footprints or tire prints from forklifts or anything else indicated that this facility had been left untouched for a substantial period. Aiming his flashlight up, he looked for some sort of signage to give an indication of how the racks were organized. Above the racking, he saw a series of QR codes on triangular coroplast signs and a sequential series of numbers from sign to sign. That was not going to help. Shining his light down the length of the warehouse, he spotted what looked like an office and started making his way toward it.

After a minute or so of walking, he came to a twenty-by-twenty-foot office with a door in the center that let him in. Three computer workstations sat on three different desks – all covered in the same fine layer of dust. With the power having been out for over a year now – obviously none of them were going to boot up and reveal the contents of the warehouse to him. He sat heavily in one of the desk chairs. I don't want to spend days picking through racking to find what I need, he thought. Just then, as he was immersed in thought, the sound of breaking glass far away inside the warehouse jarred him out of his thoughts. More glass audibly fell on the floor as someone continued breaking a window or a glass door. Caleb stood and did a quick check of his primary weapon and then a check of his secondary. He reached across his waist and felt for the coffin-shaped handle of his Laredo Bowie in its sheath. Although it was not a necessary check, the big blade soothed his nerves; its reassuring presence had helped him out of some scrapes in recent months. Knives did not malfunction or need reloading, and in close quarters could wreak horrendous damage on an opponent.

He moved to the door leading into the warehouse and looked through the window in the direction the sound had come from. No movement and no sound, nor any light from a flashlight. Caleb opened the door and moved through quickly, covering the open space between the office and the closest set of racking as efficiently and quietly as he could. At ground level under the racking were pallets of large cardboard totes – Caleb had no way of knowing what was inside and whether they offered cover as well as concealment. Moving fast and light on his feet, he traversed to the end of the aisle and stopped. Once again, he looked and listened. Squatting down, he took a look around the last tote towards the direction the sound had come from. About 75 to 100 feet away, he spotted light streaming into the warehouse, which revealed broken glass on the floor from the window that had been smashed – presumably to gain entry. Caleb paused. This could also be a distraction tactic to get him moving towards the sound and glass damage. Checking his six (behind him), he scanned around where he had come from. Nothing.

Standing up with his rifle butt shouldered in the pocket just under his collarbone at the low ready, he advanced towards the window. Stopping about two meters away, he looked and listened again. Nothing. Shuffling forward, he spotted boot prints on the far side of the broken window leading away from his current position. Someone was in the warehouse with him! Caleb quickly looked left and right and decided to move in case he was being targeted. Backing up a few feet, he entered another row of racking and squatted down again. The pallets under this racking had layers of paint cans stacked and wrapped with stretch film – Caleb had no idea if they were full or empty. Concealment, yes; cover – who knew? Decision time. Begin the hunt for whoever was in the building with him or use the broken window to leave and set up an ambush for whoever was tracking him. Caleb made up his mind and stood. At that exact moment, he realized he had made a blunder. Assumption is such a dangerous thing, he reminded himself – I am assuming he, my opponent, is alone. The window exit created a fatal funnel for Caleb, who by using it as an exit made a single aiming point for another shooter to hit him. Caleb squatted again. There had been no sign of a second or even third opponent, but assholes tended to travel in packs, he told himself.

I could climb the racking and get to an overwatch position, Caleb thought, but in doing so would negate any mobility. Plus, my rifle would be slung, and my back exposed for whoever came at me from the rear. Not a good plan. Caleb continued thinking - I wish I had a partner or small team to help out, and I also wish I had paid more attention to small unit tactics classes. If wishes were fishes… Caleb thought. Enough bullshit – time to move. Holding a low-ready position, Caleb moved to the end of the row and looked left and right. He followed the boot prints in the dust in pursuit of his foe. At the corner of the racking, the space between the prints had widened considerably and the heel prints had vanished – the guy had sprinted. Obviously, quietly, as Caleb had not heard a thing.

Going deeper into the warehouse in pursuit seemed like a good opportunity to get ambushed. Caleb spun around and ran for the open window. Yes, he might be running into another ambush, but he liked the odds better and could set up his own ambush outside. In a few short seconds, he approached the window and, with a small jump, cleared the six inches of wall underneath it and emerged into the sunny day outside. Tacking hard left immediately upon exiting, he gritted his teeth in anticipation of a shot. No shot rang out. He was behind the warehouse where the loading docks were located on a broad asphalt yard. Still running, he headed for the traffic barriers between the open area and the chain-link fence on the far side of them. Hopping over a barrier, he dropped to the ground and got the barrier between him and the warehouse.

Laying his rifle on the cement barrier, he got his eyes behind the optic and began surveying the warehouse. Again. Nothing. Since nothing seemed to be happening, he took a pull from the camelback, which was part of his backpack. Whoever invented this device should get an award, he thought. Being able to access water without reaching for a canteen or bottle of water was helpful and allowed him to maintain his focus on the warehouse. Caleb checked his watch – 1415. Getting here had taken the whole morning, and now all this farting around was costing him valuable time.

Caleb reflected for a moment – why had this guy shot at him? Was he simply out foraging for himself and Caleb's arrival shocked or scared him? Was this guy here for a similar reason to his own – looking for some sort of supplies or tools? Was he simply trying to drive Caleb away so he could continue his own search? Maybe this could be sorted out another way than reducing it to violence. This guy had knocked over the stack of pallets, but perhaps that was to isolate Caleb on the roof and allow the shooter time to search the warehouse for whatever he was looking for. Shrugging off his pack again, Caleb dug inside for something white. Sadly, the other thing he could find was a pair of his tighty whities – man, would his previous girlfriend ever mock him for his current underwear choices, but in the aftermath of the fall of civilization – old man underpants had been all he could find. Tying them to the end of his rifle, he raised them up and called out. "Hey!" "You inside!" "Hey!" He waved the underwear back and forth but kept looking around in case the guy inside had come out another way and was flanking him. "What do you want?" A voice answered from inside the building. Caleb responded, "Why were you shooting at me?" "I thought you were going to ambush and shoot me," retorted the unseen guy inside. "Can we work something out or does this have to end badly?" yelled Caleb. "What do you propose?" came the voice. "I have no beef with you, I only need something from inside this building and then I will be on my way," Caleb yelled. "How do I know that isn't bullshit?" responded the mystery man. "You shot at me first," said Caleb. "I haven't done anything to you."

Minutes passed. "I suppose that's true," said the hidden man from inside the warehouse. "If I step outside, are you going to put a hole in me?" Caleb understood the lack of trust. In this version of the world, trust was a rare commodity – always earned and rarely given freely. More moments passed. "Well, we could keep hunting each other, and eventually one of us would likely die," came the voice. "I'm hungry and tired. How about we take a pause, have a drink, and eat something? If it turns out we don't like one another that much, we can go back to trying to kill one another." "Sounds reasonable," Caleb called out. Caleb lowered the makeshift white flag and undid it. A bit of a brown streak in that underwear he noticed grimly – time for laundry. Securing the underpants back in his pack, he stood up. Keeping his rifle at low ready, he stayed put in case treachery was at hand.

Stepping into the sunlight came a man much like himself. Wearing what looked like hunters' Realtree camo, his possible erstwhile enemy had the typical lean and rangy build of those who had survived the fall of society. Fatties were a thing of the past. Easy calories were only a memory, and anyone unable to run at a good clip or hike for hours with a pack on was easy pickings for those who remained. A brown bandanna covered whatever hair he had, and a pair of Oakley sunglasses or a knockoff version of the same covered the eyes gazing at him. Leather boots completed the bottom end of the picture, but it was the rifle in his hands that caught Caleb's eyes. In a world dominated by AR-15s and their clones, Caleb's Springfield M1A was a rarity — considered too heavy and bulky by most, whereas this guy appeared to have a Russian or Yugoslavian SKS as his primary weapon. Running 7.62 x 39, the popular AK-47 cartridge lacked the reach or terminal foot pounds of Caleb's M1A in 7.62 x 51 but was a popular piece among gun aficionados.

Seeing his opponent's barrel pointed at the ground, Caleb slowly advanced towards him, maintaining his vigilance in case this was all a setup. He could see the other guy was scanning left and right as well – probably equally suspicious. A little healthy paranoia keeps you healthy, Caleb reminded himself. Stopping ten feet short, Caleb peered past the shooter and then checked his own six – looking for unseen affiliates, he maintained his vigilance. "Caleb Johnson," he offered. "Mitch Greenly," came the response. Both men assessed one another. Greenly was about an inch or two shorter and maybe ten pounds heavier, Caleb observed. Under the brown bandanna, he could see some red hair sticking out, a ginger, Caleb thought. Like that meant anything of value these days.

"So how are we going to do this?" asked Caleb. "I am guessing we are both here looking for something and the daylight is going to go away." "Taking pot-shots at each other is not going to help find what we came for." Mitch Greenly smiled. "I wasn't taking pot-shots – I had you squarely in my sights. If I had wanted you dead, you would not be having this conversation right now." Caleb did not like the sound of that. "So why didn't you?" Mitch smiled again. "I figure we have all seen and done enough killing for a lifetime. I am not turning into a pacifist or anything equally stupid, but sometimes I just don't have the stomach for it. Give peace a chance – I think John Lennon said that."

Caleb stood silent for a long stretch. "Don't take it personally," Mitch said. "Everyone has had someone get the drop on them from time to time; today just happened to be your day." "So, you not killing me makes us friends now?" Caleb replied. "Well, I wouldn't go that far," Mitch responded. "Maybe just not enemies – for today at least." "How about we sit for a bit, out of the sun and parley?" Caleb nodded his agreement, "inside?" Turning and heading back into the dark opening of the warehouse, Mitch made his answer known.

Following Mitch, Caleb walked back to where the office was. Passing through the door, each man took up a desk chair and sat down. Both held their rifles across their laps as their respective levels of trust had not graduated to laying down their weapons yet.

"What do you need out of here?" asked Mitch. "I'm looking for an AC transfer switch," shared Caleb. "You?" "Nothing so exotic," offered Mitch. "I need a length of stranded copper wire." Caleb considered the response from

Mitch. "Copper wire, huh?" "Should be easy enough to find, if you don't mind me asking – what's it for?" "Replacing some of the wiring in a Dodge Power Wagon I am trying to get back on the road." "What's an AC transfer switch for?" inquired Mitch. "I need it for my solar system – the one I have burned out," replied Caleb.

Both men sat quietly for a minute. Caleb took the quiet time to take a more detailed assessment of his acquaintance. The camo jacket and pants Mitch wore looked slightly worn but clean. The belt knife looked like a Finnish-style puukko knife with a sheath covering most of its length. There were two leather pouches that looked like ammo pouches for the SKS. Lastly was a pair of well-broken-in Wrangler leather gloves completed, the gear Caleb could see. Compared to what Caleb had on his person, it seemed quite sparse. "Live close?" he asked Mitch. "Why do you want to know?" replied Mitch. "You don't seem to have much kit to be wandering around in the world," offered Caleb. "I like to travel light. Too much gear weighs you down and tires you out," expressed Mitch. "You look like you are out on the town for a couple of weeks with all that stuff!"

Caleb laughed. "Yeah, I tend to overpack. I'm always worried about possibilities. My approach is based more on concealment and conflict avoidance than on interacting with unknowns. It keeps you alive longer."

Mitch stood up. "Guess we had better get after it. How about we look for your switch thing first and then my roll of wire? Teamwork makes the dream work." Caleb laughed, "I have not heard that in years. Can't remember where it comes from." "Deal. Without access to the inventory system, I can't think of a fast way to find what I am looking for. The brute force approach is probably going to be the only way." "Let's start at opposite ends of the warehouse and meet in the middle. Cover twice the area in half the time," suggested Mitch. Caleb nodded and reached for a pen and a piece of scrap paper. He quickly sketched out what he was looking for. "It should look like this or close. If you find anything even remotely similar — call out and I will come over and have a look."

Mitch said, "Sounds good." Both men exited the office and headed to opposite ends of the warehouse. As Caleb walked, he took out his flashlight from its belt holster. Like many other prepper-type guys, he was a bit of a gear nut. He loved his Streamlight and trusted it. A flashlight was one of the most used bits of his kit. The lumens produced by his flashlight did an excellent job of illuminating the way as he walked to the north end of the building. Arriving at the last row of racking, he began making his way along the rows. He swept up and down with his light, looking for the item he sought. The racking went three high, and he couldn't really see what was on the second or third levels. Caleb decided to survey all the ground-level stuff and see if he could find what he came for. If not, he would have to devise a way to get to the second and third levels and look inside the boxes or totes located there. Caleb groaned inwardly — this could be a long and boring process.

At the other end of the warehouse, Mitch was coming to the same conclusions. Scanning the ground-level pallets under the racking, he moved along slowly. He wanted to ensure he did not miss anything that could possibly be what they came for. Three rows of racking later, he had seen nothing that resembled what either he or Caleb were looking for. "Hey!" Caleb's voice echoed from the far end — "I think I might have found your wire." Mitch turned and headed in the direction of the voice. Presently, he arrived where Caleb stood, shining a light up into the racking. "I was focused on the ground-level stuff, but something caught my eye, and I looked up," said Caleb. On the back pallet of the second level was a pallet with spools of wire. They had plastic stretch wrap over them, but the wire was visible nonetheless. Mitch looked around. "I don't see a ladder anywhere." Leaning his rifle against a nearby pallet, he grabbed an upright and started to climb. Before pulling himself up, he suddenly stopped. "Are we good?" he asked Caleb. "I don't want to get up in the racking to see my rifle pointing at me." Caleb looked at Mitch for what seemed like a long stretch. "Yes, I would have the drop on you, and yes, there would not be much you could do about it. I'm tired of looking at everyone as a foe and potential enemy. This is the longest I have interacted with someone I randomly ran into that did not turn into a fracas of some sort. If it's all the same to you – I'd like to go along to get along for now." Mitch nodded and returned to his climb. Working his way up, he managed to squeeze between the uprights and survey the contents of the pallet. It was a pallet of miscellaneous rolls of wire – copper as well as aluminum and some other materials. "I can't get at it from here. I need some space," Mitch advised. Caleb suggested, "Why don't you throw the stuff off the first pallet onto the floor and create some space for yourself?" Mitch nodded and took out his puukko knife and began hacking away the stretch film. As soon as he got the stretch film partially removed, he began tossing items off the pallet onto the warehouse floor. A couple of minutes of throwing items down, and he had room to stand next to the pallet of wire spools.

Next, he removed the stretch film from the pallet of wire spools. Starting at the corner, he tossed the rolls he didn't want down. The first roll onto the warehouse floor was shockingly noisy. The sound reverberated throughout the abandoned warehouse. Following up with more rolls, the sound became a cacophony of metallic ringing and clanging. He continued with his knife work and fought with more plastic stretch film. A couple of minutes later, he exclaimed, "This looks like it!" Lifting and then carrying a twelve-inch-high roll of wire, he moved to the edge of the pallet he was standing on. "Pass it down," Caleb said to Mitch. "Do you need wire for anything?" Mitch asked Caleb. "No, I'm good, but if I do, I will remember this place," responded Caleb. Mitch sat down on the pallet and then swung his legs around and climbed down. Once down, he bent over and hefted the spool off the floor. "Too heavy to carry and too awkward a shape – here, help me unroll some of this." Caleb grabbed the offered end of the wire and began walking backwards. "That should do it," directed Mitch. He then produced a set of wire cutters from an inside pocket. Cutting off about a twelve-foot length, he began winding the wire segment into a manageable coil. This disappeared into an inside pocket of his camo jacket along with the wire cutters he had brought.

"Now we go find your switch and get the heck out of here," suggested Mitch. Caleb nodded and returned to sleuthing the racks for his switch. Mitch walked behind him, aiming his flashlight on the second level so he could potentially spot something. After four rows of searching, Caleb stopped in front of a half dozen similar-looking pallets in a row. The packaging on the outside of the boxes appeared to be in Chinese or Korean characters – Caleb had no idea. Also stamped on the brown cardboard boxes, in English, was the word 'switch' among the other descriptors. Caleb pulled his folding Cold Steel Voyager from his pants pocket, and cut away the plastic stretch film. Next he started slicing open some of the box tops. Mitch moved to an adjacent pallet and performed the same process. "Is this it?"

called Mitch, holding a switch aloft. "Nope," replied Caleb, unceremoniously dropping the incorrect switch he had pulled out of his box on the floor behind him. "Is this it?" called Mitch again. "Nope" came the response again. This went on for fifteen minutes or so as the men dug through the boxes on the pallets. "Holy shit! This might be it," exclaimed Caleb. Holding a white and green mechanism he dug out of a box with packing materials still clinging to it, Caleb examined his prize.

Setting the switch down, Caleb swung his backpack off and opened the top flap. The switch went inside, as well as two more of the same he pulled out of the open box. "Don't need to come back here if I can avoid it," he said. "Crack! Crack! Crack!" Suddenly, gunfire reports came from outside the warehouse. Caleb swiftly closed the flap of his pack and slung it over his shoulders. He saw Mitch perform a chamber check on his SKS, and as he watched, Caleb did the same on his own weapon. "What the heck was that?" Caleb whispered. "I don't know the point of whispering after all the noise we just made," Mitch replied. "Let's get to the opening I made and see what's going on." With their scavenging missions now complete, both men moved toward the previously broken window, securing their flashlights away as they hurried over.

Approaching the broken window which led outdoors, they stopped to listen. Wind whistled past the open window, but nothing else made a sound. "So, what now?" asked Mitch. Caleb replied, "My habit has been to wait before moving whenever I hear gunfire. See if I can figure out where it's coming from and then head the other way." "Then you never know what happened or is happening," retorted Mitch. "True that," replied Caleb, "But a big part of me doesn't give a shit. Keeping my nose out of other people's business has been a winning formula so far." Mitch scratched under his bandanna as he considered Caleb's position on this matter. "Crack! Crack!" came the gunfire again. Mitch looked at Caleb. "I don't know about you, but I'm going to go out there and see what's going on." Taking off, Mitch hit a dead run as he exited the warehouse and immediately veered left and then right as he carried his SKS at a high ready. Getting to a parking barricade on the opposite side of the asphalt, Mitch shoulder-rolled to a prone position behind the cement barrier and laid his rifle atop it. He then looked for targets. No shots rang out. Caleb peered right and left out of the opening in the side of the warehouse, looking to see where the shooting was coming from.

"Crack! Crack! Crack!" shots were fired again. Sounds like something smaller, caliber-wise, Caleb thought – a twenty-two maybe. It wasn't the throatier report of a thirty-caliber weapon. Caleb made his own exit from the warehouse and joined Mitch. The repeated shots told both men the direction they were coming from. It was the opposite direction of the large propane tank where Caleb first encountered his new acquaintance. Looking over at Mitch, Caleb hand-signaled moving towards the shooters' position. Mitch got up and moved alongside Caleb. "We don't know what we are walking into, so let's be careful," suggested Mitch. "Stay frosty," replied Caleb with a tight smile. The two men trotted the length of the warehouse hearing more gunfire as they approached the end of the building. Stopping at the corner, Mitch squatted and peered around the edge of the building, keeping his weapon back to not reveal his presence. The end of the warehouse looked like employee parking as there were several cars still sitting there. Looking a little more closely, Mitch noticed fleet markings on the vehicles suggesting they were company vehicles abandoned here when society unraveled.

"Crack!" Both Mitch and Caleb could see the source of the gunfire. Kneeling between two vehicles was a woman with two young kids. The youngsters were squatting alongside the woman. A girl and a boy, each with small backpacks, looking scared and wide-eyed. The woman held a Remington Nylon 66 rifle in her hands as she panned the trees across the parking lot from her. "Are they gone?" asked the girl. "I don't know. I don't think so," replied the woman. I haven't seen any movement for a while now." She turned, sat, and pulled the magazine rod out of the butt of the Nylon 66. From a jacket pocket, she produced a handful of .22 shells and began feeding them into the magazine of the old-fashioned rifle. A semi-auto rifle that came out in the late 1950s, the Nylon 66 held 14 rounds of twenty-two and was surprisingly accurate but especially noteworthy — it rarely malfunctioned. The woman finished feeding the gun and replaced the magazine rod in its proper position. Caleb called out, "Hey lady!" The woman frantically spun to bring her weapon to bear on the newly perceived threat. "Relax, lady," yelled Mitch. "We are not with whoever you are shooting at. We heard the shots and came to have a look-see. We're no threat to you." The woman kept her rifle trained in their general direction. Looking over her shoulder at her previous field of fire and back towards the two men, she clearly looked stressed. "Seriously, ma'am," called Caleb. "We mean you no harm." "Ma'am? Who says ma'am anymore?" asked Mitch. Caleb shrugged. "I didn't want to keep calling her lady. Can't say girl anymore. Who knows?" The men focused on the woman again. "We are going to step out so you can see us. We are armed but will keep our rifles pointed away from you," Mitch yelled.

"They're still over there," called the woman. They might shoot at you. How do I know you aren't with them?" "Good point," said Caleb to Mitch. "We are making an assumption here," Caleb continued. "A woman with two kids doesn't automatically mean she's one of the good guys." "Fair point," replied Mitch. Playing the hero had gone wrong for him a couple of times in the past, he painfully remembered. "What about the kids?" he asked Caleb. "Is she kidnapping them or protecting them?" "This is why I avoid conflict," said Caleb. "Too many unknowns and too many motivations." Time stood still for a while as the men mulled over the situation.

"Why are you shooting at whoever is in the trees?" Caleb called out to the woman. "Because they're slavers!" yelled the woman. "Slavers?" Caleb looked at Mitch. "Did I hear that right?" Mitch looked perplexed at Caleb. "Ma'am – did you say slavers?" Caleb asked. The woman yelled back, "What, are you hard of hearing? Yes, I said slavers." Mitch – "I guess she said slavers." Caleb sighed with exasperation. "What has it come to that we have slavers now?" Mitch said, "At least she didn't say cannibals." Caleb smiled grimly – "Oh, just wait for it – that's probably what's coming next."

"Ma'am – do you require assistance?" Caleb called to the woman. Looking around the corner, he could see her squatting down between vehicles talking to the children. Further away in the trees, he, for the first time, spotted movement going on. "Ma'am – whoever is in those trees is moving. You might want to make up your mind a little more quickly." Just as he finished speaking, a dozen people emerged from the trees in a skirmish line, weapons leveled in the direction of the woman and her children. With Caleb and Mitch's positioning, those weapons threatened them as well. "Mitch, we have bogeys heading our way – a dozen of them." The woman rose up and viewed the group coming towards her. Heading her way were ten men and a couple of women. This was a rough-looking group of individuals. Everyone carried a long arm of some sort, and several had handguns on their hips or in leg holsters. None of the firearms matched one another. They had a hodgepodge appearance, ragged-looking jeans, dirty t-shirts, untied boots, and a mixture of ball caps, watch caps, and unkempt loose hair added to the incohesive appearance of the group.

"Okay – decision time," said Caleb to Mitch. "Do we throw in with a woman and kids or some rag-tag band of possible slavers?" "I've always been a women and children first kind of guy," Mitch replied with a smile. Caleb grinned back, "Okay – its go time."

"Hey lady, run this way with your kids and we'll provide covering fire," yelled Caleb to the desperate-looking woman. Mitch and Caleb stepped out from the corner of the building and started laying down fire in front of the advancing group. The M1A, equipped with its bigger 7.62mm round, produced a distinctively different bark compared to the less powerful SKS. Mitch and Caleb fired rounds into the ground past the parked cars but in front of the now-stopped group. Seemingly stunned by the new fusillade of shots from unexpected adversaries, the slavers split up and ran in several different directions. Untrained and undisciplined Caleb thought. Mitch and Caleb kept firing but didn't actually try to hit anyone as they ran. As the two men fired their rifles, the woman and her kids wove their way through the cars towards them. All three were bent over at the waist to avoid being caught in the hail of bullets flying overhead. Rounding the corner at a run, they pitched themselves against the wall and slid to the ground. The dozen slavers across the way had retreated to the safety of the woods and melted from sight.

"Okay, we have a couple of minutes while they regroup and start coming back at us again or send out flankers to get behind us. We need to move now!" expelled Caleb in a single breath. "We can do introductions later – any of you hurt?" The woman and two kids looked at him and shook their heads. Mitch nodded his agreement. "Let's make book and get out of here." Caleb looked him in the eye. "You take six?" Mitch nodded again. Caleb headed out in lead with the two youngsters right behind him, then the woman with Mitch pulling up the rear.

The newly formed collection of two men and their three additions ran single file the length of the warehouse to get away from the slaver gang. As Caleb led, he began checking their back trail – the gaggle he led was leaving a noticeable trail as they fled. This was not going to throw off the woman's pursuers. Looking further into the industrial park they were heading through; he saw building after building. He paused them momentarily – "See that tall building with the old water tower on top of it, way over there?" He pointed for Mitch and the woman to see. They looked in the distance and then acknowledged what he was talking about. Caleb – "They know there are at least five of us. Our trail is clear as our boot tracks are leaving an obvious path behind us. If Mitch and I each carry a kid on our back and we head in different directions, there will be three different sets of tracks for them to follow. This might confuse and slow them down a bit as they try to figure out where the other two have disappeared to. They might think we are laying an ambush for them. Thoughts?" The woman spoke first, "Where are we supposed to go again?" Caleb pointed at the water tower on the building in the distance. "Head for there and we can regroup. Mitch and I can head off in different directions and, with our higher ground speed, get there close to the same time even if we take a longer route." Mitch spoke, "I think it might help. Splitting them into three groups of pursuers might make an actual ambush easier if we decide to set one up." The kids didn't have much to say. They just looked scared. The girl was slightly older of the two but couldn't have been much more than eight. The boy was six or maybe seven, but both already had a hard look in their eyes from having seen far too much at too young an age.

The woman looked at Caleb and Mitch, "I'm trusting you with my children and I have known you for what - maybe five minutes, but I see little choice. I pray you are who you appear to be and don't hurt either me or my kids." Caleb spoke and Mitch nodded his agreement, "Lady, we won't hurt you or your kids." The woman took the head of each of her two children in turn and kissed them on the foreheads, "Mummy loves you both very much." With that, Mitch had the boy climb up on his back, whereas Caleb shifted his backpack to the front of his torso. Caleb looked the woman in the eyes – "Head towards that building but don't make a straight line. Check your back trail and if you can, double back a couple of times and switch directions without putting yourself in danger. If you find a stretch of cement or asphalt with little or no dirt or debris on it, use it to change direction and hopefully throw your pursuers off. Run for three or four minutes if you can and then walk for a minute to catch your breath. Doing that will help you cover the most ground and not exhaust you. Do you have any water?" The woman shook her head as did the kids. Pulling the tube of his CamelBak free, Caleb offered a drink to each of them. "No more than a mouthful each," he instructed. Caleb saw Mitch take a pull from his own canteen. Once the woman and kids finished, Caleb took a drink himself. I need to top that up again when I get a chance, he thought. Looking at the young girl, Caleb motioned to her, "Come on." He then helped the young girl get positioned on his back.

"Go," said Mitch, and the group broke into three. "What's your name?" called Caleb after the woman as she began running. Shouting over her shoulder, she yelled back, "Abigail," and then continued directly away from the group.

Caleb looked at Mitch. "Abigail it is," and headed out east of the building. Mitch hitched his kid a little higher on his back and started west. Caleb settled into what could most accurately be described as a trot. The girl on his back wasn't overly heavy, but the pack on his front was in the way and awkward. He kept changing his rifle from hand to hand, trying to find an efficient way to run with the ungainly load. No more than five minutes passed, and already he felt sweat beginning to form as he heated up from the exertion.

Minutes passed. Caleb followed his own advice of periodically doubling back on his trail and watching for dry, clean areas to cross to leave as little trail as possible. He remembered the tracking course he had taken at the Tom Brown Jr. Tracking School and how much information a trail could leave. He doubted any of his pursuers were trained trackers, which lessened his anxiety somewhat. The youngster on his back asked to be let down to walk after a while, as piggyback was inherently an uncomfortable place to be. Caleb compromised and let the child walk when the asphalt was dry and empty of debris. It gave him a break from the load and helped him get his breath back. After about thirty-five or so minutes of travel, he and his companion spotted the agreed-upon building. Caleb stopped at a corner and checked his back trail. No pursuers were visible. The young girl asked him for another drink. As she was sipping, Caleb spoke to her, "What's your name?" "Rebecca," she replied. She looked him in the eyes with a level of assurance that belied her young age. Five minutes later, the other members of their party came into sight. Mitch looked fatigued from his journey, and the woman, Abigail, Caleb reminded himself, appeared to have survived her run. "What now?" was her greeting upon arrival. Amusing how quickly she had deferred to his leadership, thought Caleb. "Yeah, what now?" parroted Mitch. Before answering, Caleb took a good look at their respective back trails. No sign of any pursuers.

"How long have these 'slavers' been chasing you?" Caleb asked Abigail. "They came in the night to our camp. We were part of a larger group heading to the coast. Just before dawn, they entered our camp and attacked us," replied Abigail. "I grabbed my kids and took off. It was chaotic with people shooting and running in all directions. I don't know what happened to the sentries we had in place." "Is this group the entire party that attacked your encampment or just a portion of them?" inquired Caleb. "I don't know. It seems likely they are a portion, as we had forty or so in our traveling party, and I imagine someone has taken control of those who didn't get away," responded Abigail.

"Look!" said Mitch as he pointed in the distance. Caleb could see figures several blocks away headed in their general direction. Too soon to verify if they were the same group following the woman but potential adversaries, nonetheless. "We need to keep moving," instructed Caleb. "Obviously they were slowed down by our tactics but not stopped." Mitch asked, "Do you think we should set up a hasty ambush?" Caleb remembered his training while in the military — a hasty ambush is made when a team or unit makes visual contact with the enemy and has sufficient time to set an ambush without being detected. By suggesting such, Mitch had revealed something about himself and his training or knowledge. Caleb filed that note in his mind for later consideration. "No. Too many of them and too few of us. We might be able to halve their number if things went well but that still leaves us significantly outnumbered and outgunned. I think E&E is still our best bet." "Escape and Evasion," Mitch verbalized for Abigail's benefit.

"Yep, you're right," remarked Mitch. "Time to beat the feet." Caleb looked at Rebecca. "Can you run for a while, honey?" Rebecca nodded as she looked at her mum. "I think I can." "What's your boy's name?" Caleb asked Abigail. "Trent" she responded. "Ok, Rebecca and Trent. We are going to run and walk for a while. Carrying you was a short-term plan, but our pursuers seem more determined than I originally thought. We need to create space between us and them and figure out how to lose them at the same time." Both kids looked at Caleb and nodded. They looked scared but agreeable. "Can you run?" Caleb asked Abigail. "You bet your skinny white ass I can!" she retorted. "I have no intention of being a slave to someone else for any reason. Let's go!" "Lead off, Mitch; I'll bring up the rear," suggested Caleb.

The group headed out at a slow run with Mitch out front. Caleb scanned either side of the streets as they ran, remembering that threats could also emerge from buildings they were passing. He regularly checked their back trail as they ran in case their followers started catching up with them. Each corner Mitch randomly selected to make either a left or a right, but Caleb could tell they were slowly angling towards the northeast. As they ran, residential neighborhoods came into sight, a good number of which were burned out and abandoned-looking. As they emerged from the industrial area, Caleb called a stop. Everyone was breathing heavily, but no one had started falling behind, at least not yet. Caleb looked towards the sun going down in the west. Holding his hand at arm's length, he counted the fingers between the bottom of the sun and the horizon – four. Each finger counted as 15 minutes. Caleb had been using this method to measure the daylight remaining since his dad taught it to him when he was a kid.

"We have about an hour of daylight left. I don't want to be stumbling around in the dark looking for somewhere to bed down for the night." Caleb looked at the rest of his small group. Everyone looked weary to varying degrees, but no one objected to his suggestion. Rebecca piped up, "I'm hungry, Mum." "Me too," added Trent. "When are we going to eat?" "I don't know, kids. I don't have any food to give you right now," replied Abigail. The kids looked pained but did not whine. There was a resignation in their eyes which told Caleb this was not the first time they had gone hungry. Their slender builds also confirmed this fact. In the year that had passed since things fell apart, a lot of the world had missed many meals. Being alive to complain about hunger meant you were one of the 'lucky ones', if being alive now was indeed lucky. "I might be able to help you out a bit," Mitch shared. From under his camo jacket, he produced what looked like beef jerky or at least some sort of jerky, thought Caleb. Beef might be a bit of a stretch in this situation. Caleb decided not to entertain ideas of what other possible animal Mitch had dried out. Mitch handed pieces to everyone in the party. Abigail and her kids eagerly chewed on it. "Want some?" Mitch asked Caleb. "No, I'm good," replied Caleb.

"Now we have little daylight left," commented Caleb. "I say we make our way to an abandoned house and settle in for the night." Mitch looked at him. "I'm with you on that. Any preferences?" Caleb looked in the distance. He didn't see light or movement in any of the houses in the nearby residential area. "Let's scout out a location with good lines of sight and a suitable exit if we have to leave in a hurry." Abigail and her two children made ready to move again. "I am concerned we have not seen or heard from our pursuers. It makes me think they are glassing us and watching. Waiting for us to let our guard down and then hitting us." "What does glassing mean?" asked Rebecca. "It means looking at us with a pair of binoculars or a monocular, honey," answered Mitch. "They can see us from far away and we can't see them." "Oh, I get it," she responded. "Like spies." Mitch smiled at her – "Yes, like spies."

Caleb took the lead and made his way toward the housing area. Mitch pulled rearguard duty once again. After ten minutes of walking, they were deep in the residential area. It was a depressing sight. Garbage littered the street everywhere and the front lawns of most of the houses. An inordinate number seemed to have suffered some sort of fire damage. Garage doors remained open, as did the front doors, giving the appearance of people having left hastily. To where? thought Caleb. Where did all the people go? Caleb spied a two-story brick-faced house at the end of a cul-de-sac. If the bricks were real, it might offer some ballistic protection. It had what looked like a fairly heavy wooden door with a small window in the center. "Let's make our way to that one," suggested Caleb. The group made their way closer to the house. The double garage door remained closed, as did all the windows. "Mitch, can you make your way around the back and see if you can spot any movement or lights?" "Sure," came the quick reply from Mitch. Caleb pointed to the second-floor balcony which jutted out from the building. "We can use that for overwatch of the street in front of the house and spot anyone coming toward us," he said to Abigail and the kids. "What's overwatch?" asked Trent. "A high place where you can see from," explained Caleb. "It's like being on a hill where you can see all around you," he continued with a smile. Trent appeared to understand, and Rebecca and her mother nodded their understanding as well.

At this point, Caleb actually took a moment to look at the three people who had affixed themselves to him and Mitch. Abigail was of average height for a woman and had the slender/skinny build that had become commonplace after the grocery stores stopped having easy access to food. The kids were similarly thin but not gaunt. It appeared Abigail had been managing to keep them at least minimally fed. Abigail had mid-back auburn hair kept in a ponytail. She was pleasant to look at, her features having a faint

Latino or Southern European cast to them. Rebecca had matching hair of similar length. Trent was a tow-headed blond boy with what looked like a home-style haircut probably made with paper-cutting scissors. He had the typical messy hair a young boy unselfconscious about his appearance would have. Both kids were obviously Abigail's given their features.

Mitch returned from his scouting of the house. "No signs of life. The back door appears slightly ajar. I think we could gain entry that way," Caleb suggested. "Okay, let's go." The group walked between the houses to the rear of the building. There was a shoulder-height hedge separating the two properties, but there was an opening in the hedge large enough to easily let the group into the backyard. "Stay here," directed Caleb to Abigail and her two kids. "Mitch and I need to clear the house before you come in." Caleb made his way to the back door, stepping up onto the cedar deck coming out from the back of the house. The rear door to the house was slightly open. Caleb held his weapon at the ready and did a quick chamber check prior to moving through the door; he had replaced the partially empty mag back at the warehouse after firing rounds at the opposition. Mitch was stacked up behind him, and the two of them quickly entered. The door opened into the kitchen area, which further opened into the front living room. The house was in a mild state of disarray but not the absolute wreck many buildings were these days. Mitch opened the door to the pantry and shone his light into it as Caleb opened a door to what revealed itself as stairs to the basement. "Clear," called out Mitch for his area after he had taken a good look inside. The shelves were predictably bare, but no threats existed inside the small space. Caleb pulled a wedge-shaped rubber doorstop out of a pocket and tapped it under the door with his foot to hold the door to the basement closed. “We’ll check down there after we finish the rest of the house," he said to Mitch, and they continued on. The rest of the main floor had bedrooms and toilets but no occupants. On one side of the living room was a staircase leading to the second floor which they ascended as part of their house clearing process. Once on the second floor, an open bedroom door revealed a sliding glass door to the balcony they had spotted from the ground. Looking through the glass doors, they could see a waist-high wall around the balcony which provided concealment but no real cover as it appeared to be made of wood and vinyl siding. Finishing their check of the upstairs rooms, they headed back down to the main floor. Standing in front of the door leading to the basement, Caleb removed his wedge and pulled open the door. Mitch took a handheld light from his belt as he didn't have a rifle-mounted version, and they proceeded down the stairs. The stairs were carpeted which significantly dampened their footfalls as they made their way down. Their lights intersected in the gloom of the unlit room which made ordinary objects appear eerie. The large room they came into had the ubiquitous big screen TV mounted to the wall as was common in so many finished basements as well as assorted comfortable-looking chairs and a large leather couch. A laundry hanger, otherwise better known as a stationary bike, sat in the corner.

At the rear of the room was a short hallway with uncarpeted cement flooring. The two men entered the hallway and saw a closed door. It didn't appear to match the rest of the décor as it was metal with a metal frame. The door itself had a door handle and a deadbolt just above it. The door handle and the deadbolt looked commercial grade with an anti-jimmy J-bar assembly installed as well. "Well, this is interesting," said Mitch. "Not your typical suburban basement feature." Caleb got closer and put his ear to the door – no sounds came from inside. "I don't like leaving uncleared space behind us, but at this point I don't think we have much choice," Caleb suggested. Mitch stepped forward and gave the doorknob a twist – it wouldn't open. "Worth a try," he said with a smile. Caleb chuckled – "True that." Caleb looked at the bottom of the door and saw there was insufficient clearance to insert his door wedge. Curiouser and curiouser.

Both men headed back upstairs. Once in the kitchen area, they gestured for Abigail and the kids to come inside. "Okay. The house appears empty and safe for the night. We found a locked door in the basement which could lead to something, but without some heavier duty tools, we aren't going to be able to get into it," Caleb told the group. Looking at Mitch, Caleb said, 'Can you set up overwatch from that balcony? Make it our observation post." "Check," Mitch responded as he turned and headed towards the stairs. "Right – we need to get settled. Abigail, why don't you pick out a room upstairs for the kids and yourself to spend the night? I am going to close and somewhat barricade the main floor doors to slow down anyone who might want to come for a visit in the night," said Caleb. He pulled his flashlight from his belt and handed it to her so she and the kids would have some light to see by. Abigail nodded her agreement and headed for the same staircase Mitch had just gone up. Caleb put his rifle in an accessible location and put on his headlamp. Next, he began dragging furniture in front of the back and front doors to block them from easy entry. He also closed all the curtains and blinds to aid in light discipline and make the house dark to the outside world. Once this set of tasks was complete, he took off his backpack. Inside were a half dozen freeze-dried meals he kept for his forays into the world outside of home. He also removed a small collapsible wood-burning stove he carried and assembled it. Going through the sliding glass doors which led onto the backyard deck, he opened the propane barbecue and set his little stove on the grill. Looking at the still-attached propane tank, he had a sudden inspiration. Reaching down and hefting the 25-pound tank, he could tell there was still propane inside it. "Dumbass," he said to himself as he disassembled his wood stove and put it back in his pack. Pulling his stainless-steel cooking pot with the folding handle out of his pack, he considered a source of water next. There should still be some water in the hot water tank, he thought as he headed back into the house towards the stairs leading to the basement.

Upon arrival downstairs, he found the hot water tank. There probably hasn't been water pressure for ages, he thought, so the need to open a tap upstairs to relieve the pressure wouldn't be necessary. Locating the drain valve, he put the lip of his pot underneath it and proceeded to fill the pot three-quarters full. Shouldn't be a need to filter it, he thought, plus he was going to boil it on the barbecue, making doubly sure it was safe. Task completed, he headed back upstairs and then outside to the deck. Luckily, the striker on the barbecue still worked, and after a small amount of fiddling, he got the unit going and started the process of heating the water. It had gotten dark by now, but the flame inside the barbecue really didn't go anywhere, maintaining light discipline. Abigail and the kids drifted back downstairs to see what was going on and hung around the warming water. "What's the water for?" Rebecca asked. "Dinner," responded Caleb. "Dinner?!" all three of them chorused. "Yep," replied Caleb. "I have some freeze-dried meals in my pack, but they each need a cup or more of water to reconstitute." Smiles broke out on obviously hungry faces.

"I have beef stew, Pad Thai with chicken, beef stroganoff, and a couple of others sitting on the counter in the kitchen." Discussion and bargaining erupted from the small group as they negotiated who was going to get what. Shortly thereafter, the water had converted to a rolling boil. Caleb asked Abigail to rummage through the kitchen drawers to come up with some forks or spoons to eat the meals.

Caleb poured an appropriate amount of hot water into each of the pouches and instructed the mum and her kids to let them sit for at least a couple of minutes as the boiling water did its trick. Filling up a stroganoff pouch for Mitch, Caleb made sure the BBQ was out and headed up to the upstairs deck with the food and a fork. "Made you some food," said Caleb as he handed the warm container to Mitch. "Hope you like beef stroganoff." "Hot food's good food," responded Mitch. "I'll maintain lookout so you can eat," said Caleb. Mitch nodded. "We need to talk a bit," started Caleb. Mouth full of the warm food, Mitch nodded his agreement. "This morning, we were adversaries and now we are seemingly in some sort of partnership with a woman and her two kids under our protection. This is not how I imagined the day shaping up when I started out. I know literally nothing about you, where you are from, where you're going, and the same holds true for me for you. We don't know anything about this woman and her two kids, and we are in some level of conflict with a group Abigail calls slavers. We don't know if that is true or if she is merely stringing a lie for us to believe. The amount we don't know greatly exceeds what we do know." "Agreed," said Mitch in between mouthfuls. The smell of the food was getting to Caleb. "What say I stop talking for five minutes, let you finish eating, and then go get some food for myself and fill the large hole I have in my gut which is talking ever louder to me, and then we continue this discussion?" Mitch gave a quick thumbs up and shifted in his seat to look over the handrail into the darkening gloom as he kept working away at the grub in the mylar pouch Caleb had given him.

Heading back downstairs, Caleb could hear talk coming from the kitchen where everyone else was working on their respective meals. "That pretty much wiped out the food I had in my pack except for a small amount of beef jerky I keep to chew on while hiking," said Caleb. "We are going to have to come up with something new for tomorrow," he told Abigail, Rebecca, and Trent. "I put some water in your pouch for you," said Abigail. "I hope it hasn't been in there too long and made things mushy." "Hot and ready is all I care about," replied Caleb, and he pulled open the package and sat on a kitchen chair. The kids looked like they were finishing their meals. "Where were you planning on going once you got away from the slavers?" asked Caleb. "Where on the coast was your group heading?" "Did you have an actual destination or were you just heading in that general direction?" Abigail looked at him over the top of her beef stew pouch, which she had just finished emptying. "Honestly, I hadn't thought much about it. Today has been such a scramble getting away from those people, and this surprise dinner made me so happy I did not really think about it. I guess I was pretty much in survival mode – just running and trying to stay alive." "Can we stay with you?" Trent said somewhat earnestly to Caleb. Looking from face to face, Caleb saw three sets of desperate and imploring eyes regarding him hopefully. The world Caleb inhabited now was a much different one than a year ago. The world was a much harsher and unforgiving one where acts of kindness were usually punished, and cruelty was more the norm. "I don't know just yet what I am going to do. Let's just get through the night and see where we are in the morning,"

Caleb responded. Abigail and her two kids looked somewhat crestfallen after the non-answer. Caleb knew he could be taking on a lot of responsibility for people he knew nothing about and had no experience with – outside of today's events. He went back to shovelling the contents of his pouch into his mouth in an effort to quell his complaining stomach.

Just then, a low whistle came down from the position Mitch occupied. Caleb looked at Abigail. "Get the kitchen sliding glass door closed and pile some furniture in front of it quickly and quietly – can you do that?" Abigail stood and gave him a thumbs up as she marshaled the assistance of the kids. Caleb headed upstairs. "What's up?" he asked as he got close to Mitch. "I see lights moving off in the distance," Mitch replied, pointing down the street from where they were currently residing. Caleb looked to where Mitch was pointing and sure enough, he could see a number of what looked like flashlights or headlamps casting about on the ground as they proceeded forward. "What do you think?" Mitch asked Caleb. "Do we pack up and get out of here or stay put?" Caleb considered the question. "Moving in the dark with Abigail and the kids is likely to be a problem. I say we button down and go into silent mode. I don't know if they are tracking us or just heading in this direction by chance. What do you think?" Mitch rubbed the day's growth he had on his chin. "When you fired up the BBQ, I could smell the old grease on it cooking as you heated the water. I don't smell it now, but perhaps it drifted on the wind and told them someone was here doing something." Caleb looked back at Mitch, "Yeah, I thought of that as I heated the water. Smells can travel a fair way and as hungry as everyone is these days – it is a real risk to potentially betray our position. I guess I thought the cost/benefit ratio was worth it. Maybe I am about to be proved wrong."

"Do you have any force multipliers we could use for an ambush?" Caleb asked Mitch. "I have one trip-wire flare I sometimes set up when I am out and about, but nothing outside of that," replied Mitch. "What about you?" Caleb thought about it for a minute. "I have a coil of wire I could make some tanglefoot with, but not much other than that." Both men considered their options. "I am going to talk to Abigail," announced Caleb. "I'm going to give her a revolver and show her briefly how to use it." With that, Caleb stood and headed back inside. "Let me know what is happening out here," he instructed Mitch, who grimly nodded.

Descending the stairs, Caleb approached Abigail. "Put the kids in another room for a second," he directed. "Nope, not going to do it. They have seen a lot and can handle some more – if they don't stay, I don't stay," she tersely responded to his direction. "Okay," retorted Caleb as he reached inside his waistband, pulling out a four-inch barrel Ruger handgun positioned there. "This is a .357 magnum revolver," he shared. "It holds six rounds and." "Has a hefty recoil," Abigail continued for him. "It is either a single-action or a double-action depending on whether or not you cock the hammer," she concluded with a smile. "I'm not some nail salon bimbo, you know; I owned a revolver before, before all of this," she indicated by waving her hands around. "I even went to a range and practiced now and then, so I'm not some sort of newbie." Caleb realized his mouth was hanging open with this new information. "Well, I guess I underestimated you," Caleb responded. "Do you have any other hidden skills I am not aware of?" "Guess you will have to hang around and find out," she coyly teased with a smile.

"Jokes aside – we have an issue coming at us, we can see lights coming this way and we don't know whether or not it's your slaver friends or someone else. Regardless, we need to turn off all lights and get you and the kids tucked away in a bedroom. Let's go!" The coy smile vanished as Abigail became all business again. "Do you have any reloads for this piece?" she inquired. Caleb dug two filled speed loaders out of belt pouches. "That's all I've got. Use them wisely and don't forget about through-and-through damage with that thing. These sheetrock walls will barely slow down the 125 grain hollow points that thing is loaded with. Neither Mitch nor I want to be a bullet sponge, so think about where the rounds are going to go before pulling the trigger." Abigail nodded her understanding, tucking the revolver into her waistband and putting the speed loaders in an outside jacket pocket. She picked up her twenty-two-caliber rifle from where it was leaning against a wall and gathered the kids and headed upstairs.

Caleb returned to the front second-floor balcony where Mitch kept watch. Looking over the handrail, he could see lights a little more than a block away. "Go time is getting close," whispered Mitch. Caleb could see the lights arcing off from the road onto each structure as each house was passed. He could also see a single light pointed right at the ground where he and the rest of his party had traversed on their way to the house, they currently hid in. "I am going to go and cover the back entrance if you can handle the front," said Caleb to Mitch. "Sure thing," responded Mitch. Caleb headed back inside and towards the stairs. He popped his head inside the bedroom where Abigail and the kids were hiding – they were all sitting between the bed and the inside wall. Rebecca gave Caleb a thumbs up. Once downstairs, Caleb moved to the back of the house. As he got to the kitchen back door area, he heard some noises coming from the deck. There was enough moonlight that he could see a group of scruffy-looking dogs on the deck sniffing around the BBQ. Caleb grimaced as his concern about the smells of cooking permeating the neighborhood came to fruition. The mangy mutts hadn't noticed him yet as they tried to figure out where the good smells were coming from. In the next moment, Caleb heard sounds coming from the front entryway. Deciding dogs were the lesser of his problems, he moved towards the front door. Lights from flashlights were penetrating the living room window but mostly were blocked by the pulled drapes. Being careful not to get caught in their glare, he positioned himself next to a large wooden wall unit. He did a quick chamber check and ensured his safety was off. "The trail leads into here," he heard from outside. Caleb could see some lights outside of the house as people moved about. The moral quandary he suffered was whether to open fire based on what he thought to be true about them from Abigail or engage them and see what he could learn. He decided on the latter. "What do you want?" he called out. He immediately heard some movement in the front of the house. "Who are you?" came back a rich baritone voice. "Who I am is my business, and you trying to come into my house is also my business," Caleb responded. "We just want the woman and the two kids. We know you have them, and they belong to us. Send them out, and we will have no quarrel with you," replied the same voice. Caleb could hear some movement along the side of the house as men moved to the rear of the house to flank him. "I hear your guys moving around back, mister. You have no right to enter my residence or to this woman and her kids. People can't own people, or have you forgotten that?" The voice came back at him, "In case you haven't noticed, the world has changed. The old rules no longer apply. You get what you can take and keep what you can hold. Either you hand them over, or we are going to take them, and that, sir, is a fact!" Caleb shouted through the front entryway, "You are making a mistake, and it's not going to end well. I suggest you forget about this woman and be on your way. She's under my protection now, and I'm not going to just hand her over!"

Just as he finished his last words, Caleb could hear the door being impacted at the rear of the house as men tried to force their way in. "Mitch! Go time!" he shouted. Gunfire erupted from the front balcony as Mitch fired downwards towards the attackers. The SKS made steady cracking noises as the rounds went off. Sporadic return fire started as the men out front scrambled for cover, then the back door burst open as the men there slammed into it with their full weight. Caleb sent a couple of rounds from his Springfield through the center of the doorway, and judging from the falling body, he must have hit something vital. Fire and move, he reminded himself as he changed position. The gunfire from the front of the house picked up as Mitch engaged targets and their adversaries got more organized in their resistance. The sliding glass door to the right of the kitchen smashed open as intruders made another avenue of entry inside. Caleb swiveled and opened fire through that opening but was unable to determine whether he made any hits or not. Rounds impacted the wall near his head from behind the house. "Fire and move," he said again as he changed position. Going into the kitchen, he fired five rounds while moving, all through the now open back door. He heard a muffled cry as another body was impacted by his 7.62mm round. "Coming down!" called out Mitch to Caleb. "I have the back," yelled Caleb. Squatting down behind the kitchen island, Caleb considered his options. He could hear the mewling sounds of injured men outside as a result of his shots. Mitch sounded unhurt as of yet, and the gunfire was dropping off from both the front and the back of the house. "I think I got at least three," called out Mitch. "I count two," responded Caleb. If there were ten or twelve in the group, they had cut their active members down by almost half. The sound of smashing glass reverberated throughout the house, followed by the whoosh of flames. Another smashing sound in the kitchen as a Molotov cocktail crashed into the kitchen and exploded in a ball of fire. The first gasoline-filled bottle had crashed through the side window next to the front door. Evidently, the men outside decided burning them out was the right idea. Upstairs, another smashing sound of glass and the now familiar whoosh of flames came as the burning gas splashed across a room. "I'm going to get Abby and the kids," Mitch yelled. Caleb could see both the front and rear entrances were obstructed by rapidly growing fire and smoke. Gunfire from outside started again as rounds impacted the walls, light fixtures, and appliances in the house. Pieces of sheetrock and wood flew all over. Abigail and the kids came quickly down the stairs, followed by Mitch, and all were beginning to cough from the expanding smoke of the fires. "Follow me!" called Caleb as he yanked open the door to the basement. He then led the group down the stairs to the basement. Mitch closed the door behind them as he was the last to go down.

Caleb figured the closed door would hold back the flames and smoke for a few minutes as they searched for a basement window to escape from. Mitch held his flashlight, and Abigail held the light she had gotten from Mitch. The group clustered at the bottom of the stairs. "What now, boss?" asked Mitch. Even in the flurry of activity, Caleb noticed the implicit denoting of leadership to himself. "We need to find a way out of here fast before the house burns down on us." No sooner had he spoken those words than a bright beam of light fell upon the group. Both Mitch and Caleb spun with their weapons to bear upon the direction the light was coming from. "It's okay, fellas," came a voice.

"No danger from me." Both men advanced towards the light, rifles pointing forward. The holder of the bright light directed his flashlight towards the floor. Behind the light, they could make out a smaller and much older man. The locked metal door! Caleb suddenly remembered. He had forgotten all about that! "Come, come with me," gestured the man as he turned and headed through the doorway. As the roaring of the fire upstairs grew in volume and smoke more forcefully penetrated the basement door, the men, Abigail, and the children had little choice. Caleb led the kids and woman, and Mitch took up the rear. As they passed the old man at the metal door, he closed it behind them. They were on a staircase leading down, and electric LED lights mounted on the ceiling overhead illuminated the way. The old man turned a wheel mounted on the back of the metal door, and one-inch thick flat metal rods extended into holes in the brick walls on either side of the door. "Keep going," said the man as he waved them forward. After about twenty steps, the stairwell ended, and Caleb could see another metal door. The old man passed the group and opened this door, leading them inwards. They walked into what appeared to be a twenty-by-twenty subterranean room. There were cinder block walls on all four sides painted a cheery shade of yellow. Beds lined one wall, a long couch divided the space, creating a living room with a couple of large chairs and a desk in the corner. End tables and a coffee table completed the rest of the decor. "What is this place?" Abigail asked the old man. "Our hideout," answered what looked like a ten-year-old girl sitting on the couch across from them. "That is my granddaughter," explained the grey-haired man. "We live here."

Crashing sounds came from upstairs as the building above started to fall in on itself. "We used to live upstairs," the girl commented with a hint of sorrow in her voice. "I'm sorry, but where the heck are, we, exactly?" exclaimed Mitch. "This is a shelter I had built five years ago," explained the old man. "I saw the way the world was going and wanted a safe place for my children and grandchildren should the eventuality I foresaw come to pass." "Children and grandchildren?" asked Abigail. "Where are they?" The old man looked dour. "My little Angeline is all I have left," he replied, looking at the young girl on the couch. Angeline looked back at him with obvious sadness. Caleb realized he and everyone in his group were standing when they could be sitting. "Do you mind if we sit down?" he asked the old man.

"No, not at all, please sit," the man gestured towards the chairs and couch. The two men, Abigail, and her children all sat. This was going to be interesting.

CHAPTER TWO
COMPLICATIONS

"Gerald, my name is Gerald," said the older man. Caleb introduced himself, followed by the rest of his companions. "Nice to meet you all," replied Gerald. "Can I offer you something to drink?" Trent and Rebecca put up their hands as the adults nodded their agreement. Gerald walked to the other end of the room to a hallway leading away. "I can't believe our good fortune," Abigail said. "I thought for sure we were going to burn to death." "Or get shot," Rebecca added. "It does seem strangely fortuitous Gerald was able to help at just the right moment," Caleb added. He looked to the desk against the wall. On it was a pair of computer monitors, showing screens of gray fuzz presently. "I have a feeling our host was watching us from down here," Caleb added. Gerald returned with a serving tray holding several glasses of orange liquid on it. He handed them out to the group, who each eagerly drank them. "Tang! I haven't had Tang in years," Mitch exclaimed. "I am afraid it's the best I can do under the circumstances," offered Gerald. "No, no worries," answered Mitch. "I used to love Tang!" The kids were mystified by the discussion between the adults but were quickly guzzling down the orange-flavored drink.

"Gerald, if I'm not being too nosey. How is it you are here a year after the crash, in apparent comfort, enjoying Tang and who knows what else when the world above is practically eating one another to survive?" asked Mitch. Gerald smiled at Mitch. "Well, that's a bit of a story. Two years before the crack-up boom, I saw the red flags of a society at the end of its rope. The endless accumulation of debt and deficits with no apparent way to pay them off. The degradation of our society where deviancy more and more became the norm, and a world at large tired of being bossed around by the West." Gerald continued, "I couldn't see any way out of the direction we were going and realized there was going to be a period of dislocation. I wanted to both survive it and at the same time help my family survive. It appears I fulfilled the first part of my plan but not the second part. Other than you, sweetie," Gerald said as he smiled warmly at his granddaughter. "I made good money as I owned a pair of car dealerships. I used those funds to hire contractors to build this underground shelter in my backyard. My property is actually a quarter acre with a wooded area behind us leading down into a ravine. I put up temporary fencing in my backyard so the neighbors couldn't see what I was doing. It did generate a lot of curiosity among them. With what ended up happening, I wish I had taken more measures to keep the construction a secret. It's too late for that now." Gerald sighed as he relived the memory. "You can't see it, but I have a 500-gallon cistern outside of these walls which collected water from the roof of my now burned-down house. I put away a year's food for my daughter and her husband as well as Angeline and her brother. The toilet you can't see leads to a septic field and is pumped out with battery power. Batteries powered by the solar panels I had on the roof of my now ruined home.

"Were you watching us from down here?" asked Caleb. "Yes, I had surveillance cameras set up inside the house to check if it was safe to go upstairs when we needed to. Other than the occasional small animal poking around, it's been pretty quiet this last year. We would often go upstairs to get some sunlight as living underground can be depressing." "I guess those cameras are gone now too," Gerald noted as he looked at the computer monitor screens of gray fuzz. Caleb looked at Gerald. "It seems our arriving in your house has impacted you negatively in a number of ways." "It is going to force my hand quite significantly," replied Gerald. "I was listening and watching you as I have a dilemma." "What dilemma is that?" Mitch asked. "I am dying," replied Gerald. "I don't know when, but it isn't too far away. I have Type I diabetes, and I am running out of insulin. I managed to keep my supply refrigerated until now, but that is going away once my battery bank runs down and the solar system that charged it is now gone." "I was thinking of approaching your group and asking you to take my granddaughter with you as I have no one else to watch over her and she is all I have left in the world." Mitch, Abigail, and Caleb all exchanged glances. This is not what they had expected. Who knew what was expected, but taking on the young child of another man was certainly not it. "I have things I can give you," said Gerald. "Things that would make surviving much easier." "The only thing I do not have is time." Gerald smiled again at his granddaughter. "And time is all she has. Lots and lots of time. Time without me." Abigail spoke up. "We'll take her." "Whoa, whoa, lady," exclaimed Mitch. "Not so fast. What do you mean we?" "Only earlier today we met by chance when I was on a scavenging mission, and now we're what? A big happy family?! I have other people counting on me. I can't be taking on more responsibility for a kid I just met with a woman and kids whom I just met!" Mitch turned and looked at Caleb. "Where are you with this?" Caleb stared at the floor for a while before answering. "I was just thinking of an old movie I watched years ago. Life is like a box of chocolates. Sometimes you just never know what you are going to get." "What the hell does that mean?" asked Mitch. "It means I'm tired and need a rest. We have been going all day, running, surviving a firefight, and a house burning down around us. I say we turn in and sleep on it," responded Caleb. He looked around the room. Everyone from his group looked exhausted. Gerald and his granddaughter looked stressed but otherwise fine.

"Agreed," Abigail replied. "Things will look different in the morning after a good night's rest." "What about our friends upstairs?" Mitch inquired, looking upwards. Caleb considered the question. "I think they are going to assume we perished in the fire. More than one of their team is gunshot and probably needs medical assistance or burial. From the sounds we heard, the roof and walls collapsed, covering the basement area up. Who knows – maybe the fire will burn for a couple of days. I think we're okay for the night." Gerald had moved to one of the couches and pulled a handle. It was a pullout bed with sheets already on it. "Abigail and her kids can sleep here," he offered. "You gentlemen can figure something out. I have more blankets and pillows I can get." Having slept in his jacket and poncho more times than he could remember, blankets and a pillow sounded pretty good to Caleb. The group settled in after making themselves comfortable. Both Caleb and Mitch took out bore snakes to pull through the barrels of their respective weapons and did some perfunctory breach cleaning with gun brushes. Caleb hand-loaded some cartridges into the magazine he had used upstairs to top it off and replaced it in his weapon. He cycled the action, putting a round in the chamber and then engaged the safety.

An empty gun is just a stick, his dad used to say. A straight finger is the best safety, his Warrant Officer in the military used to say. Caleb saw Mitch doing roughly the same routine. You need to take care of your weapon for it to take care of you. No matter how tired you were – weapons maintenance took priority. Gerald had put his granddaughter to bed and moved to turn off the lights. "Night all," Gerald said to the group at large.

A good eight or nine hours later, people in the room started waking up. Mitch could smell smoke from the fire. It had made its way downstairs via whatever ventilation system Gerald had in place. That gnawing sensation was back in his stomach despite having enjoyed a full meal last night. Everyone started to get up from where they were sleeping and stretch out the kinks. "I have to go to the bathroom, Mum," said Trent to his mother. "Me too," agreed Rebecca. "Me three," said Mitch with a laugh. "Me four," thought Caleb. Despite all of the sweating and running/walking yesterday, he still had urine to expel. The body is a funny thing, he thought. Gerald pointed to the hallway – "the toilet is at the end. Whoever needs to go the worst can go first." The two kids leaped to their feet and made a run for it.

"No fair, no fair," yelled Trent as Rebecca edged him out at the end of the hall.

Gerald surveyed the group – "who's interested in breakfast?" Immediate smiles broke out giving him the answer he expected. "Anyone want to help me put something together?" Abigail looked at the two men. "Expecting me to rustle something up for you big strong men?" "If it wouldn't be too much of a problem, ma'am," Mitch said with his best shit-eating grin. Abigail rolled her eyes and followed Gerald to the kitchen food prep area. Caleb looked at Mitch. "Can I talk to you privately?" Mitch nodded and headed to the stairwell they had come down the night before.

"We have ourselves a bit of a situation here," Caleb started. I left my retreat to scout for an electrical switch I needed. Now I am getting roped into an instant-family. I'm not set up for an increase in my headcount. I'm a solo operator, a lone hombre if you follow." Mitch considered. "While I'm not a single individual in my circumstance, I'm not in the adoption business either. We have limited resources. Additional mouths to feed are only a drain on lessening resources." Caleb continued, "So we just walk away? Is that ok with you?" Walking away from these kids and their mother, not to mention the granddaughter who is now looking at us with those yearning puppy dog eyes saying – help me, mister, please help me in the most pathetic way possible, is nothing short of a death sentence for all of them." Mitch stared at him. "You think I don't know that?" Caleb asked. "So, what are we going to do about it?" "Damned if I know," Mitch shot back at him.

A while passed, and then Gerald returned to the main room. "Breakfast is ready," announced Gerald. Everyone could smell the aroma of eggs and even bacon. Five minutes later, all conversation ended as people were busily chewing. "So, where did you find bacon and eggs, Gerald?" asked Mitch as he finished his meal. "Freeze dryer," replied Gerald. "Come again?" said Mitch. "The power of freeze drying. I paid someone to freeze dry hundreds of pounds of meat, eggs, and a few other essentials as part of my supplies. Once you remove the water, they weigh next to nothing and take up a whole lot less space." Caleb spoke up, "The meals I served you guys in the pouches – remember? Same thing, except I bought mine at an outdoor store. Light as a feather until you add water and let the reconstitution happen." He continued, "If Gerald had as many pounds freeze-dried as he says he did, it would have cost him thousands of dollars. Buying your own freeze dryer saves you a ton of money outside of buying the raw materials themselves." Mitch looked dutifully impressed. "Freeze drying – who knew there was such a thing?"

Mitch resisted the urge to lick his plate. He could not remember the last time he had had bacon. As he looked around, he could see everyone else scraping every last bit off their plates. Except for Angeline, who appeared to be just picking at her food, and Caleb, who was adhering to his OMAD (one meal a day) regime. Gerald noticed too, "What is the matter, honey? Don't you like your bacon and eggs?" "You know I do, Gramps, but I am scared about what is going to happen to us," said Angeline. "Our house burned down, and the solar stuff won't work anymore, and you're going to get sick without your medicine," she said, stifling a cry that tried to escape her throat. She looked very unhappy, stood up, and went down the hall. Gerald got up and followed her.

Caleb looked at Mitch. "Do we need to talk some more, or have you decided what you want to do?" Mitch – "I don't have the answer right now. I say we defer making any decisions and see about getting out of here." Mitch addressed Gerald, who had come back from consoling his granddaughter. "Is the stairwell we came down the only entrance to this underground realm you have created?" Gerald, "I was concerned about getting trapped down here, so I had a hatch built at the far end which opens up into a garden shed I have in the backyard. I have not tried it yet but am hoping the fire didn't spread there and consume the shed." "Great. Let's go and see if we can get it open," replied Mitch. Caleb looked at Gerald, "Gerald, do you own a firearm?" Gerald, "As a matter of fact, I own several. What do you suggest for our foray into the land above?" Caleb replied, "Anything semi-auto, maybe a shotgun in 12 gauge for the immediate circumstance — can you accommodate that?" Gerald smiled. "Does a Benelli M4 clone do the job? I have a good Turkish-built version which was less than half the cost of an actual Benelli." Caleb replied, "As long as it is reliable and functional, it'll be fine. I presume you have ammunition?" Gerald stood and walked to a corner of the room which held what appeared to be a wooden wardrobe, but when the door was opened, Caleb could see a gun safe inside. Gerald punched in a combination and swung the door open. Inside was a number of long arms standing on their butt ends and shelves with handguns, ear defenders, and other miscellaneous shooting gear. Gerald withdrew a semi-automatic shotgun from the safe and performed a breech check on it. The black shotgun appeared to be equipped with ghost ring sights and a synthetic sling. A sideshot carrier was attached to the left side of the receiver, which gave him easy access to another six cartridges when filled. He turned and grinned, "Good to go." Caleb looked at Abigail. "By virtue of being a mother and specifically their mother, you get the babysitting duties. You might be a whole lot more capable than we understand at this point, but that will reveal itself later. For now, your primary help will be watching the children, including Gerald's granddaughter, as we scope out this hatch and the ground above. Are you okay with that?" Abigail smiled and nodded her agreement.

Gerald, to everyone's surprise, slid himself into a plate holder vest and put a bush hat on. Mitch looked at Caleb, "Perhaps there are more surprises yet to come." The three men, with their firearms, headed down the hall towards the spot where Gerald had indicated the hatch was placed. Sure enough, there was a steel rung ladder bolted into the brick wall leading upwards. "There's a combination lock in the hasp up there, so I need to go first," said Gerald as he snapped on a headlamp he had added to his gear. The other two men nodded. Gerald began his ascent of the ladder with his shotgun slung across his back. At the top of the ladder, Gerald worked the combination lock until it opened and then dropped it into a pocket. Sliding the locking bar out of the way, he slowly lifted the hatch. As the hatch was inside a shed, no light spilled in from above. Gerald continued pushing until the hatch was completely open and out of the way. He climbed further up the ladder and disappeared into the shed. Caleb went up next, followed by Mitch. Moments later, all three were inside an eight-by-twelve garden shed. The hatch had a set of four plastic milk crates glued or fastened in some other way to it, with what looked like miscellaneous junk inside them to hide its existence. The shed had a wheelbarrow, rakes, shovels, hoses, and other obviously gardening-oriented materials placed around inside it. The front doors were closed, but light spilled inside through the crack where they came together. Caleb advanced to the doors and, after confirming the other two men were ready, slid one open a crack. Looking out, he could see a smoldering hulk where the house used to be. The adjacent houses on the neighboring properties did not appear to have sustained any significant damage. The brick stairwell leading down to the survival bunker was fairly visible with the remainder of the house burned away, which meant future concealment was sketchy at best. In addition to his existing problems, Gerald now had another one added to his plate.

Not seeing anyone, Caleb slid the door fully open and stepped out into the morning sun. The smell of the fire strongly pervaded his nostrils as the remnants of wood, plastic, rubber, and other materials hung in the air. Smoke drifted upwards from a number of spots in the debris as there was no fire department anymore to come and put things out. "Guess we are lucky the whole neighborhood didn't burn down," remarked Mitch. Caleb and Mitch surveyed the area as their arrival yesterday had been at daylight's end. A wooden fence ran along the property line encompassing the large backyard. The deck where the BBQ had stood was entirely gone, but Mitch could still make out the shape of the grilling unit in amongst all the other wreckage. There were some trees standing in the yard behind the garden shed which led to the ravine Gerald had mentioned. Leaves from the poplar trees rustled in the light breeze that blew across the yard. "It doesn't look like our problem people are here any longer," Caleb commented. "Yeah, they must have left after thinking we burned to death inside," replied Mitch. "Nice folks, I am sure." Gerald looked at them both and then raised the topic that was occupying his mind: "Gents, what about my granddaughter?" Mitch and Caleb looked at one another and then at Gerald. "I have to tell you, Gerald, we are conflicted. I run a solo operation, and Mitch has a group he is part of, and if I am not speaking out of turn here, Mitch — he is not the sole decision maker for that group," responded Caleb. Mitch nodded his agreement. "She will die without me. I am running on borrowed time, and without me, she has zero chance. You both seem like decent men. I know the world has become a hard place and many have lost hope, but I would rather go to my grave knowing someone is willing to at least give her a chance of growing up," Gerald said. He looked defeated and dejected. Caleb stared at him a long time. "You didn't ask Abigail to take her on, why?" Gerald looked back at him. "I would have considered that in the time before the crash, but in this reality, we live in, strength matters more than compassion. All ideas of feminism and women's liberation went out the window about a day after things fell apart. She seems like a fairly capable person, but Angeline's odds of survival in the care of a lone woman are practically zero. You know that as well as I do." Caleb shrugged. "I can't argue with that. I think when we go back down into your refuge, Abigail is going to make a similar request to yours. She understands the ways of the world now and needs protection. I'm just not sure I am the best one suited to provide it."

Caleb looked at Gerald again. "Okay, as reluctant as I am to make this choice, I can't simply walk away from your granddaughter. Adding one more person to my situation would be a challenge but not an insurmountable one. I'll take her with me to my retreat." Gerald stepped forward and wrapped Caleb in a full-body hug. "Thank you, sir, thank you. You have no idea how much this means to me." Caleb could see tears forming in Gerald's eyes. Mitch looked at them both. "So, does this mean I am stuck with Abigail and her kids? That dog won't hunt!" he exclaimed. At the mention of dogs, perhaps coincidentally, there came a snarl from a direction none of them were looking. Turning on their heels, they could see a large mastiff-type dog snarling with its head down, advancing in their direction. Behind it was a pack of different breeds, mostly mongrels from the looks of them, forming a group of a dozen or so. The big dog's ribs were readily apparent as the pack looked to be starving from lack of food, which reinforced their courage in approaching humans. It was probably the same dogs that were around the BBQ last night. Gerald slipped off the safety and fired a round from his 12-gauge over the heads of the pack and yelled at them, "Get lost!" The pack retreated a short distance but then stopped. Caleb said, "I kind of wish you hadn't done that, Gerald. Now every ruffian, scavenger, and low-life in the area knows someone with a gun is here." Gerald shrugged. "Got any better ideas?" The pack of animals started inching towards the men again. None of the dogs had been injured by the loud noise, and hunger drove them mercilessly. Mitch reached inside his jacket and dug out a Barnett folding slingshot after slinging his rifle. "Cover me," he said to his companions as he loaded a steel ball bearing he obtained from somewhere on his person. Pulling the rubber tubing to full draw, he took aim at the mastiff. "Thwack!" The projectile made a loud smacking noise, hitting the growling animal right in the mid-chest. The dog yelped in pain and fear and spun to run a short distance. Already reloaded, Mitch nailed the next dog in the face and then released another ball bearing after that. Mitch kept drawing and releasing steadily. The impacted dog's bit at the sudden and unexpected pain hitting them, and the rest of the pack understood something bad was happening to them. Mitch kept up his barrage until the collective willpower of the pack broke and they fled past the burning wreckage of the house.

Caleb was impressed by the marksmanship and ability of Mitch and said as much. "Handy device for dealing with dogs, skunks, and other critters that have taken an interest in me," Mitch commented. The ball bearings are hard to come by, so sometimes I use marbles when I find them. "Handy indeed," agreed Gerald.

With the dog pack dispersed, at least for now, the men's attention returned to their original purpose in returning to the surface — surveying the damage and deciding what to do from here. There was no sign of the attackers from the night before, and the only sound audible was the wind blowing through the various trees in the area. Caleb turned to Mitch — "Okay, decision time. What is going to happen with Abigail and her two kids? I have agreed to take on Gerald's granddaughter — is there any possibility of those three returning with you to your location?" Mitch grimaced, "Yeah, I'll take them with me and make a case for them, but I can't guarantee anything. We have a council to decide things, and I am not technically even on the council. I act more as a ranger on the outside, scavenging for items we need. I don't like politics, and I don't like being indoors all day – I would rather be out in the world on my own." Caleb, "okay, it's settled – Angeline goes with me and the rest with you. What about you, Gerald? What are you going to do?" Gerald sighed and looked off into the distance. "I knew this day was coming, but now that it is here, I'm not happy about it. This world is merciless to the less than able-bodied, and I'm lucky to have lasted this long. I don't know how many Type I diabetics are left in the world, but there can't be many, and those that do exist are living on borrowed time. Let's go back into the shelter. I can give each of you some things that may help. I don't know how long I have before the insulin shock kicks in, but I do have some insulin in my refrigerator that probably has not spoiled yet. Let me get you equipped and on your way, and I will make my peace with my maker. I have a bottle of Jim Beam that I have been saving for a long time that might see the light of day."

Mitch and Caleb nodded their agreement to Gerald and headed back toward the garden shed. Minutes later, they were back down inside. "What did you see?" asked Rebecca. "We heard a gunshot – what was that about?" "Gerald tried to scare off a pack of dogs, and then Mitch really put the run on them with his slingshot," Caleb answered with a smile. "They won't be hanging around here again any time soon." "We were worried," Abigail commented. "Maybe those men from last night were still looking for us." Caleb replied, "There was no sign of them but that doesn't mean a whole lot. Since this shelter is no longer viable, we need to get moving. Mitch has agreed to take on you and your kids, and I am going to take over custody of Angeline." "Okay," responded Abigail. "I guess the kids and I have no voice in any of this. We are just helpless burdens to be carried about and have no say or choice in anything any longer. Welcome to the new world of women and children as mere property." She glared at Mitch and Caleb but spared Gerald any of her wrath.

Caleb had mixed feelings. On the one hand, he didn't want to be party to any of this and thought about just walking away. He had come into the city to hunt for a part he needed for his solar array and had gotten into a gunfight, a house fire, and suddenly had become guardian to a small child. Not at all what he had planned for. He had spent the last year on his own and liked it that way. Adding a young girl to the equation would dramatically change things for him. On the other hand, he reflected on all of the pain and suffering he had seen since the inward collapse of modern society and didn't know if he could live with adding to it. One small girl wouldn't eat much and would help get him through those days when loneliness made an appearance.

Caleb said, "Sorry, but you really don't have any say in this matter Abigail. Neither Mitch nor I am obligated to do anything for you and your kids or for Gerald's granddaughter. The fact that we have agreed to take you on is a gift and should be seen as such. If this is unacceptable, you can certainly be on your way and figure out your next steps." Abigail frowned and looked quite unhappy. The reality of her circumstances settled in, and her frown changed to a look of determination. "I guess it is what it is," she remarked. "Kids, let's get ready to go and see what our new home looks like." Gerald spoke up, "Gentlemen, I can provide each of you with some beef jerky and energy bars for the road, as well as other miscellaneous supplies if you would like." Both Caleb and Mitch acknowledged his offer and followed him to the small hallway where materials were stored.

Fifteen minutes later, everyone had ascended to the surface. With their beverage containers topped up with water and beef jerky in their pockets, Caleb and Mitch faced each other. Caleb addressed Mitch, "We started out as adversaries and now are parting as something resembling friends. Odd how things work out." "Odd indeed," replied Mitch. "Take care of yourself. Maybe someday we will run into each other again." "Thanks, you too," said Caleb. Caleb turned to Angeline, "Say good-bye to your grandpa. We're going to be on our way now." Angeline's eyes were red from the tears she had shed earlier but seemed to steel herself for the imminent departure. "I love you with all my heart, little one, but I can't take care of you anymore. Caleb is a good man and will watch over you. I have a date with destiny which I am going to keep," Gerald said to the little girl as he knelt in front of her. "Bye Grandpa," came the whispered response from the obviously distraught child. The two embraced for a long hug and then Gerald stood up. "You have the last of my family in your possession now; I hope you can raise her to adulthood and help her remember her family and where she came from," Gerald said to Caleb while looking straight into his eyes. "I will do my best, sir. Hopefully, we can dig our way out of this mess that has been created and return to something resembling what we had before," Caleb responded. At this point, Mitch, Abigail, and the two children headed out in the direction Mitch set, and Caleb and Angeline headed west. As Caleb walked, he looked over his shoulder and saw Gerald standing and watching his granddaughter leave for the last time.

CHAPTER THREE
THE RETREAT

Caleb and Angeline continued west. Their flight from the slavers had taken them far east inside the city and out of the industrial district Caleb had first entered in search of his burned-out part. Now he was forced to retrace his steps westward to his retreat, which meant going through the city again with the incumbent risks of doing so. Caleb looked at Angeline's footwear. She had white court shoes with red laces on. Definitely not the best thing for walking long distances. Fortunately, Caleb knew about an outdoor/workwear store just past the center of the city. If it wasn't too thoroughly pillaged, it might offer up a pair of hiking boots in her size and maybe a couple of sizes up from there for future use. Thinking like a parent already, he thought. Caleb continued walking with the young girl in tow behind him. She didn't say too much either due to the shock of her changing circumstances or perhaps being quiet was just her nature. Hoping for the latter, he thought. If she was a constant chatterbox, he would likely begin to resent her presence rather quickly. After a couple of hours of trudging, Caleb called a break. Spotting a couple of office chairs sitting on the road, who knows why in the heck office chairs were on a road, but 'whatever' he thought, they sat down. His water supply was in his CamelBak, and offering her drinks from his mouthpiece was not the most sanitary of options. She surprised him by sliding her child-sized backpack off her shoulders and taking an olive-green canteen out of it. She twisted off the cap and took a drink for herself. "Do you know where your mum and dad are?" he asked her. "Grandpa said they are in heaven waiting for me," she responded. "What about your brother?" he asked her next. "Oh, he's there too," she said with some confidence. "Do you know where heaven is?" he asked, continuing with the same line of questioning. "It's the place where all the good people go," Angeline replied with some conviction. Caleb sat pensively for a few minutes. If that answer served her purposes, he was not going to mess with it now.

Looking around, he scanned the road ahead and the streets heading north and south of where they sat. It amazed him how much debris had scattered about. Seemingly random bits of furniture and household materials lay about as if, in its final death throes, civilization had vomited the contents of people's homes and businesses outdoors onto the streets. Oddly, there did not appear to be any corpses in sight. You would think that with the 'big die-off,' as he tended to think of it, there would be bodies or at least skeletons everywhere. Where did everybody go? He remembered when the hyperinflation had gotten really bad; there was a lot of panic and people loading up vehicles and leaving. Leaving for where? he thought. The market collapse had been global in nature, and nowhere that had escaped the consequences. At least that he was aware of. He remembered being unsurprised by the failing of the modern economy as debt levels had gone parabolic and the central banks did the one thing they knew how to do – create more currency. Interest rates on the long end of the curve had risen steeply as the market demanded a higher and higher return on their capital, and governments demanded the Federal Reserve lower rates so their interest payments stayed manageable. When the black swan event arrived, and everyone knew there were several black swans circling, things just fell apart. Exponential debt growth had created exponential reactions to the failing system, and rapidly society came apart like a cheap suit.

Caleb believed it was the payment systems that had really accelerated the collapse. The lynchpin to society in Caleb's mind was 18-wheel tractor-trailer trucks. Practically everything everyone ate, wore, used, or worked with came on a truck. In the final days as things unfolded, there had been an issue with the payment system, and truck drivers couldn't access diesel for their trucks. Politicians were issuing one emergency order after another, but it was truck drivers' inability to put diesel fuel in their tanks that had really put the final nail in the coffin. Their company-supplied fuel cards stopped working completely. Without fuel, all transportation of goods just ended. Food didn't make it to grocery stores, fuel itself was not transported to gasoline stations, and cardlocks for farmers to get diesel for their equipment, and on and on. Everything ground to a halt. Truck drivers unhooked the trailers behind their rigs and abandoned them helter-skelter. They used what fuel they had left in their tanks to drive home to be with their families.

In his time in the military, Caleb remembered a lesson from one of his instructors — 'the rule of threes': three weeks without food, three days without water, three minutes without oxygen — all three led to death. He was pretty sure about the three minutes without oxygen rule — that was certain. Three days without water or three weeks without food — well, those were debatable, but he got the general idea of the expression. Using the number three made it easier to remember. Without a constant supply of new goods, the shelves emptied quickly, and the rule of threes became a reality for many people.

Seeing what was coming about two years prior after a long conversation with a good friend of his, Caleb decided to hedge his bets and do some preparation in case things went south. An early adopter of Bitcoin, he had made an embarrassing amount of money off what seemed, at the time, to be a silly if not outright foolish idea. Once the reality of his windfall had set in, he quietly resigned from his position where he worked and began prepping as his full-time job. He spent six months in his apartment reading article after article online and watching YouTube videos in an effort to rapidly ramp up his knowledge. In the same time period, he traveled south to attend a tracking school, a famous shooting school, an escape and evasion school as well as some others. His time in the military served him well, but he had only spent three years in that organization; he had acquired some skills but not nearly as many as he now wished he had.

During the upskilling and educational period, he purchased a small acreage on the edge of Harmony, a bedroom community outside of the city. Many of the 'preppers' online advised being at least an hour away by vehicle to escape the masses, but Caleb wanted access to materials he thought would continue to be available inside a city after a collapse. He invested a good amount of money in making his retreat less noticeable or nondescript so if looters or marauders came through, they would not see anything worth investigating. With the cessation of fuel deliveries and now the complete end of oil drilling, refined fuel production, and all other parts of the gasoline/diesel distribution system, getting fuel for a motorized vehicle was an impossibility. Caleb realized he was going to be on foot or bicycle for a long period, so being way out in the boonies was a no-go for him. In addition, he figured if society somehow got on its feet again, it would be in or near a city as opposed to somewhere out in the bush.

After offering some beef jerky her grandfather had given to him to Angeline, they got on their feet and started moving again. The sun bore down on them in a cloudless sky, and Caleb realized a head covering for the young girl was also in order. He didn't need her getting sunstroke in this situation or even a bad sunburn. The outdoor store he had thought about earlier was still an hour away. "Hey. Let me put this on you. It will keep the sun off your head." Caleb fashioned a triangle out of the bandanna he normally wore around his neck, making a bonnet to cover her head. She repositioned it slightly to make it more comfortable on her head. She smiled at him for the effort. Resuming walking, Caleb scanned ahead of them and every so often their back trail. Other than the occasional bird overhead, he didn't see any signs of life. After another hour of walking had passed, they stood outside of the outdoor/workwear business. Some of the windows were broken, and the front door was propped open. Caleb looked at Angeline. "Stay here. I am going to have a look. If anyone comes, call out to me from the doorway. Don't go anywhere else." She looked at him and appeared to understand his directions.

Caleb did a quick mag check and chamber check of his rifle. All good. As he approached the entryway, he was looking and listening to the best of his ability. The inside of the store was largely visible from the front door. Boxes with and without shoes and boots were strewn about. Obviously, he was not the first person to think of coming here for footwear. Scanning the store, he didn't see any immediate threats. Cautiously, he made his way inside as he worked to clear the room. Passing through the main portion of the store, he came to the doorway leading to the back of the store. It was a bit darker here but not worthy of his flashlight just yet. The rear of the store was much like the front. Boxes tossed everywhere and shoes littered the floor. Somewhat ironically, he saw a lot of what could be described as 'fashionable footwear' lying about. I guess in a societal collapse, fashionwear does not figure as highly, he thought to himself with a chuckle. Not finding any threats in the back of the store, he returned to the front and looked outside to see Angeline standing exactly where he left her. He called out to her to come into the store and join him.

Once inside, he had her sit down and take a sneaker off. Looking inside it, he found her size and then hunted for something appropriate. A few attempts and a couple of near misses later, he found a stack of boxes containing Adidas Terrex hiking boots for kids. They seemed to be comfortable for her, and luckily, her size was available. Caleb kept her sneakers, as she would only wear her new boots for an hour or so before blisters showed up. Her new boots would definitely need breaking in. He put the next two sizes up of hiking boots into his backpack for her. She was undoubtedly going to be growing bigger as she moved into her teen years. Angeline looked happy with her new footwear. "I like the green highlights," she commented as she admired them. "Good," replied Caleb. "Let's get out of here." "I'm hungry," came her reply. Caleb paused and unslung his pack again. Inside were some of the protein energy bars Gerald had given him. He opened a couple and handed her one. She polished it off quickly and looked at him. "Still hungry." He smiled and opened another bar, some sort of yogurt-covered bar with raspberry flavoring, and handed it to her. She accepted it and continued eating. Caleb re-slung his pack, took a drink from his drinking tube, and headed back outdoors. Angeline trudged along behind him, chewing on her bar. Looking at his watch and the angle of the sun, he figured they still had plenty of daylight hours left. They were averaging half the speed he normally moved at with the child-sized strides and child energy levels currently being expended. They were making progress nonetheless. There was no way they were going to make it all the way back to his retreat today; it was just too far. With this thought in mind, Caleb started looking for a place to bed down for the night before it got dark and avoid searching in the dark.

Continuing west, they passed the university buildings. He could see a column of smoke rising from inside the campus and took that to be a sign of life. He thought of coming back into the city at some point and perhaps taking up residence on campus. There were plenty of brick buildings that afforded some ballistic protection. Several of them were quite tall which would allow good overwatch by a sentry. The problem was – he was only one man. How would he recruit or attract others when there seemed to be so few people left and those who remained were fearful almost to the point of paranoia? His interaction with Mitch had been refreshing in how quickly they had overcome the fear that gripped most people these days. Mitch had made mention of heading to his acreage which was northeast of the city in a small bedroom community. Mitch had been short on details about exactly where it was, how many were there, and other salient points. Presumably, he was being careful as the world they now inhabited paid for caution and punished carelessness.

"Are we there yet?" asked Angeline, knocking Caleb out of his internal thought processes. "No, sweetie. We won't make it there today. Maybe tomorrow." She screwed up her face in displeasure. "I am tired of walking. Can't we take a car?" Caleb laughed out loud. "I would love to, Angeline, but working cars and gasoline are hard to come by these days. Plus, the batteries in any of the cars you see are long dead." She frowned. "I hate walking. It's boring." Caleb was about to reply when he spotted something. It was a wheelbarrow lying on its side on a patch of overgrown grass in front of one of the university buildings. Walking closer, he saw weeds and grass had grown up around it, obviously it had been there for a while. Up righting it, he kicked the pneumatic tire – it still had air in it! He looked at Angeline. "Want to ride for a while?" She laughed her agreement. "Well, get in," he replied. He picked her up and set her in the wheelbarrow. She lay back using her backpack as a pillow and put her feet with her new boots on the bottom of the barrow. Caleb laid his M1A across her lap and told her to hang on to it for him. He checked to ensure the safety was on before laying it down to avoid any unexpected mishaps. With that, he grasped the handles of the wheelbarrow, picked it up, and started walking. Due to her small size, it was surprisingly easy for him, and after a short distance, he became quite comfortable with his new transportation method.

The kilometer passed. As dinner time approached, Caleb's upper back was starting to protest loudly. The burden he was supporting in the wheelbarrow was wearing on him. Numerous times he had stopped to stretch the kinks out, but it was getting to the point of needing a longer break. Light as she was, the constant carrying of her weight and the wheelbarrow added up for the involved muscles. Angeline had definitely enjoyed the ride. At one point she had even fallen asleep. Now at the westernmost edge of the city, Caleb could see rolling hills of prairie grass with the periodic clump of trees ahead of him. The neighborhoods they had traversed were somewhat uniform in their destruction. A good number of houses had experienced fires, and one whole block was burned to the ground, but Caleb went around it on side streets as he did not want to inhale whatever toxic fumes might still be lingering about. He did see stray dogs once in a while and coyotes a couple of times. Caleb surmised coyotes were one species that would have taken advantage of the demise of the city – moving in from the surrounding area to hunt mice or stray house cats or whatever was still living in the city confines.

On the edge of the grasslands, Caleb saw a house that fit their needs for the night. He retrieved his rifle from Angeline and then unceremoniously poured her out of the wheelbarrow. "Hey!" she protested, but not too emphatically. Her legs were a bit wobbly after having ridden for so long, but within a minute she was moving about with ease. "We need to bunk down for the night," he told her. "That house over there looks like a good candidate." "You stay here, and I'll check it out. If anything happens here, call out." "Okay," she replied.

Doing his usual mag check and chamber check, Caleb walked towards the building. It was a long dark blue rancher-style house with big glass windows in the front and an attached two-car garage. The front face had a blend of river stone and flat rock along the base as trim. It was a style Caleb particularly liked. Its state of repair did not look too bad, and there was a lack of garbage or debris in the front yard. The grass was heavily overgrown of course, and there were no obvious trails or tracks in the grass, suggesting wild animals had not taken up residence. Caleb walked between it and the neighboring house to have a look in the backyard area. Oddly, neither property was fenced, which in the city was somewhat unusual. In the backyard, a green metal children's swing set hung idly with no breeze to move the hanging seats. The windows into the house were dark and still reflective of the west-setting sun. There were a number of large red pots in the backyard where someone had once planted flowers, but due to inattention were long dead. Caleb approached the back door, which was closed. A screen door was in place and not locked when he pulled it open. The door into the back of the house opened easily. He entered the quiet stillness of a long empty house. Once inside, he could see Angeline through a window standing on the road out front. There was a musty smell, dead air with too little ventilation for too long. The house was in some disarray but not overly much. Someone had left in a bit of a hurry but not a panic. Not hearing or seeing anything to give him concern, Caleb moved through the living room to the front door and opened it. "Come on in," he called out to Angeline. "What about the wheelbarrow?" she asked. "Just leave it. It isn't going anywhere," he responded. She made her way across the yard and onto the front stoop. "It's okay inside – come on in," he told her and ushered her into the house.

The far wall of the living room had a white brick fireplace built into it. "I'm going to check out the rest of the house and then we are going to look for some firewood," he told her. She plunked down into a living room chair and began waiting. Following his normal process, Caleb made his way through the three bedrooms, a couple of bathrooms, and to his surprise, a walk-in pantry. A pantry with canned goods still on the shelves! "Guess no one has looted this house yet," he said to himself. Going back to the living room, he removed his pack and put it on a loveseat in front of the windows. "What do you say we go get some firewood and make a fire in that fireplace and cook some hot food? I saw some interesting cans in the pantry." Angeline pulled herself away and wiped her eyes with her sleeve. "Ok."

An hour later, the two had accumulated enough firewood to keep the fireplace going for several hours and had retrieved some cans from the pantry. Caleb was amazed to find several cans of Irish stew on the shelves. There were no punctures or rust on the cans, and when he opened them with his travel-sized can opener, they smelled unspoiled. A long-handled, copper-bottomed pot from the kitchen cupboard and with a good bed of coals in the fireplace, soon the smell of simmering stew entertained their nostrils and made their mouths water. Caleb had not smelled anything so good in a long time. A little more searching for bowls and spoons, and the pair were soon enjoying a good hot meal. Caleb dumped another couple of cans in the pot, and both enjoyed tasty seconds. After sitting back and digesting for a while, Caleb got up and drew the mauve-colored curtains in the living room closed and went back into the kitchen and placed a chair under the doorknob of the back door. Not foolproof by any means – it would make a racket at least if someone tried to force their way in. With that idea in mind, he dug out some stainless-steel bowls he had seen and stacked them on the chair so if anyone decided to force their way in via that route, they would make a lot of noise, giving Caleb and his young charge time to get up and deal with whatever was coming through that point of entry. Caleb also drew whatever blinds and curtains he could to minimize any light coming out of their temporary abode.

. "Okay," he said to the young girl. "This would be good time to begin your education." She looked at him attentively. "If I pat the top of my head like this," Caleb started patting the top of his head, "that means you come to me. Get it?" She nodded. "If I raise a fist like this – you freeze where you are and don't move. Get it?" She nodded. "If I lower my hand like this, you get down on the ground and get out of sight as best you can. Understand?" Once again, she nodded. "Okay, we are going to do two or three new ones every day, so I don't have to call out to you for you to know what to do. Sometimes we have to be quiet. You get me?" "Grandpa told me sometimes children need to be seen and not heard," Angeline replied. He also said, "Silence could be good medicine, but I don't know what that means," she said with some seriousness. Caleb smiled. "Your grandpa was a wise man, young lady." Angeline looked like she was holding back tears at the mention of her grandpa. "It's ok, Angeline. If you want to cry, you don't need to hold back." With that permission, the tears began to flow as sobs escaped her. She came at Caleb in a rush and clutched onto him as sobs wracked her little body. Caleb knelt and hugged her for a long time until she had cried herself out.

"I think we should sleep in the living room," he said. She agreed. "I'm going to hunt down some blankets." Down the hallway, he found a linen closet with some cleaner-smelling blankets inside. He was surprised to find a Hudson's Bay wool blanket inside. "Going to be taking that with us," he said to no one in particular. Genuine wool blankets were a rare find and highly desirable. Wool kept you warm whether it was dry or wet — unlike any of the more modern fabrics. Most of Caleb's undergarments were made of merino wool. He had specifically purchased those after watching some videos on outdoor adventurers. 'Cotton kills' was a common refrain from those individuals. He had a few pairs of cotton briefs, which he wore in the summer to save his good ones for the colder months. Heading back into the living room, he set up a bed for himself on the couch and for Angeline on the loveseat. He placed more wood on the fire and was about to sit down when he had a sudden inspiration. "I wonder if they have anything else interesting in the kitchen cabinets?" Angeline looked at him.

"Nothing," he said. "Just talking to myself." Caleb headed into the kitchen. Over the sink or over the fridge, he thought, and reached up to the less accessible cabinets. "Jackpot," he said out loud. Inside were a collection of half-filled and unopened liquor bottles of various sorts. Gin, rye whiskey, vodka, schnapps, and others filled the space. "Hmmm," he said to himself. "What goes well after Irish stew?" Deciding on some apple brandy, he found a glass in the cupboard and wiped out the inside with a tea towel he found in a drawer.

Walking back into the living room, he sat down with his prize and poured himself a glass. "What's that?" Angeline asked. "Something you're too young for!" was his immediate response. "Why?" was her next and expected query. "It's alcohol, and you are not old enough for alcohol. Maybe someday you will be able to have some, but not today." She pouted her displeasure. "I'm tired of just drinking water all the time." "Well, let me see," said Caleb as he headed back to the kitchen. As luck would have it, he found a can of drink crystals. "Do you like Wild berry?" he called out into the living room. "Yes, please," came her response. "Then bring your canteen as there is no running water in this house." Minutes later, they were both sitting in front of the fire enjoying their respective beverages.

After a while, the fire began to die down, and fatigue caught up with them. Caleb got up and led Angeline to the love seat where she was going to sleep. He helped pull off her new boots and then covered her with a blanket. "We'll sleep with our clothes on in case we need to get up and leave suddenly," he told her. At this point, she was tired enough that she didn't care anyway. Settling into the pillow he had found for her, she smiled at him and quickly drifted off. Caleb walked to the front door of the home and set some objects against the door that would fall over if anyone tried to force their way in. He made his way to the couch after putting a few more pieces of wood on the fire to bank it. He then closed the chain-link spark arrestor in front of the fireplace. Pulling his own boots off tired feet, he sat back on the couch with his remaining brandy. Not the manliest drink, he thought, but it was tasty. Laying his rifle alongside the couch, he settled into his own pillow. Tomorrow would be a long, hard day. The only easy day was yesterday, was his last thought with a chuckle. Sleep quickly ensued.

Daylight and the need to urinate woke Caleb in the morning. Full bladder awareness broke into his dream state, and slowly he opened his eyes. Across from him, Angeline slept soundly in the carefree slumber of the innocent. Caleb looked past her to the divide in the curtains where daylight shone into the house. Swinging himself up and putting his stocking feet onto the floor, he stretched and rubbed the sleep out of his eyes. Reaching over, he grabbed a boot at a time and pulled them over well-used but not particularly odorous socks; gotta love that merino wool. Not bothering to lace his boots, he picked up his rifle and made his way to the front door. Being careful not to make a racket, he unstacked the pieces of pottery and glass bowls he had placed in front of the door and then went outside. It was another near-cloudless day. He felt the back of his neck, and sure enough, there was some angry red skin there from yesterday's journey in the sun. Stepping a few paces away from the door, he unzipped and provided the shrubbery alongside the house with some much-needed moisture. Just as he finished, he heard his name being called from inside the house. "Caleb. Are you there?" He finished, turned, and headed back in. "Yes, I'm here. Just having a look outside."

Angeline had gotten up and put her boots back on. "I have to pee," she announced to him. "So, what do you want me to do about it?" he asked. "Where do I go?" she asked him. "Anywhere you want. It's a big world. Dealer's choice." She stared at him a bit perplexed. "Should I go in the bathroom?" Caleb could see she hadn't fully learned to appreciate the vastness of the great outdoors yet. "Sure, the bathroom sounds fine." "Where do I get toilet paper?" she asked. Caleb – "First, see if there's some left in there and if there isn't, then I have a partial roll in my backpack," he told her. She headed down the hallway, seemingly satisfied with his answer. Five minutes later, they had themselves sorted out and walked back to the road where the wheelbarrow used to be. In the night, someone had removed it. Caleb studied the ground where it previously sat. He could see boot tracks approach it and then wander around a bit before starting off in a new direction behind the single track the tire of the wheelbarrow made. The trail did not return to where it had come from but headed south. Caleb could tell from looking at the tracks a size ten-or-eleven-man's boot belonged to the individual who had taken their wheelbarrow. Caleb did a slow three-sixty examination of the area. There was no motion or sign of life anywhere, but he had that distinct feeling of being watched. "What's going on?" asked Angeline. "We are being watched," Caleb replied to her. "By who?" she asked. "Don't know," came the reply. "We need to get a move on."

Caleb checked his firearm and adjusted the position of his pack on his back. "How do your feet feel this morning?" he asked Angeline. "Okay, I guess," came the response. "Let's get going. We should make it to the retreat today if we maintain the pace." She nodded her understanding and adjusted her kid-sized pack on her back. "Let's go." Caleb took the lead and started walking. His level of vigilance, although generally pretty high when out and about, was a notch higher today knowing someone was in their vicinity with unknown intentions. It was doubtful someone needed a wheelbarrow in the night to move something. Unless whoever took it had a burning need for a garden implement, there was another motivation at play. Unknown at this point but worrisome. Caleb had drawn the curtains last night but knew smoke would have come out of the chimney. Not visible particularly in the dark, but the smell would have carried. Things burned from time to time, but barring a forest fire, smoke was usually a sign of life or even civilization. Caleb knew he should backtrack and look for tracks around the house they had slept in, but surrendered to the desire to get out of the area. He knew once they got closer to his retreat, they were going to have to do some doubling back to check for pursuers, and that was going to take some time, and he didn't know what shape Angeline's feet were going to be in after a full day's trek.

Caleb knew from experience he was a little over four hours from home. That was walking on his own. He added an hour for bringing Angeline along and another hour to do an SDR (surveillance detection route), a fancy way of saying checking behind you for followers. Add in a short break for Angeline to eat lunch and he was looking at a full day. Assuming Mr. Murphy didn't show up and throw his usual monkey wrench into things. As in previous days, the sun was starting to bear down upon them relentlessly. It hadn't rained for at least a couple of weeks, and the grass underfoot was looking a bit brown. Angeline was doing a good job of keeping up in her new boots, but Caleb reminded himself to check the soles of her feet when they stopped for a break. He remembered an old trick of rubbing bar soap onto the bottom of socks when walking long distances, and he had a small bar in his toiletry kit in his pack. An hour into their hike, Caleb called a stop. "Look over there," he said, pointing off in the distance. Standing at the edge of a small copse of trees was a tawny colored doe and her fawn. The fawn still had young deer spots, and it stayed close to its mother's side. "I thought they were going to be hunted out when things first fell apart," he said to Angeline. "People were desperate for food, and every Tom, Dick, and Harry with a rifle and a truck was out looking for deer." "What does deer taste like?" Angeline asked him while staring at the two beautiful animals. "Well, it doesn't taste like chicken. That's for sure," he laughed. "It's kind of like beef but it really depends on how you cook it," he shared. "It has been a long time since I had any venison; that's the correct name for deer meat," he told her. "I don't really remember all that well." "Are you going to shoot them?" she asked, looking concerned for the fate of the deer. "No, honey. We have a long way to go and we have no way to carry the meat and I think I'd rather see that fawn grow into adulthood and make more deer," he answered. "Good," she replied, looking somewhat happier. As if they had heard about their possible destiny, the two deer flicked up their white bushy tails and disappeared into the trees.

The pair walked for another hour, and Caleb called for a stop. He had been taking sips from the tube of his CamelBak, but Angeline had yet to take her canteen out. "Need to hydrate, honey," Caleb said to the young girl. Dutifully, she unslung her pack and took the canteen out. "Have a good drink; the water is better inside of you than inside of the canteen," he told her. "I have a good well with clear water at my place, so we don't need to save any right now. It shouldn't be too much longer until we get there." "Let me see your feet," Caleb instructed her. Angeline sat down on the ground and pulled off her boots and then her green and yellow socks. Caleb gently examined her feet one at a time. There were some slightly red areas, and one heel looked a little suspect, but so far, no blisters. He had already taken his bar soap out. "Put your socks back on, and I am going to put some soap on the bottoms." "Why?" she asked. "It will help prevent blisters. Have you ever had a blister?" Caleb asked her. "Not yet," she said with a small smile. "Good," said Caleb and dug out a couple of energy bars for her to snack on. Ten minutes later, they were walking again. The rest of their journey passed uneventfully outside of a coyote checking them out for a few minutes.

As they got to the top of a rise, Caleb stopped and sat down. Angeline sat beside him. He dug his monocular out of his belt pouch and began to examine their back trail. There had been some weaving and winding as they avoided obstacles, but the line was overall pretty straight in the direction they had come. Laziness had overcome him, and the thought of spending an hour doubling back to check for pursuers did not appeal to him. He decided to scope out the trail behind him for a half hour as he sat down and rested. Angeline was proving to be a good traveling companion as she sat still beside him and made little to no noise as she looked at their surroundings. After carefully viewing their back trail and all of the visible spots an adversary could be waiting in, he was satisfied they were in the clear. He turned and looked at his young charge. "Extend your arm and put your fingers together like this." Caleb demonstrated with his own arm. "Now put the sun on top of your fingers and make them horizontal under the sun. Next, count the number of fingers between the sun and the horizon. Each finger counts as fifteen minutes. Four fingers equal an hour. Understand?" She made the same action as him. "What if your fingers don't fill up the space?" she asked. "Well, then you estimate by moving your hand down once or twice and adding up the fingers. Right now, I see one, two, three, four handspans until the sun meets the horizon or about four hours. Is that what you get?" Angeline moved her hand up and down a few times, obviously counting under her breath. "Yes, four hours. I get it!" she exclaimed. "It's harder the higher the sun is in the sky, but it gives you a rough idea at least. In case you don't have a watch, you can make a good guess." Caleb smiled at her enthusiasm. Having someone to teach all of his various survival skills could be a fun project. Angeline seemed to be more on the serious side, which suited him well. Too much whining or crying would get on his nerves and make him regret agreeing to bring her with him.

"Ok," he said. We're about fifteen minutes from home. "Let's go." They both got to their feet and began walking. Sure enough, within fifteen minutes he could see his place. Caleb had taken the approach of 'hiding in plain sight' for his retreat. The last house on the road they trudged down, his place was certainly nothing to look at. From the outside, it looked ramshackle and unkempt. He had piled a bunch of lumber and tires in the front yard behind a leaning fence he had built. The fence was only waist high and more of a definition of a property line than a means of keeping anyone either in or out. The tires were actually buried on edge and were taken from large tractors. The way he had them placed; they would provide stout resistance to anyone trying to ram their way in with a truck. The side yard had barrels standing on end – most appearing fairly rusted out and several dead cars parked among them. What couldn't be seen was the contents of the barrels. He had filled each of them with rocks and placed them seemingly haphazardly, but in reality, were carefully placed to create a barrier against vehicles. The other side of his yard was bordered by a narrow strip of grass and the high fence his neighbor had built in disgust to hide the mess that was Caleb's yard. The back yard was not much better with a couple of run-down sheds sitting out back and some twisted trees growing out along the edges of the fence line. The house itself was a single story of faded and peeling white paint with only a few windows. It was one of the most unappealing houses he had ever seen. Bits of trash lay about, and the gravel driveway was pitted with potholes. It was exactly as Caleb wanted it to be. Standing at the end of the driveway, he looked at a number of carefully placed pieces of debris. None of them appeared to have moved. Moving closer he looked for his other early warning signs he had placed to detect whether or not his residence had been visited in his absence. Nothing looked out of place. Arriving at the exterior door of his house, he flipped up a wooden cover which concealed a keypad. Typing a nine-digit code into it, he heard the hidden deadbolt within the door slide out of the way. Looking over his shoulder at Angeline, he beckoned, "Come on in."

Angeline followed him into the house. Caleb closed the door behind her and bent down to take off his boots in the mudroom. Angeline just stared. The inside was the virtual opposite of what the outside portrayed. Caleb smiled. The craftsmen he had hired from a number of different trades had earned their pay.

CHAPTER FOURTH
Mitch

As Caleb headed west, Mitch led his small band to the north. Abigail and her kids fell into a line walking behind him. This is a mistake, he thought to himself. Looking over his shoulder as he walked, he examined his new responsibilities. Abigail was attractive, with the accentuated slimness most women had these days, with the reduced calories everyone suffered. The kids seemed all right as far as kids went. Most of the really obnoxious kids had not survived this long in the new world. The degree of entitlement and spoiled behavior the obnoxious kids displayed tied right into the type of parents who would not be ready for this new existence. Overly weak or sickly children had been the first to go after a number of various illnesses swept through surviving populations. The resilient and robust had survived the culling, and only the healthiest had endured. When he got back to his acreage, Mitch was going to have to explain the new additions to the group. 'This might not go over well,' he thought. When it came right down to it, every mouth wants to be fed, and the differential between calories consumed and the ability to generate calories was the calculus all were subject to. On the other hand, there had been a lack of children being brought into the world over the past year, and no one had the extra resources needed to care for them. Without children, there was no future to fight for, and although these two kids were not babies, they were young and essentially represented the next generation. As he walked, Mitch formulated arguments for adding these three to the population at the acreage and also tried to anticipate the arguments he knew would be posed to refuse their entry. So far, the group had not had to push anyone outside of their gates. They had largely avoided contact with outsiders, in part to avoid disease but also to avoid the type of decision he was going to be forcing them into now. Mitch wondered if the group had the necessary steel in their spines to make this kind of hard decision. It's fine when it's theoretical, but when you have to look in the face of young innocents and knowingly push them out to their demise, it wasn't going to be all that easy. He knew he had already failed personally when faced with the decision regarding the three following him now. He couldn't bring himself to turn his back on them and walk away knowing what awaited them. The world might be a much crueler place than it was, but at what price did he surrender his humanity?

Mitch was pulled out of his internal dialogue by Abigail. "Where are we going and how long will it take to get there?" she inquired. "For me, alone, it's about a six-hour hike," he replied. "With you and the kids – I don't know. Probably at least a full day." "What are you going to do about food?" she asked. Mitch noticed how quickly food had become 'his problem.' "I don't know, what are you going to do?" he fired back at her. "Well, the kids are going to get hungry and need to eat something," she replied without offering any solution. "Did Gerald not give you energy bars and jerky?" Mitch asked. Abigail stared at him. "Right," came out of her mouth. She had probably forgotten about that. Mitch turned his back on her and kept walking. He could hear some grumbling but ignored it. Looking off in the distance, he could see another pack of dogs. He wondered what they ate every day and how daring they were going to get. Starvation drove animals to extreme behaviors as well. When you were hungry, rational thought and reasonableness diminished for both people and animals. The pack of dogs, as if they had heard his thoughts, stopped and turned to look at him and his companions. The lead dog looked to be some sort of Labrador or similar breed; Mitch wasn't really a 'dog' guy and had a hard time distinguishing the various breeds. In unison, the pack turned and started moving towards him, Abigail, and the kids. "We might have a situation developing," he said to the woman and her kids. "Do you still have that handgun Caleb loaned you?" he asked Abigail. "No, he took it back," she answered. "I have my twenty-two, but I'm almost out of ammo for it." "Ok, let's head towards that building," he replied, pointing at a small strip mall immediately in front of him. "Don't run," he told them. The dog pack will interpret that as prey behavior, and it will incite them. The small group walked steadily towards the convenience store on the end of the strip mall. The dogs were still a couple of blocks away but approaching nonstop.

Pushing open the glass door, they entered a store that had been completely looted. The shelves were bare except for old magazines, phone cords, and other equally useless items in the world they inhabited. Mitch spotted a desiccated corpse on the floor in front of a drink cooler, the first dead body he had seen in a while. The man, as best he could tell from his size and attire, was missing a portion of the back of his head. I guess he really needed that Slurpee, he thought to himself with a little dark humor.

He turned and pressed the glass front door closed and looked for something to barricade the doors with. "Here, help me push this" he said to Abigail and started to shove a wooden lottery kiosk in front of the doors. "Kids, find stuff to pile in front of the doors" he directed. Outside, through the glass windows, he could see the pack approaching. With Abigail's help they dragged some other display racks and piled them in front of the doors to reinforce their barricade. The kids brought smaller items and tossed them on the pile. As they worked the dog pack arrived. Between sixteen and eighteen dogs gathered outside of the store. Their constant movement made them hard to count. All of them looked mangy and dirty. Some had open wounds in their fur and most wore collars from previous owners. They moved to the doors sniffing and nosing around in an effort to gain entry. Mitch had his rifle at the ready and was considering putting rounds through a few of them but was also aware of the scarcity of his ammunition. It became obvious after a few minutes the dogs were not going to be able to get inside. Mitch relaxed in his posture and turned to Abigail and the kids "They can't get in, but we can't get out." "What about the back door?" asked Abigail. "Yeah, I was thinking about that myself – let's go and take a look."

Mitch wove his way through the store with Abigail, Trent, and Rebecca following him. The back room was as much of a mess as the front part. Knocking boxes out of the way they made their way to the solid-steel door at the end of the small hallway leading outside. The door was deadbolted shut. Mitch gripped the door handle and threw open the deadbolt. Slowly he opened the door and managed to get it open about three inches before it stopped. Something was on the ground outside of the door preventing it from fully opening. Backing up a bit Mitch slammed his shoulder into the door to get it to move. No such luck. Abigail moved closer "I can help." Together they both threw their weights into the door in an effort to get it open. Whatever was on the opposite of the door was either bigger or heavier than they were. "Hang tight" Mitch said to Abigail and headed to the men's room. Inside he saw a mirror mounted on the wall over the sink. Pulling out his knife he slid it under the edge of the mirror and pried. With a little effort he managed to pry it off of the wall. Carrying the mirror with him he returned to the back door. Abigail got out of the way so Mitch could get close to the three-inch opening. Holding the mirror in his hand Mitch extended his arm out the opening and turned the mirror so he could what was blocking the door. As soon as he had the angle right, he saw a vehicle, some sort of a delivery van parked right outside of the rear door. Someone had backed the van to where it was. Due to the angle at which it sat; he was unable to see the driver's door. He very much doubted anyone was inside of it! Pulling his arm back in he set the mirror down against the wall. "We are blocked in by a delivery van" he told Abigail. "There is no way we can push it away with the door. This option is out."

Abigail suggested, "Maybe the dogs are gone by now. Let's go have a look." Mitch nodded and walked back out to the front of the store. The pack was still there milling about. With the return of people to the door, the dogs began barking again. "How many bullets do you have?" asked Abigail. "Rounds," Mitch replied. "Bullets are what come out of the end of the barrel, and I have ten in total." She spoke again, "Why so few? Shouldn't you have more?" Mitch said, "I had more but used some of them before I met you. I also used some in dealing with those slavers who were trying to gain entrance to the house we were in, or have you forgotten that? Ammunition has weight, and when you are walking cross-country, you try to minimize how much you carry." "What about a warning shot to scare them away?" she asked. Mitch responded, "That might work, but if it doesn't, I have just wasted a round. I have thought of shooting one of them and reducing their number, but as they appear to be starving, it would probably set off a feeding frenzy and keep them here." Mitch said, "I have another idea. Give me a minute." Going back to the rear of the store again, Mitch began opening doors to rooms. As he was in the last store in the strip mall, there was a chance of a roof hatch being inside. Five minutes of searching and there was no sign of one. Mitch walked back out front. "No luck – I was looking for a roof hatch."

Outside, the dogs yipped, snarled, and barked. They could hear and smell their prey inside but had no way to get at them. Young Rebecca spoke up, "Why don't we hide?" Mitch and Abigail both looked at her. "We are hiding; they can't see us in here, and we're safe from them." Rebecca continued, "Not really. They can hear us and smell us. Why don't we go into the back and sit really still and close the door? That way they can't hear us and can't smell us, and they'll think we are gone." The two adults looked at each other. "Sure. Might work. It's not like we have a bunch of other options at this point in time," replied Abigail with a shrug. Mitch nodded and led the group to the back of the convenience store, and entered a small office. It was dark inside as the power had been out for over a year now, but he pulled out his flashlight and led everyone inside. There was a desk in the corner with an office chair as well as some folding chairs. Abigail and the kids opened the folding chairs and sat down. Rebecca had pulled the door closed behind her as she entered. "Ok, so now I guess we wait," said Mitch. Everyone shifted in their seats in an effort to get comfortable. "Can we talk?" asked Trent. "Trent, I think we should just sit quietly for a while," responded Abigail. "It shouldn't be too long. Besides, I heard somewhere dogs can hear forty times better than people, so we are going to need to be quiet to convince them we are gone."

Time passed. Mitch left his flashlight on, so it wasn't pitch black in the room as the group waited; he was tempted to switch it off to save the battery, but his concern for the children and the fear they were feeling changed his decision. Looking at his watch, Mitch decided to let at least 45 minutes, or an hour, go by before going outside to check. After thirty or so minutes had passed, Rebecca piped up, "I need to pee" to no one in particular. "Can you hold a little longer?" asked Abigail. "I was already holding when we came in here," she replied in the whiniest voice Mitch had heard yet coming from her. "Okay, let's go see what the bathrooms are like," her mother replied. "What about you, bud?" Mitch asked Trent. "You need to go?" Trent nodded his agreement. "Okay, how about you and I go and check out the guys' bathroom?" Everyone got up and left the office. The washrooms were just outside of the office. Mitch pushed open the door and was hit immediately with a wave of really bad smells. Trent pinched his nose with his thumb and forefinger and looked at Mitch. "Buddy, we are going to have to tough this one out. I know it smells awful, but we really don't have much of a choice right now." Each went to a urinal to do their business. Minutes later, they made their escape from the reeking room. In the hallway, they rejoined the girls. "That was disgusting," exclaimed Abigail. "No argument there," responded Mitch. "Let's go and see if we're still captive inside of here." Quietly, the small group walked to the front door. Looking through the glass windows, they couldn't see a single dog. "They could still be in the general area, so let's move this stuff out of the way as quietly as we can and then venture outside for a look," suggested Mitch. Over the next five minutes, everyone lifted and carried the items they had placed to form a barrier back into the aisles of the store. Eventually everything was out of the way. With his rifle in his left hand, Mitch pulled open the glass door of the convenience store and stepped out. No sign of the dog pack.

"Come on," he said to the others who were still inside, "time to move." With that, everyone exited and reformed. Mitch looked at his small team. "Everyone take a drink of their water and adjust your packs. We have a long way to walk, and we have wasted too many hours already dealing with dogs." All three of them did as suggested and soon were ready to go. Mitch said, "I'll take point, and Abigail, please take the rear. Everyone, keep your wits about you and watch for that pack. Who knows where they are now and whether or not they will come back? We'll seek refuge in a building again if we have to, but getting surprised out in the open by them would be bad." The kids and Abigail seemed to understand.

As the group walked, blocks passed. Luckily, the dogs did not make a re-appearance. Perhaps they had found easier prey elsewhere. As they covered ground, Mitch could see the international airport to his left. He remembered taking flights in and out of that airport before the crash. Odd, he thought to himself. Who would have known looking out of the window of the Boeing 737 he was arriving in would give him a view of this exact road he was walking on presently but in an entirely different world? In his past life, Mitch had been an Internal Auditor for a large company and would occasionally travel to other locations of the company for audits. Not a glamorous job, but a necessary one inside of the company. Mitch wondered if anyone he worked with was still alive and if so – where were they now? As they came adjacent to the end of the airport property, Mitch spotted a

Princess Auto retail store off to his right. He had planned to stop in there to look for some tools the group back home needed. He stopped and looked at his small band. The kids looked worn out already; Abigail looked fine, but that might just be a brave exterior, he thought.

"I want to stop at that Princess Auto you see over there," he said, pointing. "I'm hoping there are some things I need inside. If we can find a place to bed down, perhaps we can stay there for the night and head out in the morning." Everyone looked somewhat hopeful at the prospect of stopping for the night. Mitch realized they really had not had much to eat today, and there had been a minimum of complaining about it. This made him appreciate some of the apparent toughness that had been instilled in Abigail and the kids. Life had been hard since things went south, and people had little patience for complaining or bitching anymore. They tacked east as they marched toward the auto parts store. Mitch knew auto parts was really a misnomer, as Princess Auto had become an almost everything store — it carried all manner of tools, small engine items like cement mixers, pressure washers, and a ton of other things. It was probably more accurately described as a general store but without any foodstuffs.

Ten minutes later, they were standing in front of the building. The formerly electric doors were stuck in the open position, and the inside was a jumble. Many people other than Mitch had decided to make an expedition here in their hunt for miscellaneous items to aid in survival. Mitch edged his way in among the broken boxes and various items laying about. The store was north-facing but had a fair number of westerly-facing windows, so sufficient sunlight was streaming in to see most of the store. The racking was still standing, but many of the racking's contents had ended up on the floor, making it hard to navigate. Abigail called out to him, "Do you want us to come in or stay out here?" Mitch considered for a moment and then walked back towards her. As he approached, he pulled out a red Fox 40 whistle on a breakaway lanyard. Lifting it over his head, he handed it to her. "Everyone has one of these where I live. We have a system of whistle blows we use to communicate. I know you don't know any of them, so just give a few good blasts on it if you need help." "Would Princess Auto have whistles inside?" she asked. "I don't know, but I'll have a look," replied Mitch.

"Good thinking," he said to her as he turned to go back inside. He was stopping in at this particular store to look for some galvanized hook and eye turnbuckles. A project they were working on back at the acreage required them. He also wanted to find some rivets and a hand rivet gun — a special request from Rick, the closest thing he had to a friend at the acreage. Rick was working on a solar oven project and needed a rivet gun for some part of that project.

Abigail and the kids sat down to wait; Mitch turned and headed inside. As he had previously seen, the place was a mess. Successive waves of looters, foragers, and scavengers had made their way through. Mitch headed to the section where the items on his mental list might be located. When he got to the aisle where he anticipated the first items were, he was relieved to see a good number of products still hanging off the display rack. He pushed items on the floor out of his way with his boots and got closer. As luck would have it, there were still several turnbuckles of varying sizes there. Mitch pulled down a mixture of sizes and put them in a shopping basket he had picked up on the way in. Next, he headed over to the outdoors section and managed to find a smaller-sized backpack into which he dropped the turnbuckles. He then dug the copper wire out of his inside pocket; it had been rubbing against his rib cage as he walked. It had been annoying him. He dropped a few other items from inside pockets into the backpack as well. Next up was the rivet gun. He remembered those being near the front of the store and headed in that way. After a good ten minutes of digging through the mess, he had not located what he was looking for. Why am I thinking like a customer? he thought to himself. With that thought, he headed to the back of the store and through the swinging doors into the rear of the building.

As a customer, he had never been in the back of a Princess Auto. It was dark and disorganized. There was a lot of stuff in boxes and on pallets. Hmmm, Mitch thought. This could be a long job. He turned around and went back out to the front of the store where flashlights were sold. Luck smiled upon him as there were still some flashlights in their original packaging. Most of the better ones had been pillaged, but there were some lower-quality models available. Next up were batteries. Heading over to the battery rack display, it had been pretty thoroughly cleaned out – no surprise there. On the bottom of the shelf were some large

6V Energizer lantern batteries. A couple of the low-quality lights left on display had been lantern lights. Mitch picked up three of the batteries and headed back to the flashlight shelf. As most batteries had a ten-year shelf life, he was fairly certain he could make them work. Five minutes later, he was in possession of three lantern lights in addition to his personal flashlight.

Going out to the entrance, he approached Abigail and her kids. "Hey, I could use a hand searching; you willing to help out?" The looks of boredom on their faces disappeared with the prospect of having something interesting to do. Handing each of them a battery-powered lantern, they headed back inside. As they walked, Mitch did his best to describe what he was looking for. None seemed to really understand what he was describing, but at the least, they could open boxes and dig things out. Almost at the back, Mitch halted. "Abigail, can your kids manage a knife? They are going to need to cut packing tape on boxes to get them open, and I don't think we need anyone needing stitches." Abigail considered. "I'm comfortable with Rebecca handling something sharp, but not so sure about Trent." "Mom!" came the protest from Trent. "I can do it. I know I can."

Abigail replied, "Yeah, and if you make a mistake, who is going to sew you up? Where are the antibiotics going to come from for the infection? Remember what happened to Danny?" Trent frowned at the memory. "What happened to Danny?" Mitch inquired. "He cut his foot with an axe. We sewed him up, but the wound got infected. He lingered for a while, but eventually, it killed him. We didn't have any antibiotics to give him," replied Abigail. "In this world, even a small cut can be fatal, which is why I am not going to let either one of them open boxes. I will cut the tape and let them unpack them while searching for your item." Mitch nodded his agreement.

The group of four made their way into the back area. For the next two hours, Mitch and Abigail opened boxes, and the kids pulled out item after item with a "Is this it?" call to Mitch. Some of the items were so ridiculously not it that they burst into laughter, and it became a bit of a game to them. For the first time since meeting them, Mitch got to see smiles on their faces. Finally, Abigail hit pay dirt – "This must be it!" she yelled to Mitch. A blue handle handheld rivet gun with rivets in the packaging was held aloft in her hand. The packaging clearly identified what it was and removed any doubt. Everyone sat down with the news of the find. "Who's hungry?" asked Mitch of the group. All three held up their hands. Mitch — "When I was searching for batteries, I thought I saw some bags of chips or Doritos buried under some other stuff. I don't know if they are still good, but it might be worth a shot." All three stood immediately at the suggestion of food. A minute later they were following him out to the source of much-desired calories. Pulling some large bags of cleaning rags off of where he spied the chips, a treasure trove of chip bags was exposed. The kids made an immediate grab for bags of chips, but Abigail stopped them. "Let me check the expiry dates on those before you go eating them," she said. Mitch commented — "Those dates were really not expiry dates," he explained. They were 'optimal freshness' dates. The chips would be edible long after those dates had passed. Abigail looked skeptical but accepted his explanation. Opening her own bag of salt and vinegar chips and digging into them revealed her lack of concern after Mitch's explanation. Everyone was loudly crunching their snacks and then opening seconds and thirds. Mitch realized how hungry he was himself and admired the restraint the other three had shown in not complaining about it. His respect for Abigail and her two children grew for a second time today.

After finishing, everyone put bags of chips into their backpacks to eat later. It was amazing how such a little thing as a bag of ranch or ketchup-flavored chips could be so satisfying to a hungry belly, thought Mitch. Abigail was looking around the store. "Is there anything else we might need?" she asked. "Not that I can think of," responded Mitch. Interesting how she is thinking in terms of what 'we need' already, Mitch thought. Mitch knew there was a chance the leadership at the acreage might just send her on her way with her kids behind her. Hard decisions had to be made, and the calculation of what someone brought to the table versus how much food they would consume was part of every decision. Kids didn't eat as much as adults but contributed considerably less. They needed supervision and protection fairly consistently and tended to get sick more easily. Mitch decided to forego any more thinking on the topic as it made him uneasy. He knew the decision point was approaching rapidly and did not want to be around for an unhappy outcome.

Mitch headed toward an adjoining office off the floor of the store. Pushing the door open and sweeping the room with his flashlight, he saw a mid-sized room with a desk and chair. There was another chair facing the desk – obviously some sort of supervisor's or team lead's office. Looking over his shoulder, he said to Abigail and the children – "we can stay in here for the night." They picked up their backpacks and headed over. "I am going to wander around the store and see if I can find anything soft to lay on – to make some sort of a bed." Abigail nodded – "we'll clear the space inside a bit and get ready to sleep," she answered. Mitch went on the prowl for some sort of blankets or camping foam. Fifteen minutes later, he returned with a box of camping chair foams. They were what hunters used to sit on when they were waiting in elk blinds. "We can use these as pillows and maybe put one under our hips to make the floor a little softer," he said. The three made appreciative noises and took the cushions from him. Mitch then went back out into the store and dragged a couple of chairs he found back to the room. Abigail had set the lanterns on the desk, which she and the kids had pushed into the corner, and the room appeared somewhat cheery. Mitch put the chairs against the walls inside the office and dropped into one of them. Rebecca, Trent, and Abigail took up the remaining chairs.

"Too soon to go to sleep," Rebecca commented. "No internet to surf," said Mitch with a laugh. Everyone smiled somewhat sadly at that comment. "Yeah, right about now I would have been wondering what was on Netflix," added Abigail. "Binge-watching the latest series to come out." Trent looked at his mum. "Is the internet ever going to come back?" he asked. "I don't know, Trent; I really don't know. I think our lives may have been changed permanently." Trent looked downcast. Mitch stood up. "There might be some playing cards in the aisle leading to the checkouts. I'll go have a look and see what I can find." Heading back into the store, he searched and, as luck would have it, found a deck of cards hanging off a display hook. He scooped them and headed back to the office. Once inside, the group gathered round and managed to pass a couple of hours playing the card games they could remember how to play, although some of the rules might have been somewhat flexible. After more small talk for a while later on, everyone started yawning, indicating sleep was coming. The group assumed positions on the floor and settled in for the night. The cushions helped, Abigail thought as she looked at Mitch attempting to get comfortable with his. He's not bad-looking, she thought. So far, he's been kind to me and the kids, she continued thinking. She was worried about the upcoming arrival at the acreage. Would she and the children be accepted or turned away? She really had no plan for being turned away, Abigail realized. All her hopes for herself and her offspring were pinned on the group letting them stay. She tried not to think about the possibility of no support system or protection. She found Mitch appealing as a man but did not want to do or say anything overt. She knew she was in desperate straits and he would likely see any signs of affection as a ploy to manipulate him and gain access to his place of safety. Additionally, he had made no mention of a wife or partner or anything similar, so she had no idea if he was attached or not. Putting tomorrow out of her mind, she drifted off to sleep.

Morning arrived and everyone slowly got up. The cushions had helped, but the adults especially were feeling the effects of sleeping on the hard floor. Abigail got her kids to dig some of the energy bars Gerald had given them out of their backpacks and had a simple breakfast. Mitch longed for a morning coffee but settled for some water from his canteen instead. He had noticed the CamelBak Caleb had and had been looking for one for some time, but so far, he had not been lucky enough to find one. Canteens worked, but were more awkward and often in the way. Perhaps on his next foray into the city, he would prioritize finding one.

"Time to go," he announced to the small group. He slung his rifle over his left shoulder and led them out of the store. Today was definitely not a sunny day, he thought. There was complete cloud cover overhead and a chill wind coming in from the west. Looking west, he could see the Rocky Mountains in the distance. At this time of the year, they were no longer snow-capped but majestic nonetheless. He remembered driving out there to go hiking with his canister of bear spray on his belt. There were no firearms allowed in the park, which made Mitch uneasy with the number of bear attacks that had happened over the years, but he maintained a careful vigilance and was ready to head in another direction should he run into one of the large predators. He had little faith in the bear spray but had carried it as a last resort. Probably it was just seasoning for his meat, he laughed to himself. He had seen videos of bears licking bear spray off of the floats on a floatplane in Alaska that an enterprising pilot had sprayed on it in a YouTube video – it didn't seem to deter the bear too much. He missed those hikes in that wild country. Now he hiked more often, but the intentions were completely different.

The group headed north. Being a significantly cooler day, they would perspire less under the weight of their packs and lose less fluid, which was a good thing. Mitch scanned ahead and every so often behind them as they walked. There were significantly fewer people around since the time of the initial collapse, but the world was not completely depopulated. There were solo scavengers who dug through the debris of a failed society in their search for food or medical supplies and oftentimes were just a little crazy. There were nomadic groups who did the same thing but on a larger scale. Mitch was more worried about these groups as they could be dangerous when encountered. They were less crazy but had adopted a different moral code than he operated under. Survival situations certainly revealed character, and the character of those gangs was questionable at best. Now, after having heard tales of active 'slavers' from Abigail, Mitch's mind still recoiled at the thought of that concept. There was another type of person to be concerned about. He knew from his knowledge of history that slavery had been an unpleasant fact for virtually all of human existence, but here in the western world, it had been stamped out for well over a hundred years. It was inevitable, he thought to himself.

The kilometers passed underfoot. Mitch thought he heard the report of a rifle or a pistol in the distance but was not sure. Abigail and the kids made small talk among themselves as they walked. Occasionally, Mitch stole a look at Abigail to see how she was faring. He figured she was keeping a brave face on, but underneath the exterior, she was probably worried. He had no idea what the council would do upon his arrival with these three somewhat helpless individuals. The new world in which they existed was particularly hard on the little ones, and the fact that these two had survived this long was a testament to their durability.

After two solid hours of walking, Mitch called a break. They had walked into a Costco parking lot. There weren't many cars here, but there were two semi-trailers backed into the rear docks, he noticed. I don't think I have gone through this one, he thought. Costco had been hit particularly hard by looters. In the run-up to the collapse, everyone with a vehicle had made their way to the well-known box stores in their last-minute panic buying when the general public had awakened to the impending collapse. Chaos had ensued in those final days, and the parking lots had erupted in many fistfights and confrontations as people fought over the crumbs of a society in collapse. Mitch remembered the fear that every media outlet had revealed in those final days. Hyperinflation had taken hold, and the buying power of fiat currencies was literally melting before people's eyes. Almost no one had hard assets, and the attempt by the western governments to push people into central bank digital currencies had failed spectacularly. Decades of profligate spending finally caught up to spend-happy governments, and the central banks had lost control of the yield curve. They panicked when interest rates spiked and did the only thing they knew how to do — make more mouse-click money, which fueled yet more inflation. The BRICS nations (Brazil, Russia, India, China, and South Africa) had to effectively wall themselves off from the western economies in an effort to dodge the collapse, but with so much interconnectedness still in place — it had only slowed their decline.

Mitch still remembered that period clearly. Years earlier, a friend of his had dropped by for a beer, and the talk drifted to the state of the world. Fueled by beer and no pressing concerns, the conversation went longer and deeper than Mitch had expected. Frank, his friend, was much more worldly and politically aware than Mitch was. There were a good number of 'aha' moments for Mitch as Frank wove together all of the disparate threads of how the world really worked. Mitch heard about oligarchies and interest groups, the donor class, the deep state, and dozens of other terms and ideas. Most of these he had never heard of previously. Frank talked at length about the narrative, spin, and gaslighting. For years Mitch had thought the 'news' was simply the news. Now he knew that different versions of the news existed and things such as misinformation, disinformation, and malinformation were a 'thing.' By the end of the evening, his head was literally spinning with the enormous download Frank had laid upon him. Frank laughed at him at the close of the discussion, "Well, buddy – consider yourself 'red-pilled' after all that."

That talk with Frank had led him down a vastly different path in his life. Ultimately, he ended up joining a group with Frank who all understood the world in this way and were actively planning for the potential collapse of Western society. Not hoping for it but realistic enough to consider it a strong possibility. This group had purchased a piece of land outside of Airdrie and spent the past five years "prepping" in anticipation of the end of contemporary society. This is where he was leading Abigail and her two children towards. Frank was no longer there – he had been killed by an intruder on their property and now Mitch was somewhat close only to Rick. Frank's death had left a large hole in Mitch's life. After that long talk over beer that night, they had grown much closer as friends, spending time at the range, erecting buildings on the acreage, taking courses together, and so on. Rick was a good guy and could carry a conversation, but he had nowhere near the depth and breadth of knowledge Frank had. Mitch would miss him for a long time.

After refueling with jerky and energy bars as well as sips from their canteens, the kids, Abigail and Mitch, resumed their trek. "Do you know what dead reckoning is?" he asked Abigail. "I reckon you're dead?" she replied with a laugh. Mitch made an exasperated sound. "Dead reckoning is a process of calculating direction and speed by using elapsed time and heading," he recalled from memory. "Or something similar to that," he continued. "See that road junction way down there?" he said, pointing in the distance. She craned her neck and looked at what he was pointing at. "Yeah, I see it. What about it?" "You take point, and I am going to bring up the rear for a while. Keep that marker in sight and head towards it. Don't lose sight of it. We are on a paved road, so it should be easy to do, but this is a good chance to learn rudimentary navigation skills." Abigail agreed and took the lead. The kids trudged on behind her, and Mitch took the rear position. In his head, Mitch calculated there was a 60/40 chance of the people of the acreage accepting her into the fold. With these odds, Mitch thought it was a good idea to begin instilling useful skills as they walked along. "So, what did you do before the collapse?" he called out to her. "I was a dentist," came the reply. "Seriously?" asked Mitch. "Why didn't you say something before this?" he asked. "Didn't seem relevant," she responded. "I don't have an office or anesthesia or even basic dental tools – what good are my skills without any of those things?" Mitch thought to himself – 'hmm a dentist.' They didn't have a dentist in their group, and they desperately needed one. Abigail didn't know it, but her chances of acceptance to the group just went up 1000%. Dental tools and the rest could be found. The knowledge from years of training could not.

The rest of the day continued much as before. Walking punctuated by short breaks. The kids were flagging as the miles elapsed, but eventually, after a couple of turns down different roads, the acreage came into sight. There had been much debate among the group about whether to go full camouflage and build deep inside the woods or clear an area around the acreage on all four sides to establish clear fields of fire and make it nearly impossible for anyone to sneak up on them. The hide in the woods side of the argument eventually lost. Mitch could see a couple of hundred yards of chain link fence running parallel to the road and a double gate near the center of it. A short driveway off the main road led to the first gate. As they got closer, Abigail and the kids could see the main house atop a low rise in the center of the property. "Is that it?" Rebecca asked. "Yes, that's it," Mitch responded. "Home sweet home, at least for now." A pair of large shepherd-type dogs spotted them and came running towards the gates. "Are those German Shepherds?" Abigail asked.

"Close," said Mitch. "They are actually Belgian Shepherds. Close to the German variety but with fewer breeding-induced health problems. Strong, loyal, smart, and highly trainable," he shared. Frank, in his seemingly endless wealth of knowledge, had selected the breed. The dogs made it to the chain link fence and barked furiously at the unexpected guests. "Good boys," called Mitch to the dogs. "Doing their job," he commented to the three of them. "They are our eyes and ears here. They are not pets, but rather working dogs. Do not give them food at any time. We do not allow them to accept food from strangers." Abigail and the kids nodded their understanding. "Right now, there is a set of eyes behind a rifle scope looking at us," he told them. "We keep overwatch in place 24/7. If you get accepted here, you, Abigail, will likely be part of that rotation. It is boring and repetitive but needs to be done. I will fill you in on that and many other things later once a decision has been made.

With that, Mitch spotted one of the inhabitants exiting the main house and heading toward them. Mitch relaxed somewhat — he was home.

CHAPTER FIVE
ADJUSTMENT

Angeline was amazed at the contrast between the exterior and the interior of Caleb's house. Whereas the outside looked passingly like a junkyard, the inside was anything but. From the mudroom entryway, she saw a beautiful white cupboarded kitchen with a kitchen island in the center, recessed pot lighting, and brilliant golden fixtures to open and close the cupboard doors and drawers with. Looking to her right, she saw a sunken living room tastefully decorated with comfortable-looking couches and chairs and an enormous wall-mounted monitor. To her young eyes, it was easily one of the nicest houses she had ever seen. Caleb ushered her in and helped her take her boots off. Caleb was unsurprised at her reaction. Inwardly, he smiled. The small number of people he had brought here had all had similar reactions. He took a measure of pride in what he had accomplished with this junkyard palace he had built. Well, maybe palace was overdoing it a bit, he thought, but it was nice! Hanging her coat up and placing her backpack on a low bench, he turned to her. "How long has it been since you had a hot shower?" She gaped at him. "A hot shower? I don't know – like forever!" Caleb smiled. "I have hot water here and a powerful shower. Let me fetch you a towel, some shampoo, and a bar of soap, and you can go for a shower while I rustle up some food for us." Angeline couldn't stop smiling. "That sounds so good!"

Caleb led her to where the washroom was, picking up a pair of towels from a hallway linen closet on the way. "Do you have some clean clothes in your backpack?" he asked her. "Yes, I have some but not a lot," she answered. "Okay, I will get your pack for you, and tomorrow we can figure out how to get you some new clothes," he responded. Five minutes later, she was in the shower washing her hair for the first time in weeks, and he was back in the entryway. He had taken his boots off as well when they arrived, but now it was time to discard the jacket. Thinking better of it, he took his jacket straight to the laundry room and dropped it in the dirty clothes basket there. He peeled off his shirt next, which followed the jacket into the bin, and after emptying his pockets, he tossed in his trousers. From there, he headed to the bedroom where he changed into clean clothes, deciding to shower after dinner when the hot water tank was full again.

The hot water Angeline was enjoying was heated via the solar system he had secreted in the trees in the back of his property. There was over an acre of evergreen trees there, distinctive in their thickness and the density of the stand. That copse of trees had been part of the buying decision for this property. He wanted somewhere he could erect a solar system that would be invisible from all directions. Of course, you could see it from the air, but planes were in short supply after the collapse, so that was much lower on his list of concerns. Inside that large stand of trees, he had logged out the center portion, selling the timber for a good sum in the process, and had a contractor come in and pour cement pedestals to mount the frames for his solar panels. The eight large frames each held three panels wired in series and connected to one large, buried cable that carried the power back to his house. Each of the frames had a hand-mounted crank attached to it that allowed him to vary the angles in the winter and summer as the angle of the light from the sun coming in changed. He had them all facing south for the best possible solar gain. He had considered building pedestals that rotated in place automatically to follow the sun, but the cost exceeded the possible benefit. Plus, he had constructed twice the system he thought he needed for his purposes. The deep cycle battery bank he had in the house more than sufficed for supplying hot water, lighting, refrigeration, and so on. He had overbuilt on the expectation that someday he might add more house guests or even a family to his situation and did not want to be underpowered. He also had a half dozen spare panels in storage in case hail or some other event happened that damaged his system. After the install, he had planted caragana plants throughout the stand of trees as prickly underbrush to dissuade random wanderers from stumbling upon his secret solar system. Caragana grew well in this part of the world and required no maintenance. He did keep and maintain a winding trail cut through the thorny plants so he could get in there himself on occasion.

In the kitchen, he took out some meat from the freezer to thaw and dropped it into a sink half-filled with water. He didn't think Angeline wanted to wait hours to eat. He had picked out a six-pack of cheese smokies to toss into his air fryer as soon as they were reasonably thawed out. There were some powdered eggs still open from when he was last at home, which he decided to turn into scrambled eggs. He realized his dietary habits might not suit the young lady as he followed a fairly strict regime that was decidedly different from the mainstream food pyramid diet. On the other hand, 'hot and ready' was quite popular with most hungry people despite what the main course was constituted of. He took some chilled water out of the fridge and set it on the counter, and then walked to the bathroom door. "Mango or strawberry flavored drink for supper?" he called through the closed door. "Mango please," Angeline responded. He returned to the kitchen and squirted some zero-carb liquid into a glass of the refrigerated water. He made an identical glass for himself and put the remainder of the water back in the fridge. Moments after completing that, he heard the shower shut off in the washroom. Hmm, I figured that would last a lot longer than that, Caleb thought.

Minutes later, Angeline emerged from the bathroom in new clothes and damp hair wrapped in one of the towels provided. She had a big smile on her face. "That feels so much better," she commented. "Clean feels so good." "I'm happy for you," replied Caleb. "Hot water under pressure is one of the greatest inventions of mankind." Caleb stepped towards her with a glass of mango drink in his hand. "Here you go," he said, handing her the chilled drink. Angeline took a long draught of the offered beverage – "Mmm, that was really good." "Another?" asked Caleb. "Yes, please," she quickly responded. Caleb fixed her another and retired to the living room. Angeline followed him and plopped into a chair. "Tell me more about you and your grandfather and how you ended up there," Caleb suggested. Angeline's face fell at the mention of her grandfather. She obviously felt deeply for him. "Do you think he's okay?" she asked. Caleb thought to himself for a moment before answering. Did he deliver the raw truth, or sugar-coat it and create a false belief for her? He opted for a middle-ground approach. "Angeline, your grandfather, as you know, is a diabetic. That's a disease that requires strict dietary control and regular intake of insulin. Obviously, he had insulin put away for this world we live in, but it needed to be kept refrigerated. With the burning down of his house and the loss of his solar panels, his ability to keep his medicine at the right temperature was lost. He knew this and realized his ability to care for you was at an end. This is why he asked me to take you in and care for you. He really loved both you and I assume the rest of your family. He went to great lengths to prepare for this world we now occupy, spending a lot of time and money getting ready. As a diabetic, however, he understood the risks and the reality of his condition. Is he okay? I do not know. Maybe he worked something out after we left and maybe not. As this is the case, I cannot give you a definite answer. If thinking he is okay helps you, I am okay with that. If you accept, he was not able to make it – that is okay too."

Angeline chewed her lip in thought. "I am going to believe he figured something out." She smiled wanly. "Works for me," responded Caleb, trying to inject a little happiness into the situation. "Back to my original question – how did you end up there?" Angeline looked up at him and focused her attention on him. "Mum and dad thought grandpa was crazy. He kept talking about a 'big problem' which he said was coming, but they didn't listen to him. They said other stuff too, but I didn't really understand it all.

Then, when things started to go bad, they got really scared and kept phoning him and talking to him. I guess he wasn't so crazy after all," she recounted. "Your grandpa was a wise man," said Caleb. "He understood the way things were going to go. Angeline – how old are you?" asked Caleb. She smiled brightly – "I'm ten." "You seem pretty grown up for ten," Caleb remarked. "I think I have had to grow up pretty fast with way things went," she replied. "I used to play with my friends and ride my bike around my neighborhood, but that's all gone now," she continued with apparent sadness. "I don't know what's going to happen to me or where I am going to go." Caleb looked at her and put on his most reassuring look. "You're going to stay with me, here in this house. We are going to make it, and you are going to grow up and have a family of your own someday if you want. Yes, things are tough right now, but the human race is hardy and resourceful. We'll dig our way out of this, and things will get better." Angeline tried to look hopeful. "What are we going to eat? What about school? Am I going to go back to school?" Caleb considered his response for a moment. "I have enough food put away for a couple of years as long as we do not add any more people to the mix. As far as school goes – I have an extensive library downstairs, and I downloaded hundreds of videos on things like gardening, raising livestock, water management, carpentry, and on and on. Many, many topics. I think we can keep you busy learning for a long time. What is valuable now as far as education goes is quite different from what was valuable – before." Angeline looked somewhat relieved at these answers. "Yes, I guess the world has changed a lot. What was important is no longer important," she replied.

"My mum and dad and brother are dead," she said with some finality. Caleb looked at her sympathetically but didn't say a word. "I know that and I accept it. When Grandpa was alive, I could live in a fantasy that everything was going to be okay, but it's not going to be okay. This is it. This is real. I am a ten-year-old girl in a stranger's house who I don't know and who doesn't know me but is promising me everything is going to be okay," she stopped talking and put her head down. "I know you think you needed to say that stuff about everything being okay, and I actually expected it. In a weird sort of way, I think I am going to get used to the idea that things are not going to be okay and just live with it. It's the only choice I have," she said with conviction. Caleb looked at her and considered. This was certainly more than he had expected. He had no experience raising children, only the memories of his own upbringing. He had watched his friends grow up in his neighborhood, but what really happened behind closed doors was a mystery. This was definitely outside of his experience envelope. "Well, you got me. I'm not really sure what to say. I'm sorry your family is dead. If living with them made you the way you are and you seem pretty well put together, they must have been good people." She lifted her head and smiled. "I appreciate that." Caleb asked, "Can we agree to work together to figure this out? Like it or not, we are going to get to know each other. We can collaborate or we can hate each other. I don't know about you, but collaborate sounds a whole lot better than the other option." Angeline looked at him for what seemed like a long time. Even though she was only ten, she seemed to have a wisdom beyond her years. On top of that, she seemed to be a very sharp kid, he thought. I may have bitten off more than I can chew with this one, he thought.

"Collaborate." She responded finally with a small smile. Caleb smiled back. "Ok, how about I look at those thawing sausages and see if we can get supper started?" With that, he stood and headed to the kitchen. Angeline followed him.

With her assistance, they were sitting at the table eating thirty minutes later.

"What made you build this place?" she asked. "Did you think the same way my grandpa did?" Caleb replied, "It is likely he and I saw the same things coming. Actually, a lot of people saw what was coming and took steps to protect themselves. Hundreds of thousands, as a matter of fact. People who thought in this way used to talk to each other over the internet to exchange ideas and give each other support." Angeline spoke up again, "So why are there so few people around? When we walked here, we saw almost no one. I mean, someone did steal our wheelbarrow, which was kinda creepy, but other than that we didn't see anyone." Caleb continued, "I think there are more people around than you can see. I think a lot of people are hiding because they are scared. No one trusts anyone anymore, and if Abigail was right and those were slavers chasing her and her kids – staying out of sight sounds like a good idea. Another thing you have to think about is the size of the population before this. The U.S. had around 340 million people, and Canada had just passed 40 million. I don't even know how many there were in Mexico on top of that, but you are talking somewhere in the vicinity of 400 million people in North America. So, if hundreds of thousands of people were getting ready for this possible outcome, you are really talking about a tiny minority. Like less than a single percentage point. I don't know if any of those numbers are even close, but based on how many there seem to be left roaming around – the collapse hit us really hard and most people are dead."

Angeline looked glum after Caleb's monologue. "Do you really think most people are dead?" she said. "I don't know about most, but definitely a lot," he replied. Maybe some areas are better than others. It gets cold here in the winter, which makes it harder. Perhaps there are more people the further south you go." "Why do you stay here then?" Angeline asked. "Well," continued Caleb, "my house is here, my supplies are here, and I kind of look at the cold as a sort of self-defence. I know most people cannot handle the cold and will head south in search of a more forgiving climate. This means less competition for me and less direct interactions or confrontations with others. I can forage in the city for things I need, and there is a good chance they will be available. Right now, people are so focused on getting something to eat that they are not thinking about most other things. This gives me a fair bit of an advantage." "You said you have enough food for a couple of years. What are you going to do after that? Are you going to head south?" she asked. Caleb – "No. I'm going to start building greenhouses to grow food in. I am going to find or trade for chickens and rabbits and maybe some goats to raise as livestock. I have a lot of materials put away, but I am waiting for the right time to start building." Angeline asked, "How will you know when it's the right time?" "When I run into even fewer people," he answered. "You mean when more people are dead?" she said somewhat accusatorily. "Yes, you could put it that way, or perhaps most people have gone south in search of an easier climate to live and thrive in," he countered.

Angeline took a few minutes to digest that. Caleb got up to get himself another glass of the mango drink with the water jug he had put in the refrigerator. Sitting back down, he continued. "What was your grandfather planning to do?" Angeline sat up slightly at the mention of her grandfather. "He talked about farming or ranching or something like that, I think. I didn't really pay much attention at the time. We used to go to his house to visit, but when he started to dig the hole in his backyard, Mum and Dad thought he had really lost his mind, and we did not go to visit nearly as much after that. I think they were mad at him, actually. They talked about him wasting his money. Mum talked about grandpa 'pissing her inheritance away,' sorry for swearing by the way, but that is what she said." Caleb grinned. "If pissing away is the worst thing you say, we're good." Angeline continued, "After Mum and Dad and Keith were killed, grandpa didn't talk nearly as much. He seemed sad a lot of the time. Sad and worried. I think them getting killed ruined his plans for us. He had this idea about all of us surviving the crash and then coming out on top somehow." Caleb decided to ask about her parents and sibling. "How did your family die?" he asked as gently as he could. She looked at him very directly. "It was stupid," she said. "Really stupid." "It was in the parking lot of a grocery store, if you can believe it." Caleb stayed quiet to let her get it out. "Mum decided we needed to pick up some items on the way to grandpa's place. Things were really starting to fall apart. People were losing it. Grandpa had been phoning us to hurry up and get to his house as he was getting scared. The cell phones were still working then, but other things were beginning to stop working. We went to that big grocery store just a few blocks from grandpa's house. Mum told Keith and me to stay in the vehicle while she and Dad went inside to buy a few last-minute things. Keith and I were trying to look at stuff on our phones, but these emergency alerts kept going off. Warning! Shelter in place! Stuff like that. I was trying to watch TikTok to take my mind off of what was happening, but the internet was acting weird. Then Keith started yelling and pointing out the window. Mum was wrestling with some lady over her grocery cart. It was just so surreal. Mum was not in the best of shape, and here she was screaming at some woman who was trying to yank something out of her cart. Then that other woman punched Mum in the face, and she fell on the ground. Dad grabbed the woman and shoved her, and she fell down. Next thing I knew, Keith had opened his door and was running over there. Dad was helping Mum up when this big guy showed up and put Dad in some kind of a chokehold. Keith started punching the big guy in the face to get him to let go of Dad. I am not sure what exactly happened next, but all of a sudden, a great big fight had broken out with lots of people punching and wrestling around. It was all very confusing. I saw Mum still lying on the ground, and I could see blood coming out of her face. Then someone started shooting. I mean – really shooting a whole bunch. Some skinny guy in a black jacket had a gun, and he was shooting everyone. It didn't make any sense. He just kept shooting and shooting. He even stopped and put a new thing in his gun – you know that thing that holds more bullets." "A magazine," Caleb suggested. "Yeah, one of those things," she confirmed. "Anyway, this skinny guy with the gun shot a whole bunch of people and then just stopped. Then he turned and walked away. He didn't even say anything. Just showed up to shoot and then leave. It was weird." Caleb urged her to continue. "Then what happened?" Angeline took a deep breath and wiped her eyes, which had become teary.

"I got out of the vehicle and ran over there. I saw Keith lying face down with blood on his back. I knew he was dead; I just knew it. Then I saw Dad lying on top of Mum. His arm was behind him and looked funny. I think he broke it somehow fighting or when he fell. It just looked strange. He was breathing, though. I pulled him over by his jacket and he yelled. I guess his arm was really hurting. He saw me and recognized me, but his face was really gray and sweaty. His other arm was on his chest and he was having trouble breathing. He said, "Help your mother" to me, but his voice was really faint. I turned to get closer and look at Mum, but she was not moving. Her eyes were open, but they were not moving either, just looking up at the sky. I had seen dead people on the internet, so I knew what they were supposed to look like, but it was different when it was real. I was staring and staring at her for a long time, and then I felt sick and threw up. It was gross. All of my food came out. I threw up on my Mum." Angeline started to cry. "I threw up on my Mum!" Angeline was now crying harder. "My dad called my name and I looked at him. His lips were looking kind of blue and he was really clutching his chest." "Go to Grandpa's house," he said. He said it again and again, but each time was quieter and quieter. Then he died too. My Mum was dead, my brother was dead, and now Daddy was dead too." Angeline covered her face with her hands. Caleb moved over to sit beside her and put his arm around her shoulder. She turned and buried her face in his chest and cried hard for a long time.

After a while, Angeline had cried herself out. Caleb looked at her and said, "Maybe we should put you to bed." She nodded and stood up. There were two bedrooms on the main floor. He led her to one and turned on the light for her. In the room was a queen-sized bed with two hypoallergenic foam pillows and a beige duvet, and small side tables on either side of the bed. "You can hang your clothes up in the closet, but I don't have any pajamas in your size. I could give you a cotton t-shirt if you like, and you could use that." Wiping her eyes once again with her sleeve, she nodded her agreement. A quick trip to the master bedroom and back provided her with a suitable large t-shirt. It would probably hang to her knees, he thought. "Okay, good night then," he said to her and closed the door. "Good night, Caleb," she replied. "See you in the morning."

Caleb made his way back to the living room. He went to the front entryway and ensured the door was locked and placed the bar across it. Deadbolts kept the mildly intrusive out, but the two-by-four he slid into the brackets would make entry much more difficult. He knew that was also only a stopgap, but it would give him time to get up, put his plate carrier on, and get his rifle ready. Yes, the world was less populated now, but there was no one coming to help if trouble came a-calling. He had made it through the first year by being diligent and careful. In this new world, only the paranoid survived, he reminded himself with a wry grin. After securing the door and checking the windows, he carried his M1A with him and went to the basement stairs. Snapping on the light, he went down to the level where his gun room was situated. Unlocking that door with a key on his key ring, he went inside and turned on the overhead light. On one wall was a rack of rifles and shotguns standing upright on their butts. A mixture of hunting and tactical firearms covered the wall in a number of calibers, from small .22 caliber plinking rifles to bolt-action .30 caliber hunting rifles and .338 caliber long-range precision rifles. A number of shotguns were mixed in, some bird guns for geese and grouse and semi-automatic short-barreled versions more for two-legged game. He also had a breaching model for when he really, really needed to gain entry somewhere. He laid his M1A down on a workbench opposite the gun rack after unloading it. Digging out a bore snake, he made a couple of cleaning passes through the barrel and then did a quick field strip so he could gain access to the internal workings of the rifle. After using his cleaning brush to get it as clean as needed, he applied some light lubrication and reassembled it. He checked the picatinny rail and the optic attached to it to ensure none of the Loctite-secured screws had come loose and had a look at the sling. Satisfied everything was in order, he breech-checked it again and placed it in the vacant space on the gun rack. Caleb unloaded the magazine, inspected the ammo, and then put it and the magazine away. The bench got cleaned up, and then when everything was spic and span, the light got shut off; he headed back upstairs after locking the door again. With a young girl in the house, he was going to make doubly sure there was nothing left to chance.

Heading back upstairs, he turned off the hallway light and headed to his room. A quick stop in the bathroom for a swipe at his teeth and to use the toilet, and then it was bedtime for him. A shower in the morning would happen as he was just too dog-tired to care anymore. A few minutes after his head hit the pillow, he was asleep. It had been a long day and tomorrow's problems would be right there waiting for him – tomorrow.

CHAPTER SIX
DECISION TIME

Hey!" called out the woman walking towards Mitch and his companions. "Back at you," replied Mitch. "So, who are these folks?" the approaching woman asked. Getting closer, Abigail saw a tall blonde woman with her hair braided into a long ponytail hanging over her left shoulder. A brown flat-topped bolero hat covered the top of her head, matching the brown and red plaid shirt she wore. She had strong features and was particularly attractive. Like so many people these days, she was slim with a noticeably narrow waist but ample hips. She flashed a brilliant smile as she got closer and revealed teeth in which a good amount of money had been invested prior to the collapse. Mitch turned and made introductions, "This is Abigail, she's the mother of Rebecca and Trent." He continued, "Everyone, this is Kate." Abigail and the two kids said their hellos and smiled as warmly as they could muster. "Are they healthy?" asked Kate of Mitch. "I guess so," replied Mitch. "I mean, I haven't seen anything so far." Looking at Abigail and the two kids, she asked, "Do you guys feel alright?" Kate didn't look impressed. "I don't think asking them is going to give us the answers we are looking for, Mitch," she said. "They could be carrying something and look and feel perfectly fine." Mitch replied somewhat sheepishly, "Yeah, I guess so." Kate addressed him further, "What was your intention in bringing them here? What's the plan?" "She's a dentist," Mitch blurted out in hopes of defusing the apparent head of steam Kate was building up. "We need a dentist – don't we?" he continued. Kate continued to look unimpressed. "That may be so, but we can't just let them in and risk infecting all of us with whatever they might be carrying. You too. You have been exposed to whatever bug they are potentially harboring, putting all of us at risk by your actions!" Mitch realized he was not going to escape much of the famous wrath of Kate. Kate wasn't the leader of the overall group, but she was on the council and held considerable sway. Most days he just avoided her. She was a poster child for what used to be known as a strong independent woman. Mitch found her annoying but rarely challenged her head-on, as experience had taught him her reasoning skills exceeded his and he usually came out on the losing end of their exchanges.

"Stay here," directed Kate as she turned on her heel and strode away. "Well, that went well," commented Abigail. "Yeah, she is what you might call – strong-willed," replied Mitch. "She has a lot of power around here and people listen to what she says. Luckily, we have Ian on the other side of her who is a cool character and doesn't get riled easily. Ian serves as a good counterweight to Kate's energy. She is very action-oriented while he tends to be more of a thinker and a planner. Actually, they make a good team – playing off each other's strengths. Ian is also on the council, but the reality is – the rest of the members are more order takers. Kate and Ian really run the show. That being said – so far, they have been making pretty good decisions which is why everyone listens to them. We probably wouldn't be here but for the decisions they made." Abigail replied, "She seems very sure of herself. I am not sure how well I get along with that personality type. I ran my own business as a dentist, had staff and did my own hiring but I know I am more of an introvert by nature. Kate strikes me as quite the extrovert." Mitch laughed, "Oh, you got that right! She likes to be in the thick of things. Always has something to say." "Is she going to let us in?" asked Rebecca. "I hope so. I am tired of walking." "We'll have to see," Mitch replied. "I think Kate is up there talking to the group about what to do. We really haven't let anyone in before — we were always worried someone new might not fit in and then we would be stuck with them. We can't send people away who know what we have and how we are set up." Although it was unsaid, Abigail sensed some dangerous undertones in his answer. Not letting people leave who had inside knowledge made entering the acreage sound like a one-way trip. Her sense of unease grew.

A half hour passed. Two people exited from the house and walked down towards the gates. Kate was returning with a man at her side this time. He was an inch or so shorter than her, the normal lean frame of the times, thinning brown hair on a round head and wearing black-rimmed glasses. He had a solemn look on his face but not unfriendly. "Hi Ian," said Mitch as the two approached the gate area. "Hello Mitchell," he replied. "What have you brought us?" he inquired. Mitch started with, "I found that coil of double-stranded copper wire we needed for the truck plus some turnbuckles and the rivet gun Rick wanted. "It seems you picked up some other items while you were at it," commented Ian with an obvious reference to Abigail and her brood. "Yeah, well there is a story to that," replied Mitch. "I'll bet there is," responded Ian. "The question is what to do with both them and you right now." Kate spoke up, "Why don't we set them up in one of the outbuildings? We can move some cots in there and provide some of the other basics. That will give us time to make decisions and keep them isolated from everyone else in case they are carrying something contagious." "Sounds good," responded Ian. "Stay put. We will send for you when we are ready," Ian told the small group. Mitch gave Ian and Kate a thumbs-up.

As Kate and Ian walked away, Mitch turned to Abigail. "Well, that is hopeful. At least you didn't get turned away immediately." "Are you in some sort of trouble for bringing us?" Abigail asked. "I mean, they did not look happy," Mitch replied back to her. "Ian doesn't like surprises or the unpredictable. Kate is good at rolling with change but gets angry faster. Ian, I have never actually seen him angry, but I suspect it isn't pretty when it happens."

"How long are we going to have to wait?" asked Trent. "I have to pee," Rebecca complained. Abigail looked at both of them. "I don't know how long we are going to wait, but that's life – sometimes you have to wait. As far as your problems go, young lady – let's go for a stroll over to those trees across the road and we can both go pee," she finished with a smile. Mitch sat down on the ground. Trent sat down beside him. "What do you think, bud?" Mitch asked him. "I don't like waiting," Trent shared with a peevish look on his face. "Well," Mitch replied, "your mum is right, sometimes you just have to wait. Sometimes there is nothing you can do about it. Say – do you know how to play rock, paper, scissors?" Trent looked back at him. "Play what?" "Rock, paper, scissors. You don't know that game?" Trent shook his head. Mitch grinned and began to explain the intricacies of the game, and two minutes later they were having fun and a good laugh. Shortly thereafter, the two females returned from their washroom trip in the bushes looking somewhat relieved. "What are you guys doing?" Rebecca inquired. "Playing a game," replied Mitch after losing for a third straight time to the quick study Trent. "Oh, I know that game," she replied and sat down beside them. Abigail sat down looking pensive.

About thirty minutes went by, and a different pair of people emerged from the house and headed down towards the gates. The first man whistled to call the two dogs, who immediately ran towards him. He and the dogs quickly moved out of sight. The other man was Rick, the guy Mitch considered a friend from among the group. Rick was of average height, had a mess of curly black hair, and the bluest eyes Mitch had ever seen in a man. Rick also had the thickest facial hair he had ever seen. When he wasn't smiling, he could look quite intimidating, but when a smile cracked his face, all that intimidation went away. "Hey Mitch," he called out once he got close enough. Mitch stood up and answered back, "Hey Rick, how's it going?" "How did you make out on those items?" Rick asked. Mitch pointed at the small backpack sitting on the ground. "Got them in there." "Excellent," answered Rick. Rick turned and looked at the broader group. "I'm supposed to lead you to an outbuilding we have. You are not to leave the group once you go through the gate, nor are you allowed to leave the building once you are put in it. We aren't punishing you; we just want to be sure you don't have a bug of some sort that is going to make all of us sick," he concluded. Everyone appeared to understand his directions. Rick took some keys off his belt and unlocked the padlock on the gate. Rick then led the way up the slight incline while maintaining his distance from the new arrivals. As Mitch and his companions walked, the house came into clearer view. A large rancher-style house, it was considerably bigger than it looked from the road. It had a green metal roof with brick chimneys at each end of the structure. It faced south, and atop the metal roof on the southern exposure lay an array of solar panels. The front exterior appeared to be a mix of stone and black bricks. Abigail couldn't see inside any of the windows, as they appeared to be of the one-way glass variety. Getting closer, they could see the blades of a turning windmill on top of a tower behind the house. Rick led them around the house in between some other buildings. She could make out what looked like shops and various storage sheds as they wove through the yard formed behind the house. Arriving at another mid-sized building, she saw an open door with light emitting out the opening.

Rick had moved to the side so the group could pass and gain entry inside the building. A pair of wooden steps led up to the entrance. Abigail went in first, followed by the kids and then Mitch. Inside were four cots, all in a row. Overhead was a battery-powered lantern hanging from a hook in the ceiling. Mitch and Abigail could see various boxes of supplies and bundles of insulation, along with other building materials, had been stacked to create room for the cots. A small folding table with a washbasin and a large jug of water had been set along the shorter wall. "I know it's not much, but we really aren't set up for quarantine situations," Rick called out. "I don't know how long it is going to last. Hopefully, only a day or two is my guess." Mitch looked out the door at him. "It is what it is." Mitch then turned and went and sat on a cot. "What about the bathroom – what are we supposed to do about that?" Rebecca asked. "I don't know," responded Mitch. "I guess we'll figure it out when the time comes." Kate appeared outside their door. "We are going to ask you to stay here for the next couple of days. If you need to go to the toilet, you can use the outhouse we just finished building." She stopped talking and pointed for the group to see. A small building away from the main building had a pair of doors with a crescent moon cut into each. "We started that project just after you left, Mitch, which is why you don't know about that. We think the number of people staying in the main house is overwhelming the septic field, so we needed to produce a solution. It's okay now, but in the winter, it's going to be much less pleasant," she said with a smile. "We'll bring you your meals and leave them on a folding table we are going to set up just outside the door. Any questions?" Abigail looked at her kids and then at Kate. "So, we are just supposed to hang around here and do nothing for two days?" she asked. "Yes," responded Kate. "We think any fever or other symptom will have made itself known by then or not. If nothing shows up, we can move to the next steps." "And what steps will those be?" inquired Abigail. "That is what is being decided right now," retorted Kate. "Good night. Dinner should arrive shortly." With that, Kate turned and headed back to the big house.

Mitch moved to the open door and called after Kate, "Could someone at least drop off a couple of books or a game or something?" he asked. Without turning around, Kate gave him a thumbs up as she walked away. "That will be something to do at least," Mitch said to the group who were sitting on their cots. He continued, "I'd like to get out of these clothes I have been in for days now, but I guess it'll have to wait until tomorrow at the very least." Abigail looked at him, "What is this place? How is it you have all this set up when everyone else has nothing?" Mitch looked back at her, "Normally I would say it's a long story and avoid it, but as we seem to have nothing but time on our hands, I will tell you. At least what I can remember."

Mitch went to a cot and sat down. "About five years ago I got invited to join this group. My friend Frank was one of the originators and really the brain trust behind it. He was big into geopolitics, economics, and understood things I will never understand. He and I would have these long talks, but it really was more of me listening and him explaining. That being said – if I mess up any of the story it's on me and not on him. He knew this stuff inside and out. I get the basic grasp of it but nowhere near the level of detail he did. Anyhow, Frank said, "We were headed into a storm." That is what he liked to call it. Governments in the Western world had been spending beyond their means for a long time. Drunken sailor kind of spending. Now, we like to blame the politicians for all of this, but to be fair they were only giving us what we demanded of them. There were individuals who came along and sounded the alarm, 'We are spending our grandchildren's inheritance,' but they were shouted down or ignored so they never really got any kind of traction. Like the old saying goes – You get exactly the government you deserve. Frank realized this and decided to act. He had been doing research for quite some time, read a lot of books, and then decided on a course of action. He liked to say to us, 'no one is coming' in regard to us getting saved. We were on our own no matter what. He convinced a number of his friends of what was coming and got the 'group' started. We never had a more formal name than that; I guess we never needed one. In the beginning, we met twice a month – usually at Frank's. Eventually we started rotating between houses to equalize the burden of food preparation and clean-up, etc. Lots of lists were made and as we got more organized, Excel spreadsheets became the norm. It was pretty disorganized in the beginning with all sorts of wild ideas getting put forth. Some wanted to buy an island off the coast, others wanted to move to South America. In the end, we settled on staying put. We had jobs to go to and bills to pay, and families to raise. Sometimes we would get distracted by the day-to-day of our lives, but Frank was good at getting us back on track and focused."

"Eventually we decided to pool our resources and purchase this property. We knew we wanted to be out of the big city but not be so far away that getting here on a regular basis was too difficult. We are closer to the city than I would have liked, but cost and availability were governing factors. After we settled on the property, came the long process of designing the house, deciding on how to heat and cool it, septic or composting toilets, and on and on. It really was a huge project. Sometimes it was like herding cats trying to get anything done, and there were lots of arguments. Over time, each of us developed our own 'portfolio' of responsibilities, so to speak. Frank naturally provided leadership and was the deciding vote when we reached impasses. Rick took on logistics, I managed security and self-defence training, and Kate ended up in procurement and inventory. The rest of the duties fell out among the other group members. If they decide to let you stay, you will meet them all eventually."

"As time passed, we added more people to the headcount. It actually became easier to recruit as things progressed since more people saw the state of the world and the trend that was developing. Towards the end, we were actually turning people away as we had reached what we thought was the maximum carrying capacity of this place. After the feces really hit the fan, we had a few of those people show up with their families insisting we let them in. That was a really rough patch. Looking into the eyes of people you knew, and in some cases friends, telling them to leave was hard." At this point, Mitch paused and looked away. Abigail could see he was struggling with the emotions from his memories. "The way you talk about Frank, I get the impression he isn't here anymore. Did he leave?" Abigail asked. "No. He didn't leave. He was killed," replied Mitch. "In the early days, we were concerned about security but didn't give it the weight or consideration we should have. Frank was out in the yard at night doing something, we don't know what, when an intruder attacked him. We found him in the morning on the ground – dead. He had been stabbed multiple times in the back and was face down in a pool of his own blood. We don't know if he even saw it coming. There were footprints leading away from the scene to a fence line where the perpetrator had climbed over. We never did find out why it happened or who did it. It really sucked. As a result of that, we made several changes in how we run things, and so far, it has not happened again."

Abigail chose not to comment. Mitch continued, "Things settled out after that. Ian stepped into the role that Frank had, but he is not as strong a leader as Frank was. Lately, Kate has been making more and more of the decisions around here. Some are okay with that, and others are not. I sense a power struggle is coming as we seem to be dividing into two separate camps. I don't know if Kate really wants to be in charge or not, but Ian is making fewer and fewer decisions. We need effective leadership, or we are going to fall apart. We did not have any structure for replacing leadership as we all thought Frank was just going to run things. No one expected him to be one of the first casualties. I am not sure what is going to happen, but something definitely is going to happen." Abigail nodded. "Is our arrival making things more difficult?" Mitch shook his head. "On balance, it is not that big of a deal. This problem has been brewing for a while and seems to be coming to a head."

"It has been a year, and we have yet to plant any significant crops. There was a stampede of people coming out of the city. In the beginning, we simply kept our heads down and tried not to be noticed. Now that the population is greatly diminished, we need to get going on that front. We stored a lot of food, and I do mean a lot, but that won't last forever. When this summer ends, we will batten down the hatches for the winter, but in the spring, we need to get going on the planting. Our focus is really going to have to change. These petty disagreements are going to have to come to an end. If we don't get moving, starvation will take us all out. I think you joining us is going to help, as we are going to need more people to work the land. In the end, I think we are all going to end up farmers or gardeners," Mitch finished.

"Well, despite some of the problems you have outlined, the past year sounds a lot nicer than what the kids and I have been through. You have a group, you have a place to live, and you have food put away. We had none of that. I am not going to relate our whole story to you, but our lives have been a lot harsher and more terrifying. I feel envious of your group's foresight and vision. We didn't have any of that. I think it is mostly luck we are even alive. I lost my husband, and I have no idea where the rest of my family is. I doubt they are even still alive. I don't think I am showing it, but I'm really scared waiting for the decision from your council regarding me and my children. If they decide to put us outside of your gate, I am fairly certain we'll starve or come to a violent end. I have no resources or the necessary skills to keep either them or myself alive. We are totally and completely at you and your group's mercy," Abigail said. She stopped talking, and Mitch could see the glassy eyes of someone fighting to not cry. The two kids noticed and came to give their mum a hug.

Mitch got up from his cot and walked around the room. "I'm already getting restless being in here," he said. "It's going to be a long two days. I like to be outside." The two kids nodded their agreement. Mitch walked to the doorway and looked out. "Hey Ben! Can you come over here?" A man in a blue denim shirt with a pail in either hand walked closer and then stopped. "Ian says we can't get too close to you as you might be carrying something," Ben replied. "Well, I can clearly see you are carrying something, and you are allowed to wander about," Mitch said with a smile looking at the two pails. "Ha ha, real funny Mitch. It's a shame with all of the successful comedians in the world you are trying to be one." Ben got a funny look on his face. "I guess there really aren't many comedians left, are there?" "What do you want,

Mitch?" he asked with some annoyance in his voice now. "Can you ask Ian or Kate if we can get out of this box and walk around the yard if we promise to stay twenty feet away from anyone we run into? Two days of sitting in here with nothing to do is verging on torture." Ben looked more annoyed. "I have things to do, and being your errand boy is not one of them." "Come on, Ben, do me a solid. These kids are already bored, and we won't be hurting anyone." Ben stared at Mitch again and then nodded. "I suppose it won't be too much of a hassle, but you are officially indebted to me now," said Ben with a small smile. "Agreed," said Mitch and turned back inside. "Ok, folks, we might be able to get out of here for a while and stretch our legs." Abigail stared at him. "We just spent a whole day walking to get here, and you want to stretch your legs? Count me out. I am going to recline on this cot and take a load off my sore feet. If the kids want to go with you, they are welcome to do so."

Ten minutes went by when a teenage girl showed up outside of the entryway and called in, "Mitch. Kate says you are allowed out but need to keep your word about staying away from everyone else. She says if you don't, they will put you back inside and padlock the door." "Thanks, Annette,"

Mitch yelled back to the teenager, who promptly strode away. "Let's go, kids," Mitch said to the kids who looked eager to escape their temporary shelter. "Are you sure you don't want to see the place?" Mitch asked Abigail. "If we get to stay, we will see it all, and if we don't, we won't have memories of what we are missing out on," she responded. "Suit yourself," Mitch replied and headed outside with the two youngsters. Trent and Rebecca gathered outside with Mitch. "Have you ever seen a rabbit hutch or chicken coop?" he asked the two of them. Without waiting for their answer, he started walking away with the two kids following in his wake.

For the next thirty minutes, Mitch toured the kids around the acreage. He took them to the three woodsheds, which each held twelve cords of split wood in evenly stacked piles. They looked at the entryway to the root cellar but didn't go in, as it was dark and musty inside, Mitch explained. They went past a number of storage sheds, each locked with a padlock; despite their efforts, once in a while, people still made their way onto the property. In the beginning, the dogs had been brought in at night, but now they roamed the yard 24/7 in an effort to deter outsiders from gaining access. Deadbolts and padlocks had been installed on almost everything in a further effort to hang onto the possessions of the group. They had a look at the combo rabbit hutch/chicken coop, which at this time had no occupants. Mitch explained the intention to put animals inside at some point in the future to obtain a source of animal protein, but had not happened yet. He showed them the newly built outhouse, whose use was going to be strongly encouraged during the warmer months to lessen the strain on the septic tank. All of the buildings had been painted a shade of forest green to help blend them into the local foliage. The roofs were all green as well, each a metal roof to provide protection against fire. He led them to the orchard, where twenty small trees had been planted equidistant apart with the expectation of significant future growth. Straw had been piled around the base of each of the trees in an effort to capture moisture in the summer and provide some insulation in the cold winters. "We haven't gotten to the point where they need pruning yet but that's coming," he told the two kids. "We are going to try and help these trees with fertilizer and selective pruning so we can get the most fruit out of them. We are also going to try and grow more trees by taking slips from these ones. It'll be a long process but who knows how long we are going to have to live here?" Rebecca and Trent seemed to understand. As they ran out of things to look at and questions to ask, Mitch led them back to the small building where they were staying. Their stomachs had begun to growl but not too long later dinner showed up.

Later on, after dinner was finished, Kate made an appearance outside of the doorway again. "Mitch, can you come outside and talk for a bit?" Mitch got up from his cot and headed outside. Kate led him around the corner out of earshot of the inhabitants on the inside while maintaining a good distance away from him. Crossing her arms, she began to pace back and forth in front of him and started talking. "No one has debriefed you after your arrival from the mission you were on. How well do you know this woman you brought with you?" Mitch replied, "Not well at all. She was part of a group fleeing people she claimed were 'slavers,' and we sort of ended up falling in together with each other." Kate continued, "Did you see any of these supposed slavers?" Mitch replied, "Yes, they pursued us from the warehouse I was searching and then attacked a house we had taken refuge in. We had a firefight and then they threw Molotov cocktails in through the windows and set the place on fire. We retreated down into the basement to get away from the flames as we couldn't go outside because we were surrounded." Kate looked skeptical. "So why are you still alive?" Mitch related the story of Gerald and his surprise entry into the fray and how he brought them into his shelter. Mitch went on to talk about Caleb and his interactions with Mitch back in the warehouse where they had first encountered each other. "So, he was shooting at you?" she asked incredulously. "Well, more I was shooting at him," Mitch relayed to her. "And now you are friends with him?" she asked with continued incredulity. Mitch responded, "Enemy of my enemy is my friend kind of a thing. I think friend might be an overly strong characterization of the situation, but we did get over our impasse and let bygones be bygones." Kate resumed her pacing. "Do you know anything about him and his group?" she asked. "I think he's a loner," Mitch replied. "Actually, no longer a loner as he took on Gerald's granddaughter." Kate looked perplexed. "Gerald's granddaughter – where does she fit into this mix?" Mitch gave a further explanation of how Angeline ended up in the custody of Caleb and what the expected outcome was for Gerald. Kate looked somewhat downcast. "That would be hard to deal with," she replied. To lose almost the entirety of your family and then give your granddaughter to a complete stranger. Wow."

Kate undid her braid and shook her hair out. The blond tresses circled her head as she pulled her hat back on. She returned her gaze to Mitch. "There are going to be some changes in the ways things are run around here. The council is going to be talking to everyone about what that is going to look like and what it will mean for the group." Going back to Abigail, Kate continued her questioning. "She said, or you said she is a dentist. Is that true?" Mitch looked at Kate. "How would I possibly be able to verify that?" Kate frowned. "Agreed. Stupid question. Did she talk about her experience as a dentist at all?" Mitch stared at Kate again. "You mean in between shooting at slavers and surviving a house fire or at some other point?" "You had hours of walking to get here, didn't you?" she asked. Mitch responded. "Yes, but talking about our careers in the time before never really came up. We were thinking about staying alive and what was needed to ensure that continued." Kate frowned again. "I suppose it doesn't really matter what you found out. Either she is a dentist, or she is not. If she isn't, we toss her and her kids out of here. Everyone needs to bring value to stay here. We are not a charitable organization." "Yeah, I am seeing that," Mitch commented somewhat sardonically. Kate cast her gaze upon him with more intensity. "We are up against it, Mitch. The world is not the place it once was. We are well-stocked, but those stocks are not going to last forever. Come spring, we are going to have to hit the ground running, or we might all be getting a lot leaner. I would love to be more open to helping others out, but that is just not possible under current conditions."

"The dentist and her kids can stay as we desperately need that skill set. There are not too many other skill sets we are lacking, so if you are out and about on an expedition, think about that before you drag anyone else back here." Kate finished with some finality. Mitch nodded his agreement. He was glad Abigail and her kids were going to be able to stay. He had grown fond of the kids, especially in the past couple of days, and didn't want to push them out into an increasingly cruel world. "I appreciate that, Kate," he said to her. "I hope she fits in and is what she says she is." Kate gave Mitch a tight smile. "I do too," and with that, she strode away. As she walked, she called out over her shoulder, "You are still on quarantine – don't forget that."

Chapter Seven

Kate

As Kate walked away from the outbuilding, they had put Mitch and his new companions in, her mind churned. She felt annoyed, and this annoyed her. Emotions arriving of their own accord didn't fit into her mental map of herself. Every time an emotion forced its way into her consciousness against her will, she got irritated. Damned emotions, she thought. With all that she had to deal with, these intrusions were most unwelcome. She had been gradually assuming more direct control over the group as Ian noticeably retreated into himself. This forced more of the decision-making on her, which was frustrating as Ian clearly wasn't doing his part. In council meetings, she made an effort to let him have his say and even directly ask his opinion on things on which she had already made up her mind about in an effort to engage him. His responses were reduced to grunts or single words like "yeah," "ok," or "sure," with no elaboration or explanation. Kate felt this was placing more of the burden on her, and this was not what she had signed up for. The council had been formed to allow all of its members input and then voting rights under the assumption that the collective IQ was greater than any one individual's, and by approaching problems this way, they could avoid making serious mistakes. As time had passed, however, she realized she was assuming more and more of the alpha role and the remainder of the council was turning into deltas or worker bees, and now Ian seemed to be turning into a bravo. Very frustrating!

Mitch arriving with this woman and her two kids added to the 'Things to do list,' but it really wasn't that onerous. Mitch was right – they needed a dentist, and it had been a topic of discussion on more than one occasion. An abscessed tooth was not outside the realm of possibility with the total lack of dental care everyone was getting these days, and that could be either debilitating or even fatal. So, if this dentist woman wasn't sick or her kids weren't, Kate didn't see any other option than to let them stay. She would go through the motions of holding a committee meeting, but with the stagnation of that group, she already knew the outcome. On top of that, she had much bigger concerns to focus her attention on — not counting the failing leadership within the committee.

Arriving back at the house, she went in through the back door into the mudroom. Taking off her boots and hanging her jacket on the wall-mounted hook, she pulled on her slippers and headed into the kitchen. Two ladies were there working on dinner. "So, what are they like, Kate?" asked the freckle-faced redhead kneading bread on the flour-covered kitchen island. "I don't know," replied Kate more tersely than she had intended. "It's just some woman and her kids. She is a dentist, though, which does make her interesting." The redhead seemed to disregard the terse reply and continued happily, "It will be intriguing to hear their story. They are the first outsiders we have interacted with in a positive manner in a long time." Kate smirked. Interacting in a positive manner must be the new code phrase for talking to people without shooting at them. Their last few 'interactions' had all ended with dead bodies needing to be buried.

"Well, intriguing is going to have to wait. They are in isolation for a couple of days to see if they are contagious in any way. Steer clear of them until at least the day after tomorrow. Direction on this matter is going to come down from the council after tonight's meeting," she said to both of the women while they worked. Opening the fridge, she scanned for something refreshing to drink, but nothing caught her eye. "We have some lemonade in the big carafe on the counter if you are looking for something tasty," the other lady, a short-haired brunette, said to her. "Thanks," Kate said as she pulled a glass out of a cupboard and moved to the carafe at the end of the counter.

Departing the kitchen, she walked to the dining room where the council held their regular meetings. It was designed as a dining room to seat a dozen, but the population of the house had grown to the point where it was impossible to fit everyone into the same room, seated for a meal. In addition, the shift work schedule they now operated under, with the need for constant security, meant meals were taken at a number of different times in the day. The kitchen always seemed to be preparing food as people rose from bed or went to bed at differing times throughout the twenty-four-hour routine. The large dining room table was now covered in charts, reports, tally sheets, and other miscellaneous items needed to run the organization. When the council met, they pushed aside the materials and took over one end of the heavy oak table. The chairs were made to match in an Amish style of woodworking that Kate didn't really like but were commonplace in rural settings. Comfortable enough, but a bit dated for her taste. Not that it mattered anymore.

Sitting down, she reached for the latest inventory that Jean had done of their foodstuffs. Jean had organized her count into dried goods, freeze-dried goods, canned goods, frozen items, smoked meats, and perishables. It was a multiple-page document written in cursive. Kate stared at the handwriting for a long while. Cursive writing. Who knew that it would make itself useful again? In a world of laptops and voice-to-text, the skill of being able to write without resorting to block letter printing had been on the path to extinction. Ironically, it took the collapse of an entire society to bring it back. The inventory had tallies at the bottom, plus some caloric calculations. All food, regardless of how it was stored or preserved, could be counted in terms of the calories it delivered. What the tally sheet did not show, however, was the nutritional value remaining in those calories. Every day that passed meant their food stores lost some of their nutritional value and were less life sustaining. This didn't mean they wouldn't eat all of it, eventually. Sometimes just having something to put in your belly was enough, she thought, but what was apparent was the need for fresh food to be reintroduced into their diet. The group had put away enough food for three years according to their calculations, but new mouths were inevitably going to arrive – either through the front gates or out of a mother giving birth from within their midst. The three people sitting in one of the storage sheds at that moment were evidence of that, she thought to herself.

She put the inventory down. Important but not interesting, she had to admit. How had she ended up here, she thought to herself? From running her own successful business in a large, beautiful city to this country abode in Podunk nowhere. It had been a strange and surprising journey. But before she could take a walk down memory lane, Andy walked into the dining room. "Who do you have stashed in that shed?" he asked her in his overbearing and always irritating way. Andy was probably her least favorite person of the group. He had been a friend of Frank's and was asked to join before her, so he always acted as if his seniority in the group accounted for something. Reality was, Andy probably brought the least to the table of any of the group's members. She suffered his presence due in part to their need for people. Losing modern society and all of the labor-saving devices and product availability due to its efficient supply chains meant a lot more work had to be done manually. In addition, the loss of centralized control over the use of force meant they had to supply their own security, which was onerous to say the least. Staffing the overwatch tower 24/7 was an enormous drain on resources and a simultaneous drain on morale. Everyone found the duty tedious and boring and was reluctant to do it. Kate and Ian had both made impassioned speeches to the team about the necessity of maintaining security and the potential impact of having a security failure. The group as a whole agreed and understood the essential nature of the task, but the speeches had a short-lived effect. No matter how you sliced it - it was boring duty. They had thought of combining it with other duties, but that idea had been discarded as other duties would have immediately reduced the effectiveness of the overwatch, which could have fatal consequences.

"What are you doing?" Andy inquired. "Reviewing inventory," she responded with more irritation in her voice than she wanted. "Find anything interesting?" he asked. "Interesting, no. Concerning, yes," she replied with markedly less irritation in her voice. "We are over-indexed on some items and sorely lacking in others. We are not rotating our stocks properly and are running into dating issues on some foodstuffs. We have some obvious count errors as well." Andy stared at her. "I guess those are problems." He didn't offer any useful suggestions or help and instead just wandered off. No wonder I find him annoying, she thought. Just wasting my time with no useful input. She put him out of her mind and returned to the inventory.

Kate, like Mitch, was aware of the fact that the group hadn't planted crops of any significance so far and their food stocks were finite. They had some fruit trees and berry bushes planted, but they had not been in place long enough to bear enough fruit or berries. At the end of this summer, the raspberries and strawberries might produce a few pails-full, but not nearly enough to make a difference. The fruit trees, especially, were going to take years of pruning and maintenance before they began to bear fruit of any consequence. They had planted apple, plum, apricot, and pear trees in their small orchard, all variants that could withstand the colder climate of this growing zone. In addition to the raspberries and strawberries, they had put in black and red currants, blueberries, saskatoons, bush cherries, blackberries, and one other type she couldn't remember at the moment. They weren't sure which would produce the most over the long run, but the group thought they would try as many as they could and then expand the species that did the best. Nuts didn't grow in this climate at all, Kate reminded herself. She was not too broken up about that one as she was allergic to nuts, but a lot of the group moaned about missing cashews, almonds, and many other favorites. Just another thing lost with the collapse of the supply chains. Focusing on the inventory again, Kate looked at the fresh tallies from today's count. In the prep phase, the group had made some assumptions about the rate of calorie burn they would sustain once they were solely dependent on their stockpile. Sadly, they were going through the food even faster than expected. Manual labor had driven up everyone's hunger level. Most of the group had desk jobs of one sort or another pre-collapse, and the conversion to manual labor lifestyles and long days had produced a lot of sore muscles and hunger pangs. They were not at the point of locking up the food yet, but Kate could see that day coming.

Kate picked up another paper document. It was an old-fashioned street map. She and other members of the team had marked known warehouses on the map, thought to contain foodstuffs. Over the past year, they had sent foraging teams into the city investigating these locations to see what could be found. For the most part, they had found them emptied out, burned down, or a combination of both. A couple of times, they had found recoverable materials, but it was getting less and less often. Once, the scouting team had ended up in a firefight with another group apparently doing the same thing, but had luckily sustained no injuries. The distances traveled were getting longer as they worked their way outward in concentric rings from their location. The expeditions also took longer as the team had to backtrack numerous times to ensure they were not being followed when they returned to the acreage. Despite these challenges, the council realized teams were going to have to be sent further afield. Further trips also meant dipping into their gasoline supplies. All of their gas had Stabil added to it to extend its useful life, but the reality was, the octane of the gas was diminishing over time and at some point, would be unusable. So, use it or lose it was the scenario they were moving into now, and with no refineries operating now or perhaps for a long time, the gas they had was better put to use to secure more food. The group did not have any horses but had put away a good supply of mountain bikes. Hauling food by bicycle was going to be limited at best. The bikes could carry a couple of hundred pounds if the correct panniers were supplied, but the rider would have to walk alongside the bike instead of ride it. Much, much slower going. Kate told herself to worry about the fuel and vehicle problem later – right now, they had to focus on food. With the potential addition of three more mouths today, the need was only growing.

Using her hands, Kate spread the map out on the table. From their location, they had gone as far as 35 kilometers or about 21 miles in their missions to the south. The deep south of the city was where the industrial area was and most of the warehousing. With another month or so of warm weather, it was time to make some deep forays into the south and see what they could find. Kate looked at the three warehouse locations previously circled in red on the map. Generally, the teams had made same-day trips out to scout the locations, but with the distances involved, an overnight trip might be in order. It would take more vehicles and more gasoline, as well as more people, which left fewer people behind to guard the acreage and work on the daily tasks that need doing. When winter fully set in, there would be no more foraging trips. On top of that, with each passing week, the shelf life of what they could find was getting older and older. At some point approaching soon, there would be no point in foraging at all. Overnight trip it was going to be, she decided to herself. Now she just had to convince the rest of the council to make it so. That was probably not too hard, she thought. They seemed to be more interested in taking direction than giving it as of late. Ian was putting up fewer and fewer objections to her initiatives. Maybe it was time to restructure, she thought. The council had served its purpose, but it was becoming apparent to her that its usefulness had come to an end. "I can see why warlords and barons and dukes evolved in the days of yore," she said aloud. Other than natural alphas, most people wanted someone to follow, she thought. Most people don't like the weight of decision-making and are uncomfortable with the responsibility and accountability that comes with leadership. It was much easier to sit on the sidelines and complain about decisions someone had made than to make them on their own.

Kate stood and walked back into the kitchen. The breadmaking for the day was complete, and the smell of fresh-baked bread permeated the room. The two ladies were now engaged in dinnertime meal prep. The redhead, Clair, was opening canned goods and transferring them to stainless steel bowls. Kate addressed both of the women – "Please put together something for the four folks we have in the storage shed outside. It's a woman, her two kids, and Mitch. I am sure they are quite hungry after their long walk to get here, so be generous with their portions." Both of the women nodded towards Kate but did not comment. Kate thanked them and headed towards her room at the far end of the house. Once there, she sat down on her bed and pulled off her footwear. A corn on her left foot was giving her grief, and prolonged wear of anything other than her slippers made it protest loudly. She didn't feel right moving around the house and the property wearing her slippers, so she tended to wear her leather riding boots, but that might need to change going forward. She wasn't sure what to do about a corn on her foot outside of putting corn pads on it, and they were running out of those. Perhaps she should put that on the foraging list, she thought to herself. She lay back on her bed. The constant stress associated with being the de facto leader of the group was getting to her. She missed Frank and his tireless energy coupled with his can-do attitude and generally positive outlook on life. Frank had been divorced for several years and didn't seem to have any interest in pursuing a new life partner. Kate had lost her husband to pancreatic cancer and had been alone for some time. She wasn't overly attracted to Frank physically but had grown more and more enamored with him as his stalwart qualities became obvious. She wasn't sure if he felt the same way and hadn't given any sign, but she couldn't help thinking things were drifting that way. She realized now that she had put her eggs in that basket, and when he had been killed by the intruder, his loss impacted her far more heavily than she had been prepared for. Now, she felt quite alone, and the group was turning more and more towards her leadership, which by its nature was a lonely position.

For now, she knew she had to focus on the bigger picture items. Her personal relationships were going to have to wait. Right here and right now they had to focus on securing supplies, planning for crops in the spring, enhancing their security, and perhaps the biggest problem — sorting out leadership and morale. Their very existence counted on these things and had to occupy the totality of her focus. Sitting back up, she felt better. Action was the answer to malaise. Getting things done had always made her feel better. Kate dug a corn pad out of her bedside table and put it on her ailing foot. She was definitely going to add this to the next foraging list. She was not going to let her stupid foot limit her. Pulling her boots back on, she headed back to the dining room. She unclipped her Baofeng radio from her belt and pressed the transmit button. "Ian, where are you currently?" "In the shop. What do you need?" came his response. "Can we meet in the next thirty minutes or so?" she asked. "Copy that," came his response. "Thanks, Ian," she replied. Arriving in the dining room/planning area, she pulled out a couple of the yellow legal pads she liked to work on and sat down. On the first pad, she wrote across the top in big letters "Leadership." On the next pad, she wrote "Expedition." She was going to make some bullet points under each heading but decided against it. Rather than pre-empting and steering the discussion with Ian, she opted to let him initiate ideas of his own, and then she would add to them afterwards.

Just as she completed that thought, Ian walked in. "That was quick," she commented. "What happened to the thirty minutes?" Ian remarked back to her. "I paused the project I was working on as it was a good time to stop." "Ok. That makes sense. Listen, I want to talk to you about a couple of different items," she replied. Ian was looking at her yellow legal pads and taking in the information on the top of them. "I guess you are planning an expedition?" he replied. Obviously, not mentioning the one with the leadership heading on it. "Yes. We can talk about that one first if you like," she responded to him. "I have been reviewing the inventories, and we are getting into a 'situation.' It's a combination of supply shortages and my belief that the window on scavenging what is left in the city is beginning to close. On top of that is the approaching stale dates of any food materials left out there." She stopped talking and looked at him, waiting for his response. "How bad is it?" he asked her. "Depends on how we look at it. We are definitely burning through supplies faster than we expected. Adding more heads to our population will only exacerbate the problem. We can make it through another year with current stocks, but after that, our reserves would be dangerously low. Additionally, we are not particularly experienced in growing our own food, and we are assuming everything goes as planned. We could have a drought or a locust infestation or lord knows what," Kate paused and waited for Ian to respond. "I agree to all of that," he answered. "I guess my question would be – is the potential risk of going on another expedition searching for supplies worth it?" "What if we find nothing worth salvaging and lose someone or multiple someone's?" Kate said. "That is the rub, I guess. Is it worth it? Can we afford not to try?" Ian frowned. He then picked up the inventories lying on the table which Kate had left there. Rubbing the side of his nose with his forefinger, he reviewed the numbers. "When were these counts done?" he asked. "These are fresh," she answered.

Ian pulled out a chair and sat down. "I don't suppose the leadership topic is any better?" he asked. Kate looked at him dourly. "Is this a good time to have this talk?" she asked. "As good a time as any other," he replied. "So, what is the deal? It's not a secret you have been saying less and less in council meetings. You just don't seem that engaged these days. What gives?" she said to Ian emphatically. Ian looked at Kate for a while before answering. Taking a deep breath, he started, "Yes, I have been holding back. As to why, I'm not sure I can answer that fully. Part depression, part frustration, and part something else I can't really identify. You seem to thrive on taking on all these decisions, whereas I find the burden of doing everyone else's thinking for them exhausting. I just don't want to do it anymore. I mean, how did any of these people survive before all this? How did they get their kids to school or pay their taxes or even hold down a job? It really perplexes me how they became so helpless." Kate nodded her understanding. "So, what do you propose we do?" Ian considered for a full minute before answering, "You seem to be making all the decisions. I suggest we talk to the council about making you the leader with all of the incumbent responsibilities and duties. You are the de facto leader as is — we might as well formalize it. I can't see them objecting as they defer to you all the time as it is. Not an absolute leader, by the way, so if you go completely off the rails, you can be removed as you hold the position through our consent. Sound good?"

Now it was time for Kate to consider. She weighed the various pros and cons in her head. She knew this day was coming, and she also knew there wasn't anyone else suitable for the position. In her mind, she knew there really was no decision to be made. Someone had to take the reins and get task-oriented, or the group as a whole would fail. "If you think you can swing it with the council and then the larger group – I'll do it," she announced to Ian. "We have so many things to focus on, and I can hear the clock ticking in the background every day. We really need to get a move on." Ian stood up from his chair. "So, tonight we discuss this with the council?" "Yes. No point in waiting," Kate agreed. Ian continued, "We can also discuss the expedition you were thinking about. I agree we should go, and I agree time is of the essence." The meeting came to an end. Ian took his leave and returned to the task he had been working on previously. Kate picked up the pad of paper with the expedition heading and began scribing bullet points on it. In her mind, the expedition was a foregone conclusion, and if the council members agreed to her ascension, she would make the decision regardless.

The rest of the afternoon worked its way by. Kate stopped to have a snack or refresh her drink a couple of times, dealt with minor issues that came her way, and at one point completely stopped working to eat the dinner prepared by Clair and Bonnie in the kitchen. After a half hour had passed and everyone's food had settled in their bellies, the members of the council slowly drifted into the dining room. Ian still had the remains of grease residue on his hands from the job he had been working on, and despite his best efforts with soap, hot water, and scrubbing, it refused to fully leave. Rick made an appearance slightly after Ian but had no visible evidence showing what he had been doing. Sarah and Kerri arrived together after eating their dinner, and Renaldo trickled in last. Once the whole council had settled into their respective seats, Kate got up and closed the sliding double doors that separated the dining room from the living room. This was the custom for these meetings, in part for privacy and in part to keep the noise from the living room from penetrating their space and allowing for the long periods of focus required to resolve issues.

The council of six was drawn from the general population of the acreage. All were long-time members of the group, with five of them being founding members. When Frank was alive, he had set the council up with equal votes for all and his, the seventh vote, to be used only as a tie-breaker when needed. With his absence from the council, there were occasional deadlocks, but those were usually resolved by having follow-up meetings after people had taken the time to think over the subject matter. Kate had been thinking about adding another member to bring their numbers up again, but that door seemed to be closing in light of recent developments. She would see how the meeting went tonight and decide from there.

Kate opened the meeting. "Okay everyone, so here we are again for another episode of the most exciting game show in the land - how to not starve and live to see another day!" Sadly, her joke fell flat on the council. Sarah stared down at her pad of paper and Kerri rolled her eyes. The men were a little more generous with a smirk or two and even a half smile from Ian. Not a great start to the evening.

"Thanks to all of you for being so enthusiastic," she said with a dollop of sarcasm. "Can we just get on with it?" Sarah contributed. "I am sure almost all of us would rather be doing something else right now. These meetings are just going nowhere and seem to largely be a waste of time. I mean you just do whatever you want anyway. We are more of a rubber stamp committee than anything else these days," she concluded. Kate decided this might be the beginning of the opening she was looking for. Before proceeding too far down the road, she decided to make some opening gestures of reconciliation. "You say I decide everything anyway — what would you suggest we do? Is there another approach or mechanism you would like to employ to make decisions for the group? What are your thoughts or suggestions on the matter?" Kate riposted. "I don't know the answer to that," Sarah fired back. "Why is it up to me to come up with a solution when all I did was point out the problem? It's not like a big mystery around here. We discuss the problem du jour and then you decide the way we are going to handle it." Sarah slumped back into her chair. Kerri then took up the challenge. "Sarah is right. We talk and talk and talk and then we end up doing it your way. Seriously, name a time when we didn't do it the way you thought best?"

Kate responded to Kerri's accusation, "It's not my fault my solution often ends up being the best one in the end. After all, we vote on each proposal after the discussion, and each of you has a vote. If the vote has gone my way more times than not – I am sorry for coming up with so many good ideas." Kerri looked as if the wind had gone out of her sails with her attempt to take on Kate. "I just don't care anymore," Kerri said aloud. "I am tired of decision-making – I have terminal decision fatigue!" Kate looked around the table. None of the men looked any more inclined to argue the state of affairs either. Kate decided to take her shot. "Ok. I get it. Everyone is tired of doing this, tired of the arguments, and tired of all these meetings. I have a proposal which might sound a little off the wall at first, but hear me out. Instead of a council, we elect a leader who can make the decisions, hold people accountable, and drive the operation forward. The leader would need to have authority but would get it from the people who live here. Their votes for the leader would grant the authority needed by the leader to get things done. It would not be permanent, say a year or two to start, and if things go well, perhaps longer, later once we have kind of sorted things out." Kate stopped and surveyed the room. Everyone had stopped being distracted and was looking directly at her. "Like a king or something?" Sarah asked. "No, not a king or a queen for that matter – maybe a Superintendent or Team Leader or something like that. Nothing nearly so formal or lofty as a king – that just sounds silly," Kate replied. "How about 'The Boss'?" suggested Ian. "Or Hoss," said Rick laughingly. "What about Coach?" said Kerri. "A coach is the leader but in a helpful, friendly kind of way – not domineering". "Hmm." replied Kate. "Sounds a little powerless, but it might fit the bill for now. I like the idea of helping versus commanding."

"Do we take a vote now or do we wait?" asked Kate. Ian spoke up, "If we are going to make this legitimate, we need to do it right. We need to bring the idea to the whole community and let everyone have a vote. If we decide here at this table, it will be seen as autocratic and people will begin to grumble or rebel. Plus, we need to have at least two candidates to vote for, or it will be simply a win by acclamation." Exactly what I was thinking, thought Kate, but she realized she had to maintain appearances. This might take a bit longer than she wanted, but taking the route Ian suggested would establish her legitimacy as the leader. She could change the title or duties later as she saw fit – just getting there first was the main goal.

Kate – "So why don't we adjourn and see what everyone thinks over the course of the next two days. See who wants the position and then figure out a process to have an election of sorts." Heads nodded and the meeting broke up. Ian lingered around after the rest had left. "I think you want this for yourself, Kate. People who want power are often ill-suited to hold it in my opinion. I hope you are thinking about this carefully. Leadership is a lonely place and although shit rolls downhill, responsibility tends to roll uphill. You will be shouldering all of the blame for everything that goes wrong around here." "I hear you, Ian. I hear you," Kate replied. "Let's see where this goes." Kate left the dining room and headed to her bedroom. She needed some time to herself to think.

CHAPTER EIGHT

NEW DAY

Morning came. Caleb opened his eyes after lying still but awake for at least ten minutes. No alarm clocks anymore. With his blinds and blackout curtains in place, his room was as jet black in the morning as it was when he went to bed. One good thing about the collapse was there was no longer a need to be up by a certain time, and every day he slept until fully rested. Caleb recalled caffeinating himself on the way to work to drive out the fatigue when late nights translated into insufficient sleep. That, however, was no longer the case. Some upside to this life, he thought. Sitting up and swinging his feet to the floor, he stood and stretched. He stopped and listened for sounds coming from Angeline's room, but there were none. Either she was still asleep, or she was waiting for him to rise. Pulling on a housecoat, he headed for the washroom and a well-deserved shower. Passing Angeline's room, he could hear the sounds of stirring coming from within.

Fifteen minutes later, he was scrubbed and refreshed. Hot water had to be one of civilization's greatest inventions, he thought to himself, and then chuckled – I said exactly the same thing to Angeline yesterday. Later, back in his room, he donned fresh clothes and looked in the laundry bin. It was getting full and needed to be addressed sooner rather than later. Walking to his bedside table, he strapped on his Casio Tough Solar Powered watch. He had picked up a couple of these in preparation for the impending fall of society, as he figured batteries for watches were going to be in short supply. He also liked the way the watch looked and sat on his wrist. He considered it an essential part of his EDC (everyday carry) items. In his right pants pocket rode a Cold Steel Voyager with a tanto tip, pocket clipped for easy access. In his left pocket was a Streamlight, which put out 2000 lumens of bright light. He had a Leatherman Rebar in coyote brown in a nylon sheath. The Leatherman was one of his favorite tools. You could get multi-tools with more options, but he found the Rebar had just the right mix and met his needs on an almost daily basis. The last item he always carried was a ferro rod in a leather case on his belt. A ferro rod worked even when wet and never ran out of fuel. You could scrape it down to almost nothing over time, but he would replace it long before that happened. He put his whistle around his neck on its breakaway lanyard and reminded himself to get one for Angeline.

Heading out to the kitchen area, he saw the door to her room open and the bathroom door closed. He set the kettle on the stove to make some hot water for the coffee he had daily. Fifteen minutes later, Angeline arrived in the kitchen. "How did you sleep?" he asked. "Not bad," came the reply. "The bed was far more comfortable than what I have been used to, but it is still a new bed for me." Caleb sat at the kitchen table with coffee in hand. "What do you like to eat and drink in the morning?" She considered the question for a minute. "I have not had a 'regular' breakfast in a long time. We were on the move as we headed toward the coast, and every day was different. What I really want, but I don't know if it's possible, is pancakes. Is that possible?" Caleb smiled.

"As a matter of fact, it is. I think I might even have some maple syrup in the pantry." Angeline clapped her hands in joy. "Pancakes!" Caleb set down his coffee and got to work making breakfast for her.

Thirty minutes later, she finished the last of her food and pushed her plate away. "I'm stuffed! She exclaimed. "Why didn't you have any? Don't you like pancakes?" she asked. "I do, but years ago I adopted a different way of eating. I have a black coffee or two in the morning and then other zero-calorie drinks throughout the day. At dinner time, I have a large meal which is a combination of fat and protein, and that's it," said Caleb. "So, no pancakes?" she asked. "Nope. No breakfast or lunch either. Just one meal a day at the end of the day," Caleb replied. Angeline did not look convinced. "Don't you get hungry?" she asked. "At first, I did, but then my hormones adjusted, and now I don't even think about food during the day. I have more time to do other things, and I use up less of my food stocks," said Caleb. "Do I have to do that?" she asked. "No. You're still growing, and I wouldn't want to interrupt the flow of energy to you when you are in this stage of your life." She looked relieved. "Since you are finished eating, we should talk about what's next," he commented to her. "You are seriously lacking in the clothing department, and I do not have anything even close to fitting you. We are going to need to go on a return expedition to the city to hunt for some clothes for you. We also need to think about footwear and some clothes and shoes for when you grow bigger. Before we do that, however, we are going to need to spend some time going over some basics. I need to explain to you my security protocols for this place as well as moving around when we are outside. I don't need to tell you it is dangerous out there, and if we are discovered by a large enough group, it could be dangerous in here." Angeline nodded her agreement.

"Before we start with that, I should give you a tour of the place," he suggested. He took her plate and cutlery and put them in the sink for later consideration. "You have already seen the upstairs pretty much. Living room, kitchen/dining area, two bedrooms, and a bathroom. Let's go down the first flight of stairs and see the next level." Angeline followed him to the doorway leading downstairs. Caleb switched on the light and descended the stairs. When they got downstairs, he showed her his recreation room with a large wall-mounted monitor along with some gaming consoles and a large collection of DVDs featuring movies from a variety of genres. The next room over was a large walk-in pantry. Two of the walls were lined with shelves of canned and bottled foodstuffs. The third wall featured a long chest-style deep freezer. Angeline had never seen such a large deep freeze. "It was a real pain getting that down here. The guys from the appliance delivery place didn't like me much after dealing with it," he said with a laugh. Backing out of the pantry, they opened the door to another room which was fully shelved and labeled. A wide variety of bins caught her eye with bedclothes, footwear, toiletries, and many other items listed. Far too many to remember. Past that room was another pair of doorways. The one on the left was his gun room. Caleb got his key out and opened it for her to see. Angeline's mouth dropped open when she saw the gun rack with all the firearms stored inside of it and all the other equipment in that room. Caleb opened the next door and revealed another stairway going down. "What's down there?" asked Angeline. "The sub-basement," he told her with a smile again, leading her down the stairs after turning on the light. "When I had this house built, I wanted to go down instead of up like most houses. By being deeper in the ground, I reduced my heating and cooling costs.

Increased the ballistic resistance of my house as well." Angeline asked, "What's ballistic resistance?" Caleb smiled again. "That means if people are shooting at me with guns, I am safe. They can't hit me because I am underground." "Oh" was her only response.

As they arrived at the bottom of the stairs, Angeline noticed the door looked different from all the other doors in the house. This one was made of some kind of metal or steel and looked heavier. "The delivery guys didn't like this one much either," he told her. "They had to use a wheeler to get it down here as it was solid steel and quite heavy." She nodded her understanding of what he was sharing. Using the keys off his belt, he unlocked the door, and they passed through. Just inside the door was a smaller room with computers and monitors. Looking at the monitors, she could see views of the areas outside his house – all angles. "This is so I can see what is going on up there and not be surprised," he told her. "A few times I have had unwanted guests, and being able to see outside my walls has been a real advantage. The cameras are hard to see, and people don't know I'm watching them." The walls were covered in shelves, and Angeline could see a wide variety of books of all sorts lining them. They carried on through that room into a larger room. This room had more light than the previous room and was different because the floor was padded. Against the far wall was a half rack for strength training as well as assorted dip handles, a bench, bars, a chin-up bar, free weights, and other miscellaneous strength training equipment. Angeline didn't know what any of it was exactly, but she got the idea it was exercise equipment. Just past that, a long heavy bag was suspended from the ceiling with a double-ended bag mounted next to that. The walls of the room held racks on which all sorts of weapons were placed. Once again, Angeline did not recognize or understand any of them, but she knew they were weapons. "This is my training room," he told her. "I try to spend about an hour a day down here practicing my various skill sets. The world is now a dangerous place, and until you arrived, I was on my own. I need all the advantages I can get, so regular training helps me, plus it keeps me in shape, and I feel good after working out." She understood and said as much.

Passing through the gym they entered a short hallway. On either side was a door with a third door at the end of the hall. Caleb turned left and opened the first door. Inside were pallets stacked with foodstuffs. "Everything in here is dry goods" he said. "I have full pallets of rice, flour, sugar, beans and lentils among other things" he said. "Currently I don't eat a lot of this kind of thing, but it was affordable and easily available. If I get into a pinch, I can use this to eat from for a long time. Everything is up on a pallet so if water were to get in here in some way it would remain dry for a while giving me a chance to clean it out." He led her across the hall to the next room. He opened the door and snapped on the light. Inside was a shop with various power tools she didn't recognize and work benches. In a corner was a bin with various lengths of steel angle iron and pipe poking out of it and one wall had a rack of various lengths of wood and metal laying on it. "This is a combo wood/metal working and everything else shop" he told her. I don't build much currently but if I needed to, I have raw materials, adhesives and lots of different kinds of tools here. He pointed at the ceiling "see that? That is venting for when I do use the power tools. Being this deep in the ground I need to force air to the surface and exchange it for fresh. If we are using the gym, we need to leave this door open to let the air flow. It was a bit of an oversight on my part, as I didn't put venting right into the gym area. Not a disaster but definitely not smart on my part." He led her out of the room to the last door. She noticed this door was barred from the inside as well as deadbolted. He turned and looked at her "this door leads down a tunnel to just under a shed I have outside. If we were somehow trapped in here this is our escape route. I have a backpack and other supplies in a locker at the bottom of the stairs. We are going to have to put something together for you. I'm not going to open this door, but you can use your imagination. I have the keys for this door on my keychain but now that you are here, I am going to put a hook on the wall and hang a key off of it." He looked at her seriously "this door only gets used in an actual emergency. No hide and seek games or anything else. Do I make myself clear?" Angeline could see the seriousness with which he dealt this topic." "I get it" she said. "Let's head back up he suggested" now that the tour was done. As they headed back upstairs, he mentioned to her he was going to leave the door to the third level unlocked going forward so she could access it as she liked. She smiled and nodded in response.

Arriving back in the kitchen, they sat down. Caleb handed her a Fox 40 whistle he had picked up during their tour downstairs. It was bright red with a matching breakaway lanyard. He got out an index card from a box he had on the counter and wrote the following: One long blast means "Alert," two short blasts mean "Clear – everything is okay." A succession of long, slow blasts means: "advance or move forward." Several short, sharp blasts mean: "Come together," three short blasts followed by one long blast mean "Danger." He shared with her, "this is a system I adopted from the Boy Scouts. It's not exactly the same but is close. Keep the card in your pocket for now and we will practice when we are outside. A whistle like the Fox 40 can produce 115 decibels of sound, which is much more easily heard over distance. On average, a human female can only generate 75 decibels, which of course can't be heard as far." Angeline put the whistle to her lips and made a small sound with it. She smiled. "Ok. I guess this is just the first of many things I need to learn," she said. Caleb – "yeah. I have a list in mind but need to write it down. I came up with twenty items just thinking about it for a minute or two. I imagine it will get pretty long by the time we are done." Angeline smiled brightly. "So, school is going to be in for sure now!" Caleb nodded. "Why don't you go to the rec room and find something to do? I am going to install this switch for my solar system I picked up in the city. I would show you how, but you don't have the basic underlying knowledge to understand what it is for, so at this point it would not make sense to show you. Solar systems are one of the items on my list, but I want to approach it methodically." Angeline got up and headed to the rec room, Caleb heading to the control panels for his solar array.

An hour later, he was done. He put away his tools and went to the rec room. Angeline had figured out how to work the DVD player and was watching 2012, a Hollywood epic disaster film. Sitting down beside her, he picked up the remote and paused the movie. "You seem to have an awful lot of these apocalypse, end-of-the-world type shows," she said. "Was this something you were hoping for?" Caleb laughed, "No, not at all. It is something I very much did not want to happen, but here we are. I began to see a problem coming and got interested in the subject matter. I know Hollywood tends to overdramatize things for effect, but I thought to myself – I can watch these shows and maybe pick up an idea or two from each of them. I have to admit I did get some good ideas here and there. I also believe in something called 'habituation,' which is defined as "a decline in responsiveness to a stimulus due to repeated exposure." In other words – if I exposed myself to this coming bad thing enough times, it would not seem so bad when it really did come." "I don't know if you noticed it or not, but a lot – and I mean a lot – of people went into a state of shock when things fell apart. It was like their minds could not accept the "new normal." Angeline nodded and remarked, "Exactly. My mum really started freaking out and dad turned into some kind of robot. I mean they were moving and doing things, but it was really weird. I had to shout to get mum's attention a couple of times, and then she gave me these ridiculous answers which made no sense at all." Caleb said, "I do have to admit to some shock myself, but I think I got focused on acting pretty quickly. I topped up my fuel reservoirs, did a final few food purchases, and ran a security check on my premises. I did not go around during the final days as things got really hairy and scary. I think a lot of people were killed in that period." Angeline glumly agreed, "That's when my family got killed. It was crazy. We should have listened to grandpa sooner and gone to his hideout. They would still be here if they had."

Caleb stood up. "Let's not sit here and dwell on the past. What is done is done. Why don't we get our outdoor clothes

on and go for a walk? I can show you the solar array."
Angeline stood and followed Caleb upstairs after turning off
the DVD player and monitor. Once upstairs, getting ready
didn't take too long. Caleb made a trip to the gun room to
pick up a firearm for their excursion outside. "Okay, here is
one of the basic rules. Maybe I will make a 'top ten' list at
some point, but for now we can call it one of the basic rules.
Never — and I mean never — go out of the house unarmed."
"I am armed," she said. "I have a left arm and a right arm,"
lifting her arms in the air. "Smart ass," Caleb said back to her.
"Everybody is a smart ass." Angeline smiled back at him. "So,
how do I get armed to follow your 'rules?'" Caleb shook his
head. "Not yet, young lady. You need to know how to
handle a weapon before I go handing you anything. For now,
you can hit them with your charming personality." Heading
into the mudroom, he pulled on his boots and then breech-
checked his weapon, a Benelli semi-automatic shotgun with
a sling. He checked to ensure the safety was on and then
looked through the peephole in the middle of the door. Not
seeing any threats, he opened the door and proceeded
outside. Angeline came out behind him and walked a short
distance before stopping. Caleb closed the door behind them
and then turned. Addressing Angeline, he said, "Every time

you come outside, take the time to have a good look around. Has anything changed since we were last outside? Look on the ground for animal paw prints and human footprints. Has anything been disturbed since the last time?" He pulled his monocular out of his belt pouch and scanned the area around them. Satisfied with what he saw, he put it away. He looked over at Angeline. "Follow me, ma'am." He headed towards a stand of trees close to his house. As they got closer, Angeline could see the stand of trees was fairly dense. Caleb walked into the trees, following a trail her eyes could just pick out. "Stay close," he said to her over his shoulder as they walked. After about ten minutes of following a winding path, they emerged from the trees into a clearing. She could see a number of solar panels in angle iron frames mounted on pedestals set into the ground. Caleb moved to the center of the clearing and turned to face her. "This is where our power comes from. Without these solar panels, we are living in the dark. The reason you and I met was my need for a certain switch which had burned out, which enabled me to continue using these panels. Unfortunately, the switch I had was made in China and was not a particularly good one. Luckily, I was able to find a replacement as well as a couple of spares at the warehouse I went searching through." Angeline looked around. All of the solar panels faced the same direction and looked identical. "How long will these last before they wear out?" she asked. "They are supposed to last twenty years," he told her. "But I am not counting on them lasting that long. I think things will be up and going again before that," he told her. "We won't need them by then."

Caleb suddenly stopped talking. He was looking past Angeline at the ground. Walking past her, he stopped and crouched. A size 9 or 10 boot print was visible in the soft earth. Caleb wore a size 11 himself, and he knew all the tread patterns of his own footwear. Someone had been in his stand of trees looking around. Caleb stood and started following the trail the intruder had left. It wove in and among his set of solar panels and then back towards the path they had followed in. The edges of the imprint had fallen inward, indicating the tracks were old or, at the very least, not fresh. Squatting down, he gestured to Angeline – "See here – this is the overall track, and deeper in is the true track. The deepest part of the depression is the floor, and the sides of the track are the walls. Get it" Angeline nodded. "If the pressure against the wall is sufficient, you get a ridge," he said, pointing at the track. Angeline looked intently where he was pointing. "Over time, I will teach you more and more about tracking. It is both interesting and a useful skill set to have in your arsenal." Caleb could clearly see the outbound tracks that they had trampled on their way in. He was angry at himself for not paying attention. "Gaps in attention like this are what get you killed," he said to Angeline, who had been watching him with interest. "We were chatting and having a good time, and I was not paying heed to the trail," he further shared. In the world we currently inhabit, you need to be aware of your surroundings at all times, or you will get blindsided at some point. "There is no one coming to save us. We are on our own. From here on in, it's your job to remind me to stay aware, and it is my job to remind you. We need to be a partnership. Do you get it?" Angeline nodded earnestly. "We are partners," she repeated back to him with a smile. "Let's head back to the house," Caleb suggested.

Fifteen minutes later, they were in the mudroom taking their boots off. Caleb noticed the Hudson's Bay wool blanket sitting on the bench where he had set it after taking it out of his pack when they first got back – he needed to do something with that, he reminded himself. Caleb headed back to the kitchen and put the kettle on. "Hot chocolate?" he asked. "Yes, please," came the enthusiastic response. Angeline sat down at the kitchen table as Caleb got two mugs out of the cupboard. Caleb then sat down at the table across from her as they waited for the water to boil. "I never had any kids, and I am uncertain what to do with you. In my mind, I am thinking of a big list of things you need to learn, but I have not asked you what you want or expect. This is all new to me, and I am probably going to make mistakes. I don't know what ten-year-old girls like or want. I only had brothers growing up, so I was never around girls your age except at school, and they were not interested in us much at that age." Angeline shrugged her shoulders. "Everything I had is gone. My friends and family are gone, so I don't know what to say. Grandpa was nice to me, but we didn't talk much. I feel like I have been living in a dream for a long time now, and I don't know when I am going to wake up. Even this place and you feel like a dream. Life is so different now with all that has happened; I don't know what to expect or even what I want. I just seem to flow from day to day and see what happens to me. You seem nice, and your house is cool and stuff, but is this my life now, or is something else going to change? I don't know what I can count on or depend on anymore. I guess I am saying I am just going to go with what comes and figure it out from there." Angeline sighed after her longest talk yet. The kettle made itself known as the water came to a boil, and Caleb stood up to make hot chocolates for the two of them.

Carrying the mugs, he came back to the table and sat again. Looking off in the distance for a while, he focused his gaze upon her again. "I guess we're going to have to figure this out together. For the time being, let's just focus on practical matters such as – you need more clothes. I have zero ten-year-old girl's clothes, and you are going to get tired of wearing the same thing every day, plus you have nothing to wear when they go in the wash," he said with a smile. "Are we going to go back into the city to get some?" she asked. "I didn't see any ladies' fashion stores in the forest – did you?" he responded with a laugh. "If I remember correctly, there were some places on the edge of town that might still have some clothes in them which we could access. It is still a bit of a hike but not nearly as far as we walked to get here." "How are we going to carry them back?" Angeline asked. "I have been thinking about that a bit," replied Caleb. "Do you remember that wheelbarrow we had for a while?

That seemed to work pretty well. I have a couple here. We could push one back to the city and fill it up. That should do you for a while." Caleb suddenly remembered the extra boots he had put in his backpack for her. He had put them under the bench where the wool blanket was set down and forgotten about them. "We have some boots already!" Angeline nodded. "I remember." "That is a good start," he remarked.

Caleb – "Before we go to town, we need to go over a few basics. Let's spend the rest of the day reviewing them and be ready to go in the morning, if the weather agrees." Angeline took the last couple of swallows of her hot chocolate and then picked up Caleb's empty mug and took the two mugs to the sink. "What basics are you talking about?" she asked. Caleb went to a kitchen drawer and took out a pad of paper and a pen and returned to the table. "Let's make a list so we don't forget anything," he suggested and began to write. Angeline stood and looked over his shoulder as he wrote. "Are we going to do all of that today?" she asked. Caleb looked up at her. "No, but I think we need to have a list started. We can cover a few of the most essential ones before we go, but when we get back, we can continue." After a few minutes of writing, Caleb had a full page filled. "That's enough for now." Caleb stood. "Follow me." Caleb headed to the front entry where his backpack was sitting. He picked it up when he got there and headed back to the kitchen. On the kitchen table, he poured the contents out onto the table. He also emptied out each of the pockets until it was completely empty. He set her two pairs of boots from under the bench, which he had retrieved, on the floor next to the table.

"This is a 'go bag' or 'jump bag' or 'day pack' or a variety of other names people have come up with. The name really doesn't matter. What does matter is what it does and what you have inside it." Caleb continued, "For me, the daypack is what I think I am going to need on my person to deal with a wide number of possibilities but not an exhaustive number. You can't anticipate everything – it's impossible. What I try to do is ensure that what I do carry covers the widest possible range of outcomes." "Here are some examples – a good fixed blade knife. I like folding blades but they have moving parts and can fail under harsh conditions. You want to pick a blade that is big enough and strong enough but not too big or too heavy." "You need a compass to find your way. You need hydration, which is why I always carry a CamelBak. Matches or a lighter for a fire are good, but I prefer a ferro rod and steel. I don't light too many fires usually, and matches can get wet and are ruined, and a lighter runs out of fuel. You can start hundreds of fires with a ferro rod." He picked up a clear plastic pill bottle to show her – "inside this bottle are a dozen cotton pads covered in Vaseline. I can take one out to put Vaseline on a skin condition, but that is a secondary purpose. These pads are really good tinder for starting a fire. It is easy to get a fire going with a ferro rod, and they burn even when slightly wet or in the rain with the petroleum jelly slathered on them."

Caleb continued to go through the contents of his bag with Angeline, explaining the reason behind each of the items and why he selected one thing over another. They spent the rest of the morning doing this and filling her smaller bag with similar items for her to carry on the upcoming adventure tomorrow. When they were done, he picked her bag up and hefted it. "No more than ten pounds, I estimate," he said, handing her the bag. "Not too heavy," she said as she slung it over her thin shoulders. Caleb handed her a sheath knife that he had brought up from downstairs.

"This is a Pendleton Mini-Hunter. It is made by Cold Steel, which is a company I am a big fan of. The sheath is made from something called Kydex, which is strong and durable and won't let the knife fall out if you run around or whatever." "Let's go outside and do some practice with it so you can get used to it." Angeline agreed and put her small backpack on a chair. Together they headed to the exit door and readied themselves to go outdoors again. Caleb did his usual checks of his firearm and looked through the peephole to see if anyone was lurking.

Once outside, they found some sticks and the lesson began. Caleb taught her to cut away from herself, some basic knife grips, and how to use the point versus the edge. What a slash versus a hack versus a thrust was, and so on, looked like. He went over some basic blade nomenclature, showing her the heel of the knife, the guard, the spine, and the belly of the knife, and so on. Angeline cut some branches and other items. Chopped the side of a wooden pole to learn about blade shock and maintaining her grip, and several other concepts. After a good hour of knife skills training, Caleb went back inside, retrieved a compass and paper map, and began teaching Angeline some basics of navigation. Midday, they stopped for a break so Angeline could eat a couple of energy bars. After that came more lessons and skill acquisition until Caleb judged Angeline had maxed out on her ability to retain information. It had been a productive day overall, and the sun had begun its descent towards the western horizon. Thankfully, the wind had been gentle for the day, and the clouds overhead were high and thin with no signs of rain. Tomorrow looked promising weather-wise, which made them both hopeful about the upcoming journey. Once back inside, they shared a simple dinner and watched one of the movies from Caleb's extensive collection. Bed followed shortly afterwards.

CHAPTER NINE
QUICK TURNAROUND

Quarantine passed, and Mitch was able to move freely around the acreage again. Abigail and her children had been given accommodation and were in the process of meeting people and getting integrated into the daily flow of the group. Tasks were already being assigned based on their respective capabilities. These were eagerly accepted by the newcomers as they knew the alternative of being put outside of the gate was far worse than any unpleasant duties they might be assigned at this point in time. Mitch learned of the plan to make a deeper foray into the city for one last big push before the weather changed. He also learned from Kate he was going to be the leader of this expedition. With all of his forays into the city beyond the fence, he had accumulated considerable experience and had additionally survived encounters with a wide swath of less-than-friendly individuals. As military members were oft to say, 'He had seen the elephant.'

Mitch was not given the opportunity to choose his team, however. They had been assigned to him, and he was not particularly happy with the selection. Part of the reason he was often on the outside on scouting missions was his desire to get away from people. Mitch liked being on his own, ranging far and wide with minimal interference from overseers. He was also not a big fan of 'being in charge.' Trying to get others to do what they already should know how to do was endlessly annoying to him. He understood command structure and acknowledged the necessity of it, but it grated on his nerves nonetheless.

Mitch was given three men and three vehicles to conduct his mission. One was a 7-ton cab-over van with a roll-up door in the back and a dock-height bed. Two men were assigned to operate that unit, plus there was a Tacoma mid-sized pick-up truck and a GS 900 BMW motorcycle for scouting. Mitch wasn't a motorcycle guy, but one of the men assigned to him was and could skillfully operate the bike. The Tacoma was a four-door model that could accommodate all of them if something happened to the van and the motorcycle. Plus, the motorcycle could fit in the back of either vehicle if something went wrong with it. The Tacoma was a 4x4 and had some pretty aggressive tires, which meant it could handle some fairly tough off-roading, as could the motorcycle if that became a necessity. Overall, it was a rather good mix of vehicles in Mitch's mind. The van could carry a lot of supplies back and had heavy enough suspension to handle a considerable load. It had decent tires on it with relatively little wear, as it was not operated too often. The motorcycle and pickup ran on gasoline, which the group still had considerable stores of, but it was aging every day it wasn't getting used. The box van was diesel-powered, which the group had less of, resulting in their being much more miserly in its use.

Gearing up was left to Mitch's decision, and for this, he went to the armory to pick out the right mix of equipment for the job. The armory was in the basement of the house and was always under lock and key. Mitch had to find Ian as there were two hasps on the door, each secured by a different lock. Mitch had a key to the first one, and only Kate and Ian held keys to the other one. This had caused considerable concern within the overall group, as access to the room in an emergency was a prime consideration while maintaining the security of the room was of equal concern. There had been some heated debates on the subject, and in the end, the two padlock/key solution was the only compromise the group could somewhat agree on. It was not ideal, but until ideal showed up and made itself known, this was the path they took. Ian met Mitch outside the door and opened the padlock he had a key for, and Mitch opened the other one. On his shoulder, Mitch had a black bag hanging, which he intended to fill with the requisite equipment. Mitch laid the bag on the workbench inside the room and went about making his selections. All four men got Glock 17 handguns with one magazine in the gun and four spares for the pouches on their belts. That was easy. Mitch picked a Savage .308 with a muzzle brake and bipod for the designated marksman of the group. This gave the team the ability to reach out and touch someone up to eight hundred meters away with alacrity, and the Leupold glass mounted on top of the rifle had cost almost as much as the rifle itself. Next up were a pair of Olympia Arms AR-15s. These had round fore guards and heavy barrels. Mitch knew from experience these were real tack drivers up to two hundred meters but could also spit out rounds plenty quick in semi-auto mode. The group had picked up a large number of thirty-round magazines before the inept politicians and their gun-grabbing policies made their way into law and had put them safely away. Those rules meant nothing now, and Mitch was happy with the foresight the group had shown in procuring these mags. One last set of items Mitch selected were a pair of breaching shotguns in twelve gauge. These were incredibly useful in bypassing stubborn locks or deadbolts or what have you. Both were smaller Churchill models made by a company called Akkar in Turkey. Mag holders and ammunition for each of the firearms came next. Mitch added a couple of pairs of field glass binoculars and a couple of monoculars to give the team the ability to see further. Last on his list were large, fixed-bladed knives. Some of the group wondered why knives were kept in the armory, but Mitch had pressed the idea, in part, to change how people saw them. A student of the Filipino Martial Arts (FMA), he was 'blade positive' and understood bladed weapons were an intermediate system between firearms and empty hands. There were plenty of sharp objects, including knives, around the acreage, but these kept in the armory were specifically fighting knives meant for combat. All had a minimum of an 8-inch blade and a guard to protect the fingers. Mitch was partial to the bowie design and selected four of these with stout leather sheaths for the team.

Mitch put all his gear in the duffel bag he had brought and zipped it up. They were not quite ready to leave yet, but the gear from the armory was now assembled for retrieval later. Next up was ensuring the vehicles were ready to go. He closed the door to the armory behind him, closed both padlocks, and gave Ian the heads-up that he was finished so Ian would know the room had been secured. Moving outside, he headed toward the vehicle parking area. The box van was still bright canary yellow. They had purchased it from Penske trucks and never gotten around to repainting it. It was a traveling billboard for that company still and definitely did not blend in with its surroundings. Mitch committed to himself he would, at a minimum, splash a coat of some dull color on it when they got back. The Tacoma was a nice shade of lawn green. Not quite military colors, but at least not a neon color shouting "Look at me! Look at me!" The motorcycle was colorful but small in profile so it really didn't matter, Mitch thought. He retrieved the keys from the key press lockup and went and started each one of them. It had been the practice of the group to start each vehicle once a month and let them idle a while to keep the batteries up. The fuel tanks were always full in case they had to suddenly go somewhere. Keeping them full also prevented water vapor from getting inside and rusting out the tanks. There likely wasn't any new vehicles coming any time soon, so they needed to take care of what they had. All of the vehicles started easily and ran smoothly. One of the group members was a licensed mechanic, and he did a good job of keeping everything up to scratch. There had been discussion about elevating the less-used units onto blocks to get the tires off the ground, but it had yet to be done. Mitch double-checked the fuel gauges, and sure enough — all of them were topped up. He let them run for a few minutes and then shut them off.

He spent the next few minutes checking tire pressures and oil levels — none of which ended up being necessary as everything was good. As he was doing his checks, Jerry walked up to him. Jerry was the licensed mechanic who was brought into the group for his mechanical skills. "What are you up to?" he asked in his usual direct manner. Mitch turned to face the slightly greying man with the distinctive sideburns he maintained, "Getting ready for a road trip, Jerry, how are you doing?" "I am doing all right, I suppose. Is there a problem with any of these units you are looking at?" Jerry asked. Mitch suspected some personal pride in the state of the vehicles was involved where Jerry was concerned. "Not a single thing wrong. Not that I expected anything to be wrong – I know how good a job you do with these vehicles." For a long while, Jerry stared at Mitch looking for any sarcasm or bullshit in Mitch's statement. Mitch wanted to smile but sensed that would be exactly the wrong thing to do, so he stayed stoic in his expression. Jerry seemed satisfied with Mitch's response and turned to the vehicles in question. "The Tacoma has had the most use out of the three and is probably going to need some significant work soon, but not immediately. I imagine it will be fine until you get back. The other two have had minimal turns on their odometers, so they should be fine. I was surprised how unused the box van was when we bought it. Being a rental, I thought it would be at the end of its life, but I guess not." This was a long series of sentences for Jerry, who usually was sparse in his conversations. "I am interested in spare tires for all three,"

Mitch commented to Jerry. Without hesitation, Jerry responded, "The Tacoma has a spare under the bed and the box van has one inside the box secured against the inside wall. For the bike, I would advise against a spare tire and suggest a patch kit instead. Getting tires on and off a motorcycle is a pain inside of a shop, let alone out in the field. If you have a flat, either patch it or throw the bike in the back of one of the two vehicles." This made sense to Mitch, who said as much to Jerry. Satisfied with the condition of the vehicles, Mitch said his goodbyes to Jerry and headed off on his next task in preparation for the trip.

Walking back to the house, he looked up at the sky. Clouds were moving swiftly across high in the sky, but the wind on ground level wasn't bad. Looking to the western horizon, he could see some serious-looking dark clouds above the line of mountains that rose there. Not promising for the morning, he thought. He noticed the breeze was a cool one, different from the warm or outright hot breezes of the summer. The weather was definitely changing, he surmised. Arriving at the house, he looked at his watch. He had asked the members of his team to meet in the dining room at 9 p.m. as generally that space was not being used by the council or anyone else at that time. Passing through the kitchen, he said hello to the two women who normally worked there, stopping just long enough to lift the lid off a cooking pot, only to get shooed away by one of them. He did not recognize what was cooking inside the pot, but it smelled good enough to cause his stomach to growl. Ever since the collapse, there never seemed to be enough food around. Meals within the acreage had never been missed, but the adoption of OMAD by the group meant everyone lost a good portion of their body fat quickly. Mitch liked the large meal concept with all the calories in one place at one time but missed the constant snacking life had encouraged in the 'before' times. Eating had changed for everyone over the past year. Food was seen as fuel rather than recreation. It had been a hard transition for some to take, and there had been a fair amount of griping. Things had settled out, and it was routine now. Once he was in the dining room, he sat down and checked his watch again. Just before the 9 p.m. deadline, three other men made their way into the room and sat. Ryan, Evan, and Kyle took up seats across from him. Mitch knew each of them fairly well, as all three were original members of the group. Ryan was the motorcycle enthusiast who would undoubtedly be riding the BMW.

Evan and Kyle did not know it yet, but they were going to be driving the box van. Mitch favored the Tacoma pickup and did not want to be in an enclosed space with anyone else for hours at a time if he could help it.

"So, what's the deal?" Ryan asked Mitch. "Gents, we are going on a road trip to do some foraging," replied Mitch. "The council has decided we need to perform a clean sweep of three warehouses in the south of the city and retrieve as much food as we can find. I have three vehicles lined up and have picked out some shiny toys for us to take along with us." Evan and Kyle looked nonplussed. Ryan seemed less happy. "How did I get roped into this shopping spree of yours?" he asked. Mitch looked at him in a deadpan manner. "Apparently you are the most skilled motorcycle operator we have. I want someone who can scout ahead as we have no idea what we are going to run into, and your name came up." Ryan appeared unflattered by Mitch's complimentary comments. "How long is this going to take?" he asked. Mitch responded to him, "I am thinking two, maybe three days at the most depending on what resistance we run into and how tightly these places are locked up." "Resistance?" asked Kyle. "Do we have some intel that hasn't been shared yet?" Mitch shut that line of thinking down quickly. "No, nothing new. Just anticipating possible challenges." Kyle wouldn't let it go that easily though. "It seems the communication from on high has been quite thin as of late. More and more decisions are getting made and we are not being told about them. Ever since Frank died, things have changed and not for the better. Frank really was the glue that held this place together and now it seems like we are fracturing and drifting apart. Have you heard about the council dissolving?" Mitch nodded. "Yeah, I heard. I am on the fence about the way things are going. A committee of six is twelve arms, twelve legs, and one brain, so I see the sense of having a single leader, but I am concerned about ending up with a despot."

Evan had been sitting quietly through these exchanges but was now looking impatient. "When do we leave? Who's driving the box van? I'm presuming it's me as I have experience operating this sort of equipment." Mitch gave him a thumbs up. "I'm in the pickup, and you are in the box van with Kyle. Ryan is going to be scouting on the bike." "We should be on the road by 0700 tomorrow morning," Mitch shared. Let's meet at 0630 in the armory to gear up and then hit the road after that. If the three of you can now give me a hand, I want to load tents, food, and the rest of the supplies into the Tacoma, and then you are on your own until the morning." The three men nodded their agreement and got up and followed Mitch out of the dining room.

An hour later, the truck was fully loaded with the required gear and supplies, and secured in place. The sky was overcast with high cloud cover and gusty winds. A couple of small dust devils in the yard picked up loose leaves and carried them off. Mitch leaned against the loaded truck and looked to the horizon. The sun was about an hour from setting, and the temperature had dropped enough that he could feel it on his skin. Mitch was thinking back a little over a year ago when he was still seeing Ronnie. Ronnie was one of the more serious relationships he had been in, and it was looking hopeful in terms of becoming ever more committed and serious. As things in the world had turned increasingly downward, the division between them had grown. Mitch was spending more and more time preparing with the group, which Ronnie thought was crazy-town. She had put up with his "prepper bullshit," as she put it, as the time when he was not preoccupied with it was actually pretty good. Mitch had tried to give her a fuller understanding of where he saw the world going, and invariably, she had shut him down. In the beginning, he had sent her links to articles on the internet, tried showing her YouTube videos, but it seemed the harder he tried, the less interested she became. It got to the point where he wouldn't even bring the topic up. He resorted to telling her he was "going to hang out with the guys," which she knew was code for going to the acreage and working there. About a month or two before the wheels really started to come off the financial system, the subject had come to a head. She decided that giving him an ultimatum was a good idea. It was her and her lifestyle or him and his 'tinfoil hat friends.' "Veronica," he only used her full name when he was being serious with her, "I am really sad you have chosen this approach of either one way or the other. You know I love you, but I love being alive even more. I genuinely believe we are coming to a crisis situation where our choices are going to be limited. I know you don't believe that or, more importantly, don't want to believe it. As this appears to be the case, I don't think we can continue this relationship, and the end has arrived." Ronnie looked stunned at his decision, as she fully expected him to choose her over his interest in staying alive. Things devolved pretty quickly after that, and the usual accusations and emotional extortion arrived, the fury of which made Mitch more certain than ever of the correctness of his decision.

Kate approaching broke him out of his trip down memory lane. "Hey Mitch," she opened with. "Back at you, boss lady," he replied. "Not yet," she countered with a smile. "Yeah, you say that, but I think it is all over except for the crying," Mitch responded. "You know it and I know it. It's about time in my opinion. We have been drifting since Frank was killed and we need to regain our focus. All of our lives depend upon it, and we can't afford to have our eyes off the ball." Mitch looked at Kate and awaited her response. Kate said, "I am glad you think that way. I agree, we have been drifting somewhat. Hearing about these supposed 'slavers' from Abigail makes me think people are reorganizing out there into different formulations. The first year everyone was simply trying to survive but now those who did are forming new societal structures to deal with the current reality. I'm afraid we are behind the curve on this and the cost of being so could prove to be fatal for us. We need to move forward, look for other groups or individuals to form alliances with, and restructure society, at least locally." Mitch nodded his agreement with her sentiments. Kate continued, "In addition to scoping out these warehouses, I want you to do some ranging around. Don't instigate contact unless it seems prudent and sure as hell don't tell them where we are located. I am interested in learning who is doing what and where. If you and the guys do find a significant cache of food in one of those warehouses – that becomes the absolute priority but to be honest you are likely going to find a whole lot of nothing. I think they have been cleaned out a long time ago and dust is going to be the only thing on those shelves. Unless you prove me wrong."

"I hope you are wrong as we could use some additional supplies. I am also interested in what is happening on the outside. I have seen people moving about, but it has always been at a distance. I think everyone is paranoid and avoiding contact at all costs. I am also wondering if slavers are our worst potential problem. What about warlords? Or even crazier – cannibals. No one, anywhere, is planting crops that I am aware of, and the food is going to run out. What happens then? People are not willing to just lie down and die. A strong leader emerges and galvanizes desperate people into following him – how is that individual going to deal with feeding his followers? Does a warlord start raiding settlements like ours? Maybe that is already happening, but due to the complete lack of communication these days – we just don't know about it yet." Kate grimly stared back at Mitch. He was demonstrating a level of understanding of the situation he had not shown before. The council had reviewed all of the members of the group on more than one occasion in their efforts to best utilize their people as effectively as possible. Perhaps Mitch had slipped through the proverbial cracks and was an unpolished diamond who could take on more responsibility at some point in the future. She decided to file that information for now. "I agree with your overall premises on these matters," she replied. "Let's check out these locations and then begin a more urgent investigation of the other topic. So far, we have managed to deal with the drifters and lone individuals who have come at us for whatever reason. We have not been tested by any sort of group or larger force, and sadly I think we would fail." "Agreed," answered Mitch.

"We are going to head out first thing in the morning. We have three days of supplies. It shouldn't take any longer than that. I will drop off a map of the routes we are expecting to take as well as a couple of options if those do not work out. I doubt our Baofeng radios will reach back this far plus I want to keep radio discipline tight as much as possible as you never know who might be eavesdropping. If, for whatever reason, we are not back by the morning of the fourth day, you had better send a rescue mission. I don't expect any real trouble, but I don't rule it out either. I know for sure there are some pissed-off slavers out there whose friends Caleb and I put some rounds into and are presumably dead." Kate looked at Mitch with renewed interest. "What about Caleb? What did you learn about him? Would he be someone we would like to enter into an alliance with? What does he bring to the table?" Mitch considered for a moment. "Caleb seemed especially capable," Mitch replied. "He is a lone wolf and for someone to survive this long without a group or teammates to rely on – you would have to be really resourceful and careful." "If that is even true," responded Kate. "He might have told you that, but who knows what the truth is. He could be a scout for another group and under direct orders to never reveal their location or numbers." Mitch considered again. "That is true, but not the sense of him I got. He agreed to take on Gerald's granddaughter as his responsibility, but perhaps I am reading too much into that as well. Who knows? I have no idea who or what I can trust in this world."

What kind of equipment did he have? Was he well equipped or did it look like things he had scraped together after the fall?" inquired Kate. Mitch did not hesitate in his response regarding this topic: "No, his gear was top notch. His choice of firearm was a bit outside of the mainstream thinking but a highly functional piece; it was an actual battle rifle versus a carbine. His pack, boots, knife, and everything else spoke of quality and organization. He was well put together. I did notice he chamber checked his rifle regularly as well as checking other equipment every so often, which spoke to me of military experience. I have been around those guys enough to know they are obsessive about those things and have a hard time not doing them. "Hmm... ex-military you say. That could be useful. I wonder what else he is. We should reach out if we can and explore options if we can. He might have training we lack, and we might have supplies he lacks – perhaps work out a trade of some sort. Not right now as we have other priorities, but at some point, in the future. Did he mention where his retreat was located?" Mitch shook his head: "No, he didn't give any indication. I don't know if he headed north, south, west, or whatever. He headed west initially, but that could have easily changed in a couple of blocks. I have no idea where he was going." Kate frowned slightly but was not too emphatic about her disappointment. "Well, time will tell. In all likelihood, we will cross paths with him again and sort things out from there. Good luck tomorrow on your expedition. We are counting on you."

Kate strode away purposefully and headed to the main building. Mitch refocused on finalizing the remaining details still outstanding and then made his way back to his own quarters. Tomorrow was going to be a big day.

CHAPTER TEN

SHOPPING

Morning came early. After a quick breakfast for Angeline, both Caleb and Angeline geared up. Caleb gave Angeline a Nalgene water bottle as she didn't have a CamelBak like he did. Caleb put that on the list of things to look for today if possible. Beef jerky and energy bars went into their daypacks, as well as the normal E.D.C. items Caleb always took with him. He had found smaller or lighter versions of what he could for his young sidekick when they had assembled her daypack, as he didn't want to weigh her down too much. Plus, they had to be able to carry items back with them if they were successful in their hunt for needed things. He decided to bring a lighter rifle this time – a

Daniel Defense AR-15 in 5.56mm. He, like the group Mitch was part of, had put a good supply of 30-round magazines away prior to their ban by the government. He was a fan of Magpul gear and, as a result, had a good number of coyote tan and black P-Mags. Rather than a big, fixed blade, this time he decided to carry his American Tomahawk model 1. He thought he might need some chopping capability in addition to close-quarters combat capability. It was only around 20 ounces, not counting the sheath, and had considerable chopping power for its relatively light weight.

Angeline was far too young and inexperienced to carry a firearm, but he did give her a 36" polypropylene sjambok made by Cold Steel. It was quite light and fun to whip around. Designed for livestock control in South Africa and originally made out of hippo hide, the sjambok had a rather infamous past. Recognizing implements have no inherently good or bad natures of their own, Caleb had picked up a couple as part of his overall arsenal, as they had characteristics no other weapon he owned had. Swung with any kind of effort, it could raise serious welts on man or beast, and he thought she could use it against stray dogs if they came around. In addition to that was her ability to practice swinging it as they walked. He showed her the primary nine angles of attack with a melee weapon, and sure enough, once they got underway, she took the opportunity to whack innocent strands of grass, branches, road signs, and other miscellaneous objects that caught her attention. The inherent whippy nature of the device made it entertaining for her, which accelerated her skill acquisition.

"See the mountains to the west of us?" he asked her. "Almost no matter where we end up in the city, you can look to the west and know the direction you need to head. There are no mountains to the north, south, or east of here, so it's an easy direction indicator for you." He then showed her where he hid the keys to his place. Years ago, he had purchased a fake rock with a sliding bottom into which he placed keys to his house. When placed among a large pile of rocks in his yard, it quickly blended in. Angeline was duly impressed. "I would have never noticed that," she told him. It blended in so well that virtually no one would notice it. Even if they looked for it, the authenticity of the device was so convincing it would be difficult to distinguish from the rest of the rock pile. "I have another set of keys hidden near the solar panels, which I will show you someday. This is close to the house, and if there are people milling around here, it might be difficult to get to the rock. I always try to think three deep on my preparations. Keys on my belt, keys near the house, and keys far away from the house. I do this as best as I can for all things. Three is two, two is one, and one is none, I always like to say." Angeline nodded and smiled her understanding of the concept. "Three deep," she said aloud a couple of times. "Are you going to find two more girls like me to take care of, so you are three deep?" she asked with a smart aleck grin on her face. "No!" came the immediate retort, but accompanied by a laugh. "One young lady to raise is more than enough. I said for 'most things,' if you recall," came Caleb's response.

There was a Walmart Supercenter about five hours away that Caleb was thinking of. He set a steady pace that Angeline could sustain. He employed the same trick again with the soap on the bottom of her socks before heading out. Angeline seemed to be having fun as they made their way, whacking anything she could reach with her sjambok. Caleb, on the other hand, maintained his vigilance. Traveling on his own was one thing; having a young girl in his care necessarily changed things. Every so often, he called a pause in their journey and took out his monocular to scope out the road ahead. He had come this way several times in the past and knew it well. He had become accustomed to what was normal and what was not. Spying the road ahead, he saw a car parked where previously there had been none. This was cause for alarm. "What are you looking at?" asked Angeline. "It's a car," he said. "A car that wasn't there the last time I came through." "What does that mean?" she asked. "It means someone has been here or is here for some unknown reason. It could be nothing, and it could be something. I don't know. When I'm traveling, I look for signs of change, signs of someone in the vicinity. I don't like surprises as they usually don't end well." Angeline now looked concerned. "Are we in danger?" Caleb looked for a place to sit and spotted a traffic barricade nearby. He headed over there and gestured for Angeline to join him sitting on the improvised concrete bench. "There are a number of things I am going to need to teach you. Sadly, you are going to need to do some fast growing up. The time of childhood is coming to an end for you already, but it can't be helped. The world has changed, and the naivete of childhood is going to go away for a while. Here is a system I learned for being aware. Condition white – you are asleep or soaking in a tub with a facecloth over your eyes. You are completely relaxed with nothing to worry about. All is well. Condition yellow – you are aware of your surroundings. Your 'Spidey sense' is on, and if you hear a strange noise or you see something out of the ordinary, you investigate. Condition orange – something has happened which has triggered your awareness beyond the normal state. Someone is approaching, or a twig snaps behind you. There is no threat yet, but it could turn into something. You jack up your readiness in case something goes down. Condition red – the potential threat is now a real threat. Someone is attacking you; a car is heading straight towards you, or a tree is falling on you. Whatever. Something is directly threatening your health and welfare. You need to take immediate action. When we are walking along, I am always in yellow condition at the least. Do you get what I am saying?" Angeline nodded and replied, "When we are outside, I need to be aware. When we are inside, I can relax." Caleb smiled. "Yeah, that is it in pretty basic terms. You don't need to be in orange all the time, constantly thinking about threats. If you are overly vigilant, you will get exhausted and end up dropping your awareness. Like all things in life, you need a balance. I can live with your definition." Next up is the OODA loop, but not today.

"OODA loop?" she inquired. "Yeah, OODA loop. I will explain when the time comes," Caleb told her.

Caleb refocused his attention on the change in the environment ahead of them. Someone had definitely parked a car there, or more accurately, an SUV, a black Kia Sorento if he was thinking of the right make. It was a couple of hundred meters from where they stood. Presently, Caleb couldn't see any movement or anything else to give him pause. "Let's advance," he said to Angeline. "Stay frosty" was his next bit of advice. "What does that mean?" she asked. "Be on your toes," he answered her query with another idiom. She rolled her eyes, but not too dramatically, he noticed. Walking at a normal pace, they came within a hundred feet of the vehicle. Caleb could now see the passenger side door was open, but everything was still. He scanned to his left and his right. Nothing entered his awareness. The door of the house nearest the vehicle was open, but there didn't appear to be any movement coming from that area. He and Angeline came closer until Caleb could place his hand on the hood. A slight warmth emanated from under the hood. "Someone is here! Let's move. Follow me," he directed Angeline. Shifting to a light jog, they passed the vehicle and continued down the street. No contact thus far. Getting to the end of the block, he pulled her behind a red Ford F-150 and took cover. Pulling his monocular out, he scoped the open door to the house. Nothing. He turned to Angeline. "Someone or several someone's are here somewhere. I don't know what they are doing or what they want. I think we should stay here another ten minutes and see if we can lay eyes on them. I don't want to make contact, but I would like to see who is in our general vicinity. You can have a seat on the curb if you like while we wait. Maybe take a drink from your flask, but be ready to move quickly if we need to. Understand?" Angeline nodded and moved to the curb and busied herself getting her water out. Caleb turned back in the direction they had come and continued to glass the area, looking for any signs of life.

The minutes crawled by. Caleb was about to put his monocular back in its case when he heard a large bang come from the house he was watching. Then a series of bangs, or maybe more accurately, a series of impacts. The sounds were like those being made by a sledgehammer hitting a wall or something. His mind worked to decipher the sounds he was hearing. Then, as quickly as they had started, they stopped.

Angeline had gotten up and stood beside him trying to see. Another minute passed, and then two men exited the front door of the house with what appeared to be an armload of rifles or shotguns; it was too far to know for sure, but they were definitely firearms. Both of the men were in jeans and black t-shirts with ballcaps on. Caleb could see a holstered pistol of some sort on the hip of one of the men. They got to the SUV and opened the hatchback and deposited their carried items in the back of the vehicle. Caleb could see one of the men gesturing to the other in what looked like a 'go back and get something' manner, to which the second man complied and headed back inside the house. The first of the two men had lengthy hair tied in a ponytail under his baseball cap. He got into the Sorento and started it up. Another couple of minutes passed, and the second man emerged from the house with some sort of black sack or satchel, which looked heavy from the way he was carrying it. He opened the rear passenger door of the vehicle and tossed it in the back seat. Then the second man, who also had long hair protruding from underneath his cap but hanging loose, got into the open passenger seat. He quickly closed the door, and the driver pulled away from the curb and headed in the direction where Caleb and Angeline were hiding. "Get down," Caleb instructed Angeline as he squatted down out of sight himself.

The vehicle accelerated and passed their position without incident, going to the end of the block and turning down the corner onto the next street. Caleb and Angeline both stood up. "Well, that was certainly interesting," said Caleb. "Want to go to the house and see what they were up to?" he asked her. "Sure," came her response as they walked back the way they had come. A minute or two later, they stood on the porch of the house. It was a real estate developer's standard cookie-cutter-designed house, which looked like all the other houses in the neighborhood. Caleb hated the lack of architectural innovation in these areas. Developers would buy a large parcel of land and then quickly build a whole community of carbon-copied houses. Sometimes there was some variation on a theme, but it was readily apparent they were basically the same units with minor deviations from the base model. The door to this one was left ajar, so they entered. The entryway opened into a large, high-ceilinged living room. A layer of dust had settled on the furniture over the months it had been vacant. There was a trail of dirt from the two men leading to a short hallway on the way to the back of the house. Here, there was a significant amount of broken glass and what looked to be a broken mirror frame. Caleb and Angeline moved closer to examine it. Lying on the floor was a four-foot-high mirror frame, which looked like it had been attached to a mounting system on the wall. Looking at the wall mount system, it became apparent immediately there was some sort of secret compartment behind the mirror. Inside the wall was a gun rack where rifles could be stood up vertically, and below that was a shelf that looked perfect for stacking ammo boxes or magazines. Caleb turned to Angeline. "I have seen these before. Tactical Walls, a company out of Virginia, makes various devices for hiding firearms and other items around your home with easy access – usually a magnetic key is involved. If you don't have the key, you would probably need a sledgehammer to knock it off – hence the banging and crashing noises we heard earlier."

"So, the rifles they carried out were in here?" Angeline asked as she looked into the opening in the wall. "Presumably," Caleb replied. "And the black bag of stuff the long-haired guy number two carried out was probably a bunch of magazines and ammo boxes sitting on that empty shelf you can see." Angeline looked at the shelf again, "Why did they come back for that stuff?" she asked. Caleb surmised, "Either they just found out about it, had forgotten about it, or recently decided they needed it for some other reason I cannot fathom at this point." "What we do know for sure is they are either armed or better armed than they were just a short while ago. That being said – it doesn't change much. They are unknown actors with unknown intentions, so we are just going to avoid them." Angeline looked at him and asked, "Do you avoid everybody you meet? Isn't that lonely?" Caleb smiled. "My plan from long before this began was to keep a low profile. Despite what many have claimed – no one knew how all this was going to shake out. I long ago lost any belief in so-called 'experts' who rarely panned out in their prognostications for the future." "What's prognost..." asked Angeline with a perplexed look on her face. Caleb laughed aloud, "A fancy word for guessing what the future holds. Sorry about that – I am already forgetting you are ten. I am possibly the product of too much education. I'll tone it down." Angeline smiled her appreciation and asked him another question, "So why don't you get lonely?" continuing on her same tack. "I am someone with 'low affiliative need,' which is a tendency to have a reduced desire for social connection and bonding. The people who came up with that term describe it as a negative thing, but I see it as a strength. I just don't get lonely much. I am more interested in things than people generally, but once in a while I come across someone, I find interesting. Like you." He said with a smile.

"We should get moving again," Caleb said to Angeline and started walking. "We have a way to go and we're wasting time here. I don't want to be out overnight or coming back in the darkness if I can avoid it." They exited the house and, after scanning in front and behind them, carried on in their original direction. The wind was picking up a bit and the clouds had become a little more menacing. It had been several weeks since the last rainfall and Caleb hoped today was not going to be the day the trend changed. He'd be okay if it did rain, but Angeline really wasn't equipped for rain. He hoped when they got to their destination, he would be able to find what she needed. More hours of walking passed. They stopped occasionally to rest their feet and take a drink or have a snack. After several hours of walking, Caleb had Angeline remove her boots and examined her feet. The soap trick seemed to be working again as she showed no sign of blisters forming just yet. Caleb decided he would check again on their return trip. He also decided he would attempt to get her out walking for at least an hour a day to condition her feet. In a world devoid of gasoline production, at least for the foreseeable future, walking was going to be their main mode of travel. He had bicycles stored back at his retreat but disliked the need to dismount and bring a weapon to bear if they got in a situation. Additionally, bicycles, by their nature, moved much more quickly than walking and you could find yourself in a position of vulnerability quite quickly, whereas walking gave you the time to scope out the terrain ahead of you more gradually and have a better sense of what you were getting into. On top of all that – time was not really a concern as it was before the collapse. There were no dinner parties to attend, no schools to drop kids off at, and now no jobs to go to. Staying alive was the main job now and most had failed at that.

Finally, their intended destination came into view. The parking lot had a number of abandoned vehicles and even some large RVs still sitting in it. Grocery carts littered the spaces in between as did various pieces of trash and debris. "Let's walk around the entire building and take a look," Caleb said to Angeline. He wanted to see as much of it as he could before going inside. The familiar blue and yellow logo was still intact but looked weathered. No fresh coats of paint in the last year, Caleb thought. They made their way down the side of the parking lot and around back to where the loading docks were located. Two freight trucks were still backed into the docks and had their drivers' doors hanging open. The wind continued to blow and bits of paper and leaves drifted around on the ground. Death of a civilization, Caleb thought. When the eighteen wheelers stopped bringing the stuff – things unraveled quickly. He and Angeline walked past the trucks and saw the man door on the dock was propped open. Caleb thought they might enter via that route once they had completed their circumnavigation. Walking down the asphalt road behind the store, they saw stacks of blue pallets and abandoned grocery carts. As they got closer, Caleb saw a pair of booted feet protruding out from behind a stack of pallets. "Stay here," he said to Angeline as he went to have a closer look. Rounding the corner of the pallets, he saw an obviously long-dead man lying on his back. Most of the flesh from his face was gone. The crows or ravens had feasted upon his remains. Moving closer, Caleb could see a round hole in the front of the skull where a bullet entered. The man's clothes had become weather-beaten and the scavengers had taken their toll on them as well as they sought the flesh underneath them. "Walmart is your final resting place, bud," Caleb said to himself. Sad end to a life. I wonder what you did before everything fell apart, he wondered. It was not the first corpse he had seen by a long shot and it was likely not going to be his last.

Deciding it probably wasn't worth going through the dead man's pockets, he moved back to where Angeline was standing. "Dead guy?" Angeline asked. "Yeah. There is probably going to be more inside as well. Are you okay with that?" he asked her. "Sure. I've seen a lot of dead people now. It used to bother me, but it doesn't anymore." They continued on their trek around the building. No more corpses and no signs of life. A couple of crows squawked at them from the edge of the roof as they rounded the last corner, but other than that and the wind, it was quiet. "I am undecided about going in," Caleb commented to Angeline. The front doors are electrically powered and, as such, surely are not working. It is going to be dark inside, probably really dark, and we are going to have to use flashlights or, more appropriately, our headlamps to see our way around. I don't see any signs of life, but that doesn't mean there isn't any. We are going to have to be careful and stay close to one another. "See that RV over there?" Caleb pointed to a large Winnebago-type vehicle at the end of the parking lot. "If anything goes south on us and we get separated, you head to there and we will reconnect." "Got it," replied Angeline. Caleb said, "I think I want to go in through that door we saw next to the truck docks. Let's head back over there." Caleb started in that direction and performed a check on his rifle as he walked. He reached down and loosened the tomahawk in its carrying ring to ensure easy access if he should need it. A couple of minutes later, they stood in front of the open door. Caleb put his headlamp on and assisted Angeline with hers. He did a press check on his stock-mounted light as well. He had a Feyachi FL11 Tactical light mounted on a picatinny rail wired to a switch accessible to the lead hand holding the stock of his rifle. It wasn't the highest quality light by a long shot, but he had tested it a fair bit and it had held up. It had a pulse switch which turned the light on as long as he held down the switch with his hand, and it also had a rocker switch to turn it on and keep it on. He chose the latter for this application.

"Stay close," he said over his shoulder to the young girl. Stepping out of the sunlight into the darkened entry, he moved his light back and forth looking for threats. The room they had entered was about twenty by twenty feet in a roughly square shape. There was debris everywhere. Cardboard boxes ripped open with their contents spewed across the floor like vomit after a hard night of drinking dominated the space. Along the interior wall was double-high racking where more materials had been stored and rummaged through. There were no signs of life. Heading further in, Caleb and Angeline got to the receiving office and had a look inside. On the floor lay two bodies in a state of decay. They looked so bad it was hard to tell whether they were men or women or one of each. One lay partially on top of the other in a death rictus. What looked like blood was on the desk beside them and on the wall behind them. "Why don't they smell bad?" asked Angeline. Caleb considered for a moment. "A lack of moisture in here means they are probably more mummified than decomposed, which means a lot less bad smell coming out of them." As there appeared to be nothing they were looking for in this place, Caleb turned and headed for the swinging doors which gave access to the store's main shopping area. Caleb had Angeline pull one of the doors open so he could run his light over the area past the opening. From what he could see, the store was a jumble as well. Obviously, looters and scavengers had been through here – perhaps more than once. Even with that fact, there was still a lot of goods left in the store. Caleb stood still with Angeline at his side and listened carefully. He could hear the wind coming in from the doors at the front of the store, but beyond that – it was quiet. Quiet and eerie.

Continuing further, he walked towards what was left of the children's clothing section. A lot of the racks had been knocked down and the area was in general disarray. "It's going to take a while," he said to her. Angeline nodded. "Do you know your sizes?" Caleb asked her. "I don't know anything about clothes for kids." "I can look at them and then try them on, I guess," she said to him. Caleb crossed the aisle and pulled a chair out of the furniture section, which no one had found sufficiently interesting to loot, and dragged it back to where they were situated. He then sat back in the chair and placed his rifle across his lap. "Okay, get started," he said to her. He looked at his wristwatch on the inside of his left wrist and checked the time. He decided they would spend an hour here and then head back. Angeline got busy digging through the clothes that remained in the store. "Hey, look here!" she called out. It was a Fruit of the Loom cardboard display bin with a good number of t-shirts and pullover sweatshirts still in it. She began pulling them on one after another, determining her size. "Grab a couple of each in larger sizes for when you grow bigger," he told her. Angeline started to make a pile with her discoveries. Caleb leaned back in his chair and relaxed. The wind noise from the front doors was picking up, which reminded him of his desire for some raingear for her. "I am going to head down to the sporting goods section and look for a rain poncho for you. Are you going to be okay doing this? I won't be far." "No problem," came her quick reply. He stood and made his way to where he remembered sporting goods used to be.

As he got there, he started digging through the chaos that was once a store. Most of the aisles were littered with merchandise, which made walking a little tricky. He had stepped in something sticky on his way over from the kids' clothing section, and he couldn't tell exactly what it was, but now he was leaving a partial boot print as he walked. The sporting goods section produced pay dirt in terms of a couple of cheap rain ponchos, which had been overlooked. A lot of the section was empty, as it had previously held valuable items for people suddenly faced with a survival situation and little to no experience or equipment of their own. He saw that all the sleeping bags were gone, as well as all of the backpacks. Anything related to camping was mostly absent. The fishing rod and lure section had been completely cleaned out, as people thought to supplement their food supply with fish from one of the two rivers that ran through the city. He did spot a couple of packs of light sticks, which he pocketed. There was a camo ballcap in a kid's size, which he picked up for her. Realtree was the logo on the front of the cap. Not that brands would matter anymore, he chuckled to himself. The rest of the section was pretty much a disappointment. Nothing of any real value remained. He could see Angeline working away by the movement of her headlamp as he decided to head over to the area where luggage was sold. Once he arrived, he saw this area too had been pretty cleaned out. There was, however, a bright pink suitcase with wheels on the bottom. He righted it and rolled it around a bit, testing the wheels. They seemed to work well. "Kind of garish," he thought, but decided he didn't care. Maybe they could put more clothes and shoes than just their backpacks could carry and roll them back. In that moment, he realized he had forgotten all about his wheelbarrow idea that he had suggested to Angeline previously. "Well, now it was the pink rolling suitcase plan," he said to himself.

He pushed the suitcase through the mess as best he could and arrived in the shoe section. "What size are your feet again?" he asked her. "Five," she called out. He went up and down the rows until he found her pairs of sneakers, rubber boots, and house slippers. These all went into the rolling suitcase. In concert with what he had told her to do, he also grabbed one size up for each except for the slippers, which strangely were mostly gone. "Who needs slippers in the apocalypse?" he thought. Rolling the suitcase, he headed back to where she was. In his absence, she had completely changed out of the clothes she had arrived in. The old clothes were nowhere to be seen. She smiled up at him from where she sat on the floor. "I had been wearing those same clothes for almost two weeks now. I can't tell you how glad I am to be out of them!" It was Caleb's turn to smile. "I'm happy for you. I didn't mention it, but the smell told me the same thing." Angeline looked a little horrified by this revelation. "Why didn't you say something?" she asked. "No point. There was nothing I could do about it at the time, and I knew this shopping trip was coming up." "Are you about done? I found a couple of useful things and put them in this suitcase. Do you think you can push it?" he asked. Angeline got up and grasped the handle of the pink case on wheels and proceeded to roll it around a bit. "It's easy," she announced. "Good. Then let's get back on the road. We have plenty of distance to cover, and I want to be back before sundown."

Caleb helped jam all of Angeline's 'clothing purchases' into the suitcase and then had her sit on it so he could zip it closed. It was considerably heavier after adding all the pants, socks, and tops she had sourced but still not impossible — even for a somewhat thin ten-year-old young lady. It was also not completely full. Caleb had another thought. "We need a heavier jacket for you as winter is coming." He scanned around the area with his flashlight and landed on a rack of coats. He had Angeline try some of the heavier ones on until they found a suitably sized and warm enough jacket for her. Next, they searched until they found the hat and scarf display and secured some mittens and knit caps that fit her. All of these new items went into the suitcase as well, which was looking quite full. "I think we're done," Caleb said to Angeline.

Together they headed for the front entrance. As they approached, they could see outside the glass doors to where the wind had picked up and rain had started falling. Caleb stopped Angeline and dug out the rain ponchos he had found in the outdoor section. Tearing open the packaging and pulling off the price tag, he shook her poncho out and helped pull it over her head. It was a bright neon orange, which was going to do nothing for their concealment on the way home. Caleb next opened the packaging for his poncho and shook it out. He started to pull it over his head when Angeline shrieked, "Caleb! Look out!" Caught unaware by his poncho activities, someone had managed to sneak up behind him and tackle him. "Oomph" escaped his mouth as the air was knocked out of him by a tackle from behind, and suddenly, he was on the ground. The crushing weight of the attacker was heavy on his back as the shock of an unexpected impact with the ground stunned him. A flurry of punches started landing on the back of his head and neck. Instinctively Caleb balled up and covered the back of his head and neck with his hands and arms. The attacker grabbed Caleb's left wrist and pulled his arm out of the way to land punches, but just as he got a firm hold of the wrist, he yelled a loud shrieking, "aargh!" and immediately released the wrist. Caleb used this moment to turn underneath him and saw his attacker gripping his face with both hands in agony. Little Angeline had whipped her sjambok with as much force as her young arms could muster, slashing the last foot of the whip-like weapon horizontally across the face of the man attacking Caleb. It was hard to imagine how much pain he was feeling in that moment. Caleb didn't hesitate and used this moment to escape. Sitting up, Caleb posted his left hand on the ground and hipped into the attacker, turning hard to his left, rolling the man over and off of him. Seizing the pants of the attacker at the knees, Caleb used this grip to pull himself up and then retreated. Caleb's adversary displayed a large welt across the middle of his face. Caleb looked left and right to break the tunnel vision he was feeling. Somehow his rifle was more than a couple of steps away, and the man in front of him shifted from pain to rage. Snarling, he got his feet underneath him and leapt up simultaneously drawing a large hunting knife from his waist-mounted scabbard. Caleb motioned with his hand to guide Angeline back and out of the way. Swiftly reaching down, Caleb drew the tomahawk from his own belt, which luckily hadn't become dislodged.

Sliding his hawk out with his right hand, Caleb stepped back with his left leg and got behind his weapon. Immediately, he began making random circles and figure eights with the weapon to keep it moving and not present an easy target for the bulging-eyed man in front of him. Caleb's adversary made some perfunctory lunges forward, stabbing with his knife. Right away, Caleb noticed the attacker was in a mismatched stance to his own. His left side was forward and not behind the big knife. The angry man also kept his knife in relatively the same spot in front of his torso as he made small advances and tentative thrusts. Caleb side-stepped to his left and then back again to the right, seeing what his opponent did in response – not much. Assessment over! He thought and made his play. Taking a big step forward with his lead leg, Caleb raised his tomahawk high and looked directly at the man's head, simultaneously letting out his loudest shout, "Aaaah!" The man's eyes went wide in response both to Caleb blasting him with a shout and to the raised hawk, eyes locked on the raised weapon. With his big move, Caleb had closed the distance and now the attacker's knife hand was in range. The attacker had temporarily forgotten about his weapon, brain occupied with the impending doom posed by the menacing tomahawk. Still yelling, Caleb pivoted to his left and brought the hawk smashing down into the forearm of the attacker's knife hand. A satisfying thunk reverberated through the handle into Caleb's grip. Blood sprayed out of the wound as flesh was cut and bone cleaved. Shocked, the man released a tremendous shriek of pain and horror. Stepping forward with his left leg to get closer, Caleb used his left fist to hammer the forearm off the embedded blade in a checking motion and immediately sent the blade horizontally above the wounded limb into the man's neck. This was a much more grievous and final injury. Blood gouted from the massive wound in the man's neck. Caleb raised his foot and forcefully push-kicked the man back, releasing his tomahawk. At the same time, the opponent brought his free hand to his ruined neck. Falling backward onto a stack of shopping baskets, he attempted to staunch the blood streaming from the gaping hole in his neck. Caleb noticed his own breath heaving in and out. Advancing on the attacker, he saw the glassy-eyed look of someone whose life was draining out. Caleb glanced down at his tomahawk. Blood dripped off the edge and flesh clung to the top and bottom of the curved blade. Looking back to the man lying in front of him, Caleb noticed the man had dropped his hunting knife and had both hands planted on his neck in a vain last-ditch effort to stave off the blood loss. Then, slowly and inexorably, his hands slid away from his neck, completely covered in his own blood as the limp-limbed motion of death took him.

Angeline touched Caleb on the arm and he jumped at the unexpected touch. "Whoa!" she yelled at him. "It's done. He's done! It's over!" Caleb lowered his tomahawk which had somehow raised itself again. "What was that?" Angeline yelled at him. "What the hell was that?" "You shouldn't use foul language," he said to her. "It's unbecoming of a young lady." "Unbecoming?!" she shouted. "You basically just chopped someone up!" Caleb could see she was panicked and breathing heavily. "Slow your breathing down – we don't need you fainting," he said to her. She looked around at her surroundings and seemed to calm down a bit. "Who was he and why did he do that?" she asked, slightly calmer. "I don't know who he was or why he did that. Maybe he was hiding here and felt threatened, or perhaps he had been following us and decided to take his chance when we were preoccupied with our stupid rain ponchos," he let out in a long breath. Caleb looked down at the front of his poncho – the attacker's blood was on it, lots of blood. Some of the spray from the wound channels had gotten onto him. No big surprise there. Walking up to the corpse, Caleb wiped the blade of his hawk on the pant leg of the dead man and slid it back into its belt ring. Squatting down, he went through the man's pockets. A plastic folding compass, a ferro rod, and a folding knife were all he came up with. The hunting knife looked rough, with chips in the blade at several different points. It had been through a lot and wasn't worth keeping. The other three items made their way into his backpack for closer inspection later.

"We need to get going," he said to Angeline. "This ordeal only took a few minutes, but it is getting later and later in the day." Angeline intensely looked at him. "How many people have you killed?" Caleb looked at her and then looked away. "Enough. Not too many and not too few – just enough." Her gaze softened a bit as she realized he was not some bloodthirsty killer but rather a man simply trying to make it through this new world in which they lived. "Let's get going then," she said and began pushing her pink suitcase on wheels. Caleb walked over and picked up his rifle and did the usual checks on it. It was unchanged from when he had dropped it while getting tackled.

Two minutes later, they were trudging their way past the Winnebago on their way home. The rain was picking up, and the wind was now a constant annoyance. The trip back was going to be wet and dreary, as well as cold. Caleb could feel the temperature dropping as they walked and looked to the west. The mountains were shrouded in clouds and looked foreboding. He started to feel nauseous as the adrenaline drained from his system and became a little light-headed as well. He stopped and bent forward, getting his head beneath his heart. Angeline stopped and looked at him. "What's up?" she asked with some concern in her voice. "Just a little light-headed – it'll pass," he told her. "Keep going; I'll catch up." She turned and continued walking. Caleb took some deep breaths and let the rain hit him in the face. The cool drops helped him regain his composure, and the light-headedness passed, as did the need to vomit. This was not his first encounter with the post-combat shakes, and he suspected it would not be the last. It did seem to get easier over time as he gained more and more experience in the grisly task of dispatching opponents.

Hours passed as they walked, and Caleb attempted to maintain situational awareness. A great fatigue overtook him, and all he thought about was getting into bed. Angeline did a good job of pushing her suitcase on its small wheels and refrained from complaining about being wet, cold, or tired. About halfway back, he stopped for a rest and broke out some energy bars, and they had drinks from their water sources. Even though both were dog-tired, the journey back seemed shorter than the trip out. Caleb kept his head on the proverbial swivel the whole time, looking for movement and threats, of which there were, thankfully, none. Finally, hours later, they arrived back at his house. Sticking to his standard operating procedures, Caleb circumnavigated the property looking for telltale signs of trespass or intrusion. Caleb found nothing of concern, and with his remaining energy, opened the house, and they escaped the rain. Once inside, he locked up, and they peeled off their ponchos – Caleb noticed all the blood had washed off of his. After the ponchos were hung to dry, they removed the rest of their outdoor gear. Caleb looked at his young charge. "Are you hungry?" "No, just tired," came the weary reply. "I can wait till breakfast. I just want to go to bed." Caleb nodded and made his way through the house to his bedroom, leaving Angeline to settle herself in. Fifteen minutes later, after disrobing, they were each falling into deep slumbers. It had been a long day.

CHAPTER ELEVEN

LAST RUN

Mitch and his crew were up early. They met at the armory as requested. He handed out weapons to each of them and explained his reasoning for the selections. No one complained or argued as his reasoning was sound. As a group, they headed to the vehicles and started each one to give them time to warm up. The BMW motorcycle had a rifle scabbard attached as part of its normal rigging; Ryan slid his weapon inside and snapped it shut. The other men took their weapons into the cabs of their vehicles and headed toward the main gate. Mitch drove to the first gate and unlocked the padlock holding the chain in place. He walked the gate open and then drove his vehicle to the second gate.

The dogs, which normally ran freely in the yard, had been tied up temporarily so the gates could be opened and not lose the dogs. Mitch swung the outside gate open after unlocking it and pushed it aside so the team could drive out. He got back into his pickup and drove out onto the road. The other two vehicles followed him out and locked the gates closed behind them. Ryan took the lead on his BMW and headed south on the previously agreed-upon route. Their plan was to follow the route until it became impossible to do so due to opposition, physical obstruction, or whatever the case was. They had rally points on their respective maps should they become separated and agreed to rules of engagement if they ran into armed adversaries.

The first few kilometers passed uneventfully. A light rain made the riding for Ryan less fun, but he had raingear as part of his kit, which he had donned prior to departure. The other two vehicles had their wiper blades on intermittent function, as the rain was not too hard at this point. After heading west for a short period, the convoy turned and headed south. Evan and Kyle carried on a steady banter inside the cab of their truck, whereas Mitch solely had his own thoughts as company. Their first issue occurred on the main road that they had selected for the southerly portion of their trip. Kyle got there first on the bike and radioed back to the team, "Roadblock ahead. Someone has pulled vehicles together in the center of the highway." Mitch picked up his radio and thumbed the send key, "Can you get around it? What about driving on the shoulder?" Kyle responded, "I might be able to on the bike, but your larger vehicles are a definite no-go." Mitch radioed again, "Understood. Let's circle back to the previous off-ramp and see if we can bypass it." Evan got on his radio, "Understood. Backing up." Kyle turned around and quickly rejoined the group and then sped ahead back to the previous bypass. There were plenty of vehicles on the side of the road that had been abandoned when their drivers had run out of gas. When things really started to fall apart, a lot of folks decided getting into their cars and 'going somewhere' was a good idea. Many of the cars and trucks had their doors hanging open to the elements, as people had abandoned them and proceeded forward on foot. Where they ultimately ended up – no one would ever have those answers.

In a matter of minutes, the team returned to the previous off-ramp. Kyle rode up the ramp on the BMW to scout it out. Moments later, he radioed back, "Okay, this is definitely looking coordinated now. There are a number of cars piled together blocking access. I think someone is trying to block travelers from accessing this part of the city. I suggest we back up and cross over to Barlow Trail. It runs parallel to this highway and can get us south." Mitch didn't like this delay but had expected something similar when planning the expedition. "Check that – Barlow Trail it is." After a bit of effort, the team got turned around and headed north once again. It would be five or ten minutes to the next off-ramp, this time heading east towards the new route. Kyle got back out in lead scouting on his bike. Unfortunately, the rain decided to come down in greater force, requiring everyone to run their wiper blades continuously to maintain clear vision. This necessitated a general slowing of the convoy as well. The old days of having a fender bender and calling a tow truck for roadside assistance were over, and as such, extra care and attention were required to ensure no problems.

Heading up the eastbound ramp was a bit tricky with all the abandoned vehicles littering the road, but they managed to work their way through. It was early enough in the day to be heading into the sun, but the cloud cover eliminated that issue. Once they were off the main highway, the team headed east on a feeder route towards the desired secondary route. Mitch could see a group of Canada geese floating on a large pool of standing water, probably oblivious to the changed world around them. There was probably a lot more wild game now that hunting pressure has largely been eliminated, he thought. Initially, hunters had gone out of the city in search of food, and much of the wildlife proximal to the larger urban centers had been taken, but the lack of liquid fuels for vehicles had put a quick end to that. A full breeding season had elapsed since then, and Mitch thought to himself – a few years from now and the game animals would really be flourishing.

More kilometers passed, and they arrived at the secondary road going south. The off-ramp was congested but not impassable. Minutes later, they were once again making headway in the correct direction. Rain decided to come down even harder. Free car wash, thought Mitch as they made their way. After a while, they neared a major intersection, which roughly divided the city into quarters. Currently, they were in what was designated the northeast portion, and once they passed the intersection, they would be in the southeast section of the city. Evan radioed the team, "We have a check engine light on. What do you want to do?" Mitch picked up his radio, "Is it a red or amber light?" "Amber," came the response. Mitch keyed his radio again, "Let's keep going and monitor the light. An amber light could really be nothing more than a loose fuel cap. It might get more serious, but if it doesn't, we keep going." "Check," came the response. As they made their way through the intersection, the river below came into view for the first time in their journey. One of the cleanest rivers in a major city, it was reputed to have fish that you could safely eat when caught. Definitely a rarity among urban traversing rivers. With the cessation of pollution due to population downsizing, it was likely even cleaner now, Mitch thought.

Barlow Trail curved to the east until it ended and they continued on International Avenue, which Mitch found funny for this landlocked city in the interior of the continent – far away from anywhere 'International.' They were now entering the industrial part of the city as warehouses and other commercial buildings started to come into view. "Head south on 36th Street," Mitch directed via his radio.

Kyle turned down the recommended street and moved ahead, scouting the terrain. The Tacoma and box van followed southward as they began to get close to their first destination. "We need to get onto 28th Avenue and then turn south on 52nd St. to get into the loading docks of our destination," Mitch reminded the team via his Baofeng. "Check that," came back from both radio holders. The team continued on, and after a while, arrived just outside the yard of the distribution center they had targeted on their maps. It did not look promising. The yard had several trucks and trailers in it, plus it was congested with cars, pickup trucks, and SUVs. Nothing was moving. The rain pounded down and made seeing everything quite difficult. "I think I can weave my way in there, but there is no way anything larger is getting in," Ryan shared via his radio. Mitch pulled his truck over to the side of the road. "Evan, can either you or Kyle join us while whoever remains with the vehicles stays behind and guards them? I want to go in on foot and have a look," Mitch said into his radio. "Check that," came the response again.

Mitch put on his rain poncho as did Kyle. Ryan was in his motorcycle rain gear. All three performed weapons checks and put their headlamps on. Mitch locked the door of the Tacoma and gave the keys to Evan so he could move the truck if need be. All of the men had hand-held flashlights on their belts for when they went indoors to explore. The group had decided on Streamlight 88700s for their main tactical flashlight. They were quite pricey in the initial purchase, but their thinking had been focused on quality and durability, and a good light was such an integral part of being off-site searching through buildings and so on, that buying a cheap flashlight was just out of the question. Mitch headed in towards the loading docks with the other two men trailing behind. Mitch did a quick radio check with Evan before going inside to ensure they had a link. As they walked through the abandoned cars in the parking lot, they saw a lot of dead bodies. Many cars had bullet holes, blown-out windshields, and flattened tires. "Looks like a lot of bad things went down here," Kyle remarked to no one in particular. "Yeah, bad to the power of ten if you ask me," said Ryan. It appeared a lot of the corpses had died from gunshot wounds. Blood had splashed into the interiors of many of the vehicles as whatever particular version of hell had unfolded here. When they got close enough to the loading docks, they could see several of the overhead doors were open to the elements. The rain was being swept by the wind in through the doors and onto whatever lay inside. The men walked up the steel steps to the docks and surveyed what was in front of them. On the docks themselves, there were dead people in various states of decomposition. "Looks like a lot of people thought it would be a good idea to come here," Kyle commented. One particularly grisly body had a fire axe sticking out of the back of its victim. Standing in an open dock bay, Mitch could see a considerable way inside. The interior was a debacle. Chaos had reigned here, and the final acts of desperation as they unfolded had been heinous.

"Rather than splitting up, let's stick together and take a look," Mitch suggested. The interior was racked three high, and everything was a jumble. He could see pallets on the top shelves, but without working forklifts, getting them down was going to be near impossible, plus the amount of debris on the floors was astounding. Mitch led the threesome down the first aisle, weaving his way between the debris and the occasional dead body. It seemed a lot of people had fought over what was here, and many paid the ultimate price for that opportunity. Fought and died, Mitch thought to himself. The floor-level pallets inside the racking were well picked over, but there were some items that had been relatively untouched. Lawn maintenance was a category no one seemed to care about in the post-apocalypse, nor window coverings or hair care products. Toothpaste, toilet paper, and foodstuffs were obviously popular due to their absence in the pick bins. "Let's see if we can find a ladder or a step ladder somewhere so we can check out the higher slots in the racking," Mitch suggested. "You two keep going through the ground floor stuff and I am going to see what I can find," Mitch said to the other two. "You bet" came their response. Mitch looked around for an obvious direction to go. With such chaos, there was no clear direction to take. Mitch decided to head back towards the point they entered and begin searching there.

Mitch shone his handheld light along the walls looking for a storeroom or somewhere a ladder might be. He started walking along the inside of the exterior wall and searching. Ten minutes later and still no luck, Mitch stopped to rest for a minute and grabbed a metal handrail for support. He shone his flashlight in all directions looking for some sign of a ladder or stepladder. His light caught some metal tread stairs right beside him. Suddenly, Mitch realized his handrail was part of a set of rolling stairs. He laughed at his lack of observational skills and the irony of hanging onto the very device he was looking for. He turned and had a good look at the apparatus beside him. This was an eight-high set of rolling stairs used to access points located above the floor. He grasped both handrails and stepped on the metal bar just in front of the first step and pushed down. This action elevated the stairs so the wheels were free to roll. He pulled the stairs around and started back in the direction he had come from. He only got a few feet when he started to encounter debris. Letting go of the ladder, he bent over and started moving stuff out of the way. Standing, he saw he had cleared a few feet of material and could move the rolling steps again but would have to start clearing almost immediately again. Frowning, Mitch realized just getting the rolling stairs to where he needed them was going to be a bigger job than he wanted.

Leaving the stairs behind, he walked over to where the guys were working. "Guys, I have some good news and I have some bad news. Which do you want first?" he asked them. Ryan looked at him. "What is the bad news?" Mitch replied, "You only have ten left to live..." Ryan exclaimed,

"Ten, ten what?! Years, months, days? What?" Mitch replied in a monotone voice, "Nine, eight, seven, six…." "Ha ha, real funny," said Ryan. Mitch smiled back at him. "Ok, seriously. The good news is – I found a set of rolling stairs. The bad news is there is so much junk on the floors that getting them here is going to take forever." "Ideas?" The two guys looked at him. "Why don't we just climb up the side of the racking and see what is in the bin or tote or what have you and then, if it is worth it, clean a path to that bin so we can get the stairs close enough," said Kyle. "How risky is that?" asked Mitch. "We don't need you falling and breaking a leg or worse." "I don't think it's that risky. I can go slowly and carefully," said Kyle. Mitch replied, "Ok, I can live with that. We can probably see most of the stuff from the floor anyway and need to climb up only if it looks promising. Have you guys found anything of use yet?" "Not really," came the reply in unison from the pair. "Mostly stuff we already have lots of or don't need."

Mitch did some more thinking. "There doesn't seem to be anyone here and my apprehension about splitting up is a little lessened. Why don't we go on foot through the facility and see if we can find anything on the ground floor that can be carried out easily." The other two men nodded. "I'll head that way and Ryan can head the other," said Kyle. Pointing to the west, Kyle said to Mitch, "If you cover off that direction, we can see what this place has." Mitch nodded and began walking in the direction Kyle had pointed, sweeping the aisles with his light. The amount of garbage and broken packaging lying about was really amazing. It was like a swarm of locusts had descended upon the facility in a desperate attempt to find food. He did see partial bags of rice or corn starch or similar items on the floor or on the pallets in the racking, each left behind due to their damaged condition, but he really didn't see any full containers of anything much. There was some oddball stuff like gravy thickeners and chia seeds but not items that could be considered actual food. Kate had mentioned some items to be on the lookout for, but there were none of those to be found. He did pick up a bulk package of double AA batteries someone had missed, which would be useful but not more than that. As he got towards the end of the building, he saw a pair of offices along the interior wall. Approaching the nearer of the two, he shone his light in through the open door. Inside he saw what looked like two men sitting in office chairs. Getting closer, he could see they were unmoving and covered in a light layer of dust. Both men had their arms duct taped to the armrests of the chairs. Their feet were duct taped together at the ankles. The illumination from the light revealed their last hours on earth had not been pleasant ones. It was clearly apparent each of them had been tortured for some reason. Both were missing fingers off their hands. Pointing his light down onto the tabletop next to them, he spotted a pile of fingers, each with dried crusty blood where the fingers had bled out. On the table next to the pile of fingers was a pair of garden shears with blood dried on the edges of the blades. The floor around their chairs was a circle of blood spatter and footprints where their captors and torturers had stood as they performed their gruesome tasks.

Mitch wondered what information these two men could have had that resulted in this treatment. He also wondered who the perpetrators were. If they were still roaming around, they were obviously capable of some heinous behavior and likely needed to be avoided. Mitch shone his light around the office searching for clues as to what transpired here or, even more unlikely, the reasons why. Nothing revealed itself to him. He pulled some drawers open in filing cabinets and flipped through some binders of shipping manifests and the like, but there was nothing of value to be found. He turned and tripped over a shoe on the floor. It seemed out of place until he thought about the two men taped to chairs, and this caused him to shine his light on their feet. Both had their shoes and socks removed. He walked closer and bent down for a better look. Apparently, garden shears were the wrong tool for feet, as both men had blackened toes and blackened soles of their feet. Shining his light around some more, he spotted a blue propane tank torch around the 14 oz size with a nozzle on the end sitting on the floor. On a table beside it was a flint striker typically used to light a gas torch. Not a lot of deduction to figure out what happened there, he thought to himself. Mitch shuddered internally. Seeing and feeling your digits getting snipped off and then having your feet burned by a gas torch was not high on his list of things to do in life. Awful, he thought to himself, and tried to put the imagined images out of his head.

He picked up the striker and gave it a squeeze a couple of times — still lots of flint left in it and it was a useful item so into a pocket it went. Leaving the office, he went into the adjoining office to continue scouting. It, unlike the first office, had nothing of particular interest. He quickly exited and carried on. "Hey Mitch!" one of the other men shouted but not in a distressed manner. Mitch called back "On my way" and started walking towards the origin of the shout. Minutes later he arrived. "What did you find?" The two men stood in front of a pile of freshly moved cardboard. "Look! Twenty-pound sacks of pinto beans," Ryan pointed out. "We pulled a bunch of cardboard off the top and underneath were these sacks – they must have been overlooked." This was a significant find. Mitch was not really a fan of beans but they were dry goods, stored well and were a significant source of calories. "Great job guys!" "Kate and the rest of the group will really appreciate this." "Now, how do we get these to the truck?" Ryan was bent over moving the bags around a bit. "Based on a quick count we have 48 bags sitting here. If we throw two bags each over our shoulder that is eight trips to the truck each. Hard work but not impossible," Ryan suggested. Mitch said, "My dad always said work smart before working hard. What about a cart or dolly or wheelbarrow or something?" He continued, "How about we continue our search in case there was something else overlooked and then return to this pile if we don't find anything else? In our search we might also find something to transport these a lot easier than humping them out of here manually." Mitch had a sudden thought "Evan. Anything happening out there? Everything ok?" "All ok boss" came the quick response. "I am dying of boredom while you guys are in there having a good time!" Mitch turned to Ryan "Why don't you take a couple of these sacks out there and see how demanding it is? Spell off Evan and let him come in. You take a break while watching the vehicles and we will keep searching." Ryan "Yeah sure, why not. Lugging them out was my idea so I might as well find out how tough it is and simultaneously save poor Evan." Mitch and Kyle smiled at the jab and nodded. "Sounds good. Radio when you get there and let me know how it went."

Kyle helped Ryan get a couple of the sacks on his left shoulder, and Ryan headed out to the box van. Mitch and Kyle then resumed their search of the premises. After a while, Evan made his way to them. "This place sure is huge," he commented. "Have you guys found anything else interesting so far?" Mitch decided to skip telling him about his findings back in the office. "So far, just the pinto beans. This place has been pretty much cleaned out. We are going to keep looking, but almost 100% of the foodstuffs are gone. I am betting we are not the first team to come through here. Quite frankly, I am surprised no one else found those beans. That was a stroke of luck for sure." "By the way, Ryan made it out okay. He said carrying the beans wasn't too tough, and he thought we could move them all that way if we had to." Evan pointed to his right. "Has anyone checked that area out yet?" Mitch shone his light and saw a large drive-in type freezer or cooler unit. "Nope. Make sure you prop the door open in case it has an automatic closure." Evan gave Mitch a quick thumbs up. "You bet." He headed in that direction. Mitch made his way to a staircase running up the side of the wall and began climbing. After a dozen or more steps, he arrived at the landing. Shining his light back into the racking, he didn't see anything of note. Turning, he pushed open the nearest door of the upstairs offices and entered. Along one wall, he saw a number of Symbol brand inventory guns in a charging station. There were a pair of desks against the other walls and dust-covered computer stations on top of each. Must be the inventory office, he thought to himself. At the other end of the landing was the door to another office. He made his way there and went inside. There was a larger desk and a couple of chairs opposite. A bookshelf sat against another wall with some dusty volumes and a series of binders standing on a lower shelf. Warehouse S.O.P.s the binders were labeled along the spine of each. The desk had an assortment of papers on top of it in a state of disarray. Mitch went behind the desk and sat in the chair there. It was a comfortable model with tilt and all of the helpful adjustments of a chair someone spent a lot of time in. Must be the warehouse manager's chair, he thought to himself. There was a window into the warehouse across from him. Nice view, he thought. All that beautiful racking to look at all day.

While sitting in the chair, Mitch opened some of the drawers and had a look inside. In a roll held closed by a rubber band, he found a layout drawing of the facility. Unfurling it, he laid it out on the desktop and pinned the edges down with a stapler and a three-hole punch to keep it flat. He saw where he and his teammates had entered and the location of some other features of the building. Seeing it on paper gave him a different perspective of the facility, and he better understood the size of the place. It was a large building with twenty-plus loading docks along one side of the facility. "Ryan for Mitch," his radio startled him out of his concentration. "Mitch here, what's up?" Ryan sounded quite excited, "Taking fire from an unknown source. Shots fired; shots fired." Mitch stood up immediately and headed for the door. "Mitch for Kyle and Evan – are you getting this?" "Check, Mitch. We hear it. Heading to the point we entered."

Mitch went down the stairs more than twice the speed he ascended. He thumbed the radio button as he went, "Can you tell where the shots are coming from?" Ryan answered back, "They're coming from the tree line across the field. It seems like a single shooter so far." "On our way. We'll radio when we're close," Mitch radioed back. In short order, he met up with the other two men. "Weapons check," commanded Mitch. All three checked their weapons to ensure they were in battery and ready to be used. "Follow me," Mitch said and then broke into a trot towards where the vehicles were situated. "Crack," came the report of a rifle being fired. Being a single shot, it was hard to tell the direction it came from, so the men continued on towards the pickup, box van, and motorcycle. A short time later, they arrived and saw Ryan crouched down behind another vehicle close to their three. "Crack," another round came in their direction. "What's happening?" Mitch asked Ryan as they arrived. "Someone is shooting at us. The driver's side window in the box van was taken out and there are some holes in the sidewalls of the box. Other than that – not too much. It is weird. It's like he is not really trying to hit anything or maybe he is just a lousy shot. I don't know," Ryan responded. Mitch headed towards his pickup. "I am getting my binos," he said to the rest. Approaching from the passenger side, he kept low and opened the passenger door. Inside was the camouflage case which held his binoculars. He grabbed the case, slammed the door, and headed back to where the others were concealing themselves. Pulling his binoculars out, Mitch searched the tree line across the field from where they were located. He was looking for a reflection off a scope lens to give away the location of the shooter. "Clang" rang out from the side of the box van as a round perforated it again. Mitch could not see where the rounds were coming from. "Why is he shooting at us?" asked Evan. "What have we done to him?"

Mitch continued to glass the tree line. If their opponent was targeting them from inside a blind, he wouldn't be able to spot him at this distance. The other three men crowded around him. "What do you say, boss? What are we going to do?" Mitch continued to glass the tree line. The shots seemed to have stopped for now. He turned and addressed the small group. "First off, we don't know what this shooter's intentions are. He might be trying to scare us off or maybe he is trying to pin us down until reinforcements arrive. He might just be crazy and taking pot-shots for the sheer hell of it. Other than a busted window and some new ventilation in the side of the van, he hasn't done any real damage. Maybe he considers this his territory and we are trespassers. I don't know. I do know we can't drive any closer to this warehouse with all these abandoned vehicles in the way to collect the sacks of pinto beans. If we stay here, he might..." "Crack!" another shot rang out mid-sentence at Mitch. Everyone ducked in response to this latest shot. Mitch continued, "So, he's still here and still shooting. I say we saddle up, head on to our next location and then stop here on the way back and collect the rest of those sacks. Crossing that field to get close enough to take him out is far too risky and I don't relish taking the time necessary to flank him. We don't know the local lay of the land and he might have help on the way. I say we skedaddle." All three of the men agreed. "Let's coordinate our departure so we take off at the same time and make it a bit harder for him to focus on a single target. We can enter the van and the pickup from this side so he can't see us but Ryan, you are going to be fully visible getting on that bike." Evan spoke up, "We can pull the box van in front of him and shield him from the sight of the shooter." Mitch said, "Good idea. Let's get turned around and burn out of here and head towards our next stop."

The team moved according to directions and got quickly into their vehicles and fired them up. Oddly, no shots rang out. Evan pulled the box van in front of the motorcycle and Ryan mounted his bike and started the engine. Mitch pulled a U-turn with the Tacoma and with a bit of back-and-forth jockeying Evan did the same with the box van. Ryan spun the bike around and surged out in front of the group. All three vehicles rapidly accelerated and sped away from the distribution center. Evan lifted his butt off the seat as he drove and swept the broken side window glass off of his seat and onto the floor of the vehicle. The wind came in loudly through the now open window and as it did Evan suddenly realized it was no longer raining. It had been for a long time earlier but with all the excitement he had not noticed its ending. Which was a good thing as the rain would have been streaming in what was now an opening to the elements.

No gunfire followed them as they made their way out of the area. Mitch was ticked off about not loading the sacks of pinto beans and also annoyed at how little food they had found in the distribution center. They had gone there first because of the size of the place and the expected contents it could hold. There was no doubt a lot of other people had thought the same and headed there as well. The two men with the torched feet and cut-off fingers gnawed at him. Why had someone done that? What was it for? Information gathering or just simple sick enjoyment? Mitch knew there were some sickos running around in the world and now it seemed clear that some of those same sorts had survived the first hard year. Mitch also wondered if those sorts of people were more adept at surviving in this type of world. Were the evil and cruel more well-suited for the post-collapse world? Mitch had thought cooperative and collaborative types would do better as tough times necessitated team work. "Team work makes the dream work," Mitch said to himself with a chuckle — thinking back to his days working a career in business. Maybe all of that was bullshit and the brave new world wasn't all that new or brave but rather a return to a more coarse and mean existence. Mitch returned his attention to the map and their next destination. It was several miles away and the day was passing. Time to focus, he thought.

CHAPTER TWELVE
TRAINING

After a long, deep, sleep, Angeline and Caleb rose from their respective beds. Caleb felt and then saw bruising on his side where he had landed after being tackled by the man at the Walmart entrance. A hot shower helped somewhat, but a couple of Ibuprofen down the hatch helped more. Annoying, but it would resolve itself over the next couple of days. Angeline was next up in the shower queue, and after exiting, she felt immeasurably better, though the bottoms of her feet were a bit tender from the long day of walking. Breakfast in the kitchen for Angeline followed, and then the dishes were cleaned up by her. "I appreciate that," commented Caleb after she finished tidying up. Caleb made her a mug of hot chocolate and himself a coffee, and then sat down. "What's next?" she asked brightly.

Caleb sat back in his chair and thought for a moment or two. "I think I mentioned the need to get you trained in a few basics," he voiced. "Now that we have your immediate clothing problems sorted out, we should work on your skill sets. Maybe it might be a good idea to start with – wait, what do you know how to do?" he asked with a smile. "I know you think I'm helpless," she said with a good dose of sarcasm. "Well, I am not! I know how to do lots of things!" Caleb smiled again. "I am sure that you do. Snapchat, texting, web scrolling, TikTok – I bet you can do all sorts of things." Angeline frowned. "I know you think all that stuff is useless and in today's world you are probably right. But I can do other things." "Like what?" asked Caleb. "I can start a fire and I know how to use a compass for starters," she said somewhat triumphantly. "What kind of fire?" asked Caleb. "What do you mean – kind of fire?" replied Angeline. "A fire kind of fire. What else is there?" "Let me rephrase," said Caleb. "Can you light a fire with a BBQ lighter, a Bic lighter, matches, a ferro rod and tinder, a welding striker – how would you start and keep burning this 'fire' you know how to make?" Angeline chewed her lip for a minute. She didn't realize fires were going to get so complicated so fast. "I don't know what a feral rod is or a welding striker but I can make a fire with the rest of the things you listed." "A ferro rod," he gently corrected. "It's a device that you use to make sparks, same as a welding striker." "Why would you use either one of those to start a fire?" she asked. "Because they can be wet and will still produce sparks. Lighters run out of fuel or break just like BBQ lighters and matches don't work when they are wet. All of the choices I listed have their advantages and disadvantages depending on the situation. It's good to know how to use each of them and a few others I can think of. You never know exactly what you are going to be dealt and being versatile in your abilities is a formula for success." Angeline nodded.

"You said you know how to use a compass. What about a map? Can you use both of them together?" he asked. Angeline shook her head. "Nope, I know a compass will show you where north is, and because of that, you know where east, west, and south are," she proudly explained. Caleb could see he had a bit of work to do. He did like her enthusiasm, though. An eager student made the instruction all the more enjoyable. "Well, there is a little more to it than just that, but we will cover that. Do you have any other secret skills hidden inside that head of yours?" he asked. She wrinkled her brow and looked away as she thought about it. "I helped Mum in our garden, so I know a little bit about gardening, but I think that is it." Caleb got up from the table and opened a kitchen drawer, withdrawing a yellow legal pad and pen. He returned to the table and sat down. "Let's finish the list we started and put them into some sort of order. I don't want to overwhelm you, so we will space them out kinda evenly and intermingle them with day-to-day chores around here. How does that sound?" "That sounds good. Maybe we can go for more walks around this area so I get to know the neighborhood too," she suggested. "Agreed," Caleb responded.

Caleb began working on the list they had started the other day:

Mental resilience: Maintaining a positive mindset and staying calm under pressure. Maintaining perspective.

Situational awareness: Being aware of your surroundings and potential dangers, maintaining appropriate awareness levels.

Threat assessment: Understanding and assessing potential risks and dangers.

Navigation: Using paper maps, compasses, and natural landmarks to get to where you are going.

Communication: Learning basic survival communication skills, including using radios, whistles, and gestures.

Knife and axe skills: Skills for cutting various materials, building, and preparing food.

Knot craft: Knowing essential knots for building shelters, securing items, and creating traps.

Trapping & fishing: Learning to set traps and fish for food can provide food sources in a calorie efficient manner.

Improvised tools: Knowing how to make tools from natural sources.

Shelter building: Understanding different shelter types and how to build them effectively and expeditiously.

Fire-making skills: Learn different methods to start and maintain a fire.

Water collection and purification: Knowing where and how to find, collect, and purify water.

Food foraging and plant identification: Recognizing edible plants and fruits. Knowing where to look.

Self-defense skills: How to use both armed and unarmed techniques to defend yourself.

Scouting and patrolling skills: Being able to learn what is happening in your area of operations.

Tracks and tracking: It's good to understand what is in the area and how to follow the quarry.

Man-trapping and booby-trapping: How to interfere with the movement and activities of an adversary.

Caleb finished writing and showed the list to Angeline. "It's not exhaustive, but it's a good start. There are a lot of individual items that do not require a category of their own, but I will cover those as well." She read the list from top to bottom. "Booby-trapping – what is that?" Caleb looked at her a while as he collected his thoughts. "Angeline," he began, "This is not the world you grew up in. I know you can see things have changed. A lot of the old rules about how things go have changed. Right now, there are two of us. My main strategy has been to keep a low profile and stay out of sight. If, however, we get noticed, we need ways to even the odds between us and people who want to take our things or our lives. Booby traps can be thought of as extra team members who will sacrifice themselves to help us stay alive. For example, say I don't want anyone damaging our solar array. We can place traps in those woods that will maim or kill anyone who tries to get in there and wreck our electricity supply. The problem with booby traps is they don't discern. They will go off if it is an attacker or a woman or a child who just happens to be in the wrong place at the wrong time. This is why many nations on earth worked to ban land mines. Militaries place mines in many places during wars and then forget about them after the war ends, and for years innocent people find them in the most devastating ways."

Angeline asked again, "So what are booby traps?" Caleb realized he had been talking over her head. "A booby trap can be a hole dug in the ground with spikes standing upright in it and covered with plants to hide it. A bad guy comes along and steps into the hole, and the spikes go into his foot, trapping him in the hole." "Oh yuck!" exclaimed Angeline. "That sounds awful." Caleb agreed, "It is awful, and almost all booby traps do stuff like that. It is an ugly side of the way things are." "Do I need to make things like that?" she asked. "We can push that off until later, but at some point – yes, you need to learn this stuff. Like I said before – the world has changed. It is much more survival-based, and those who cannot or will not do what is necessary to survive – won't." Angeline seemed to understand this now. She looked resigned and not particularly happy. It was some uncomfortable topic material being discussed, that was for sure.

Caleb tried to put a lighter spin on things. "Why don't we start with the fun stuff first?" "You wanted to go for a walk around here – we can look for some edible plants and fruits and maybe find some water sources while we are at it. What do you say about that?" Angeline stood up from her chair. "I would like that. It could be fun. Staying in the house all day would kind of suck." Caleb rose from his chair. "Deal. Get dressed and meet me at the front door and we will go for a hike and have a look." Angeline pushed her chair in and headed to her room. Caleb took the notepad and put it back in the drawer from which he had retrieved it. Perhaps listing the booby traps had not been the best idea at this time, he thought. I guess I will leave that topic alone for a while and come back to it when she is more ready. Caleb headed back to his room to prepare for the excursion.

Fifteen minutes later, Angeline showed up at the door. This time, Caleb had only armed himself with a handgun in a leg holster. He stuck his Laredo bowie in his belt in what was known as sash carry style. The large brass pin sticking out from the thick leather sheath prevented the sheath from sliding past the belt. It was a comfortable way to carry a large blade and made for a fast and easy draw. Angeline had taken her sjambok to her room upon their return, and it was back in her hand again. "I see you have the sjambok again," Caleb commented. "Yeah, I like it. It's very whippy and fast, plus a lot of fun to hit things with," she exclaimed and started waving it around. "Whoa, cowboy! You need to be careful with that thing. When I first bought it, I gave myself a good whack across the calf to see what it could do and was rewarded with a welt the size of a hot dog, which didn't go away for days!" "Sorry," came the reply. "I'll be more careful." "No harm, no foul," he replied with a smile. Mitch pulled on his camo ball cap, and they headed outdoors.

As per his usual habit, he surveyed the area around them as soon as he exited the house. He took out his monocular and had a more in-depth look with magnified vision. There was some cloud cover today, but it wasn't raining or threatening to do so. There was a fair number of birds overhead, but they did not portend anything suspicious or unusual. The wind was largely absent today, which was nice. It was not warm enough to need a cooling breeze. Seeing everything was copacetic, he led Angeline towards the wooded area west of his house. In a few minutes, they were near a slew. He pointed at the cattails growing up from standing water. "Do you know what those are?" She shook her head. "Those are cattails, and they are pretty good to eat. If you pick them in June or early July, the new ones are pretty soft to chew and taste good. You pull them straight out of the ground, and usually the root stays behind.

Here, let's go try." He led her closer to the wetland area where some cattails were growing and bent down and grasped one shaft just above the water line. A little tug, and it came loose from its root just as promised. "See here. You can cut the last inch off with your knife and then take the next ten inches for the cooking pot." He proceeded to use his pocket folder to do so and handed it to her. "Try bending it," he said to her. Angeline gave the shaft of the plant a tentative bend while hanging onto both ends. "Not too bendy, right?" Caleb said. "Watch." Taking his knife, he cut a lengthwise slice down the center of the plant stem and peeled the outer layer away. "Now try." She gave it another try, and this time it was much easier. It actually snapped into pieces as she bent it. "Oh, oh," she commented. "No worries. That is actually what is supposed to happen. Take one of those pieces and pop it in your mouth. We have removed the outer husk, so it is clean and safe to eat." Angeline complied and put a one-inch piece in her mouth and chewed. "It's good!" she said aloud in between bites.

Caleb and Angeline carried on with their walk. He pointed out stinging nettles which, despite their name, were highly nutritious for a plant food. Dandelions, wild raspberries, and wild strawberries, as well as a number of other plants, they were able to find. The berries could be eaten as soon as they were picked, whereas some of the other plants they found required some preparation prior to being table ready. Eventually, their walk brought them to a stream bed with a six-foot-wide body of water running through it. The water looked clean and fresh, and when they bent down, it was cool to the touch. "Can we drink it?" she asked. "Sadly, no," he responded. "It looks good and probably tastes good, but there is a good chance it has Giardia or some other parasite in it. You will get diarrhea or stomach cramps or worse if you get infected with that. You can certainly fill a canteen with it but will need to either boil the water or chemically treat the water before you can consume it." "Look! Fish!" Angeline yelled and pointed. Caleb could see a small school of cutthroat trout in the center of the stream. From where he was, he could make out the red slashes under their jaws which gave them their name and distinctive look. "Good eye, little lady. Those are good eating and not too hard to catch." Caleb stood and looked along the bank of the stream. "Look over here," he said to Angeline as he walked towards some tracks in the ground. "See those? What do you think they are?" Angeline narrowed her eyes and stared at the tracks in the wet ground. "Deer tracks?" she said somewhat tentatively. "Yes, but whose deer, are they?" She stared at him. He stared back very seriously until he broke out into laughter. "Just kidding you. They don't belong to anyone. I am just pulling your leg." Angeline snickered and looked relieved. "I couldn't think of who would own them!" she said laughingly.

Caleb squatted down and traced an outline of the tracks. "These are mule deer tracks," he told her. "White tail is more heart-shaped while mule deer are larger, more elongated, and rounder shaped. Looking around, Caleb pointed out a couple of different sets of tracks. "From the looks of things, they came here to have a drink and then headed back the way they came. Water is always a good place to hunt as all things need to drink. Predators hang out around water sources for the same reasons – they know all things need to drink." "What kind of predators are around here?" Angeline asked. Caleb responded – "in this part of the world, you get bears, coyotes, and the occasional mountain lion. I don't think there are any wolves this close to the city, maybe further out near the mountains." Caleb stood and walked further down the bank. "Look here. This is not something you see all that often." In the soft ground were some much larger tracks, almost double the size of the previously viewed tracks. "Unless I'm wrong, these are moose tracks. Take a good look as you generally won't see these in this area." "They sure are big. How big is a moose?" As a city dweller, it was highly unlikely she had ever seen a moose in person. Caleb scratched his stubbled cheek. "Again, if I remember correctly, they stand about six feet at the shoulder and can easily weigh over a thousand pounds or more. The females, of course, run smaller, but they are an impressive size nonetheless."

Angeline looked up from the tracks. "Are they good to eat?" Caleb laughed out loud. "Now you're thinking like a hunter, young lady!" "You bet they are good to eat. Much better than that cattail you had earlier. Much more nutritious as well. Let me tell you a story," he said to her. "Back when we were just tribes of people roaming over the land, there were no supermarkets or convenience stores. If you wanted to eat something, you had to kill it. Yes, there were some foods you could pick or gather, but when a herd of large animals came by or you found them while hunting, the amount of food and quality of food was immeasurably better. A handful of wild strawberries might, if you are lucky, contain a hundred calories. A full-grown bison would have somewhere in the vicinity of 3 million calories. Less if you subtract out the bones and hooves and horns, etc. Depending on how you went about it – the payback in terms of effort and time expended to hunt and kill a bison versus trying to pick 3 million calories of berries is not even close to being the same. "So, picking plants is no good?" "Well, I think of it as starvation food. If you are really hungry and have nothing to eat, you can fill your belly with it until something better comes along. The effort expended in gathering it really outweighs its usefulness."

Angeline nodded her head in agreement. "What about fish? Are they worth eating?" "Absolutely," responded Caleb. "Plus, they are tasty if prepared correctly." "Can we catch some of those fish and eat them?" she asked. "Sure." He replied. "I have some rods and tackle put away, and luckily those are not brown trout, as brown trout are notoriously hard to catch. With a little luck, we can catch a mess of fish and fry them in some butter I have back at the house." "That sounds good!" exclaimed Angeline enthusiastically. "Can we come tomorrow?" Caleb considered. "I don't see why not.

Give me a minute to check my schedule. Hmm, seems I may have an opening for fishing tomorrow. I will pencil you in." Angeline beamed at him. "Yeah! Fishing!"

Caleb stood and began walking again. Coming up out of the gully formed by the stream, he could see in the distance again. He motioned Angeline to stay behind him. "Quiet for a minute." He told her and pulled out his monocular again. In the distance, he could see a line of horses and riders. He dialed up the power on his monocular and had a closer look. There were seven horses in a row. Men with various types of hats and jackets rode the horses, but the rear two men each had a horse following them with a rider being led by a rope or line of some sort; he could not tell from this distance. It appeared the riders of the horses being led were females, likely grown women based on their size. The two female riders looked down as they rode and were not looking around. Likely prisoners, Caleb thought to himself. Ranchers would have been wearing cowboy hats, whereas these men did not look at all like cowboys. Their clothing was wrong for that profession, and they did not ride with the type of ease years in the saddle produced. These people looked awkward as they rode, not connected to the animal beyond the most superficial sense.

Angeline tugged on his sleeve. "What's going on?" she asked. "Riders over there," Caleb said as he pointed. "What are they doing?" Angeline asked. "Don't know, but it looks like the two women with them are prisoners of some sort," Caleb answered. "What are we going to do?" she inquired. Caleb turned and looked at her. "I bet you are thinking we should 'do something' – right?" Angeline wrinkled her brow, suspecting this was not as innocent a question as it seemed. "I guess there really isn't anything we can do – is there?" she answered. Caleb carried on with his questions. "Why not?" "Because this is the real world and not a movie where we save everyone?" she offered. "There are only two of us and lots of them, and I am only ten, so really there is only one of us?" Caleb smiled. "You are getting it. It would be nice if we could swoop down on that party and see what is happening, but not only is there an imbalance in numbers between us and them – we have no idea what is going on. Just because those women appear to be prisoners does not mean they are either innocent or good. They could be some sort of criminals or bad people who have done horrible things.

They could be the nicest people on earth and completely free of guilt. Standing here and looking at them, we cannot tell. In this world, Angeline, assumptions can get you killed. I can teach you all about animal tracks and how to fish, but it is your ability to think critically that is going to keep you alive. It is hard, but you need to strip assumptions out of your thinking and rely on first principles. We can cover what those are later, but for now the lesson is – don't assume. You get that?" Angeline nodded. "Don't assume." "What does assume mean?" Caleb chuckled out loud. "I keep forgetting you are ten. Assuming is to think you know something is a certain way when you are lacking facts. Humans do it all the time; it is a mental shortcut of sorts and is hard to stop. With practice, however, it becomes easy to not assume things." "Check," Angeline smiled and nodded. "I think I get it."

Caleb returned to observing the riders with his monocular. They had continued the way they were headed and gave no sign of seeing Caleb and his young companion. He watched them for another ten minutes as they continued and receded from sight. I'm curious who they are and what they are up to, he thought. Are they headed home, passing through, or heading away from their homes? He decided to review his map when he got back and see if there was a logical starting point for them to be leaving from. Looking at the amount of gear they had on their horses and a lack of pack horses hauling more gear, he doubted they had come a long distance or were going a long distance. They appeared to be on a day trip of some sort, which meant proximity to his location. He considered leaving Angeline home for a day and trekking over to the trail left by those horses and heading down their back trail to see if he could scout out their base of operations. Knowing who was in the neighborhood was a definite plus in his mind. The more he thought about it, the more certain he was that this was the right decision.

"Let's head back to the house. Enough training for today. Maybe I will train you on DVD operations when we get back," he said with a smile." Angeline grinned back and started walking. As they walked, Caleb planned out the supplies and gear he would take with him on this upcoming expedition. He had a ghillie suit he had made, but for a journey of this distance, it would prove to be too hot. He decided to opt for lighter camouflage and increased mobility.

He was going to have to show Angeline more of the household functionality so she could spend some time alone while he was off. He enjoyed her company, but she slowed him down when he was traversing cross-country. On a cost/benefit analysis basis – knowing who these people were and what area they were operating in was worth it to him. He had not seen anyone in his general neighborhood for months now, so this recent arrival was making him a bit nervous.

A little while later, they arrived back at his residence. He used his monocular to glass the area around his house before approaching it. This was a habit of his which he never shortchanged himself on. He didn't want any surprises when he was opening his place up. He knew the moment when he opened the door initially was a dangerous time in his process. Once safely inside, he could button up pretty well, and with the reinforcements he had built into the structure, it would be quite hard for outside parties to get in. His doors were metal with metal frames, and he had wooden bars which he placed across the inside so breaching-type actions with a shotgun were much harder to do. He had a few other tricks up his sleeve as well if it came to that, but so far, he had escaped notice and hadn't had to test any of his preparations for repelling intruders.

Nothing seemed out of the ordinary after ten minutes of observation. He told Angeline what he was doing and why, and she seemed to understand it. "Grandpa was careful when we were in his house. We would go upstairs and look out the windows, but he was always making sure nobody noticed us. Once in a while, we would see people walking by, but if there were more than one or two, Grandpa would make us go back in the shelter and lock everything up. He said he knew he couldn't stop anyone as he was too old, so staying out of sight was his plan as well – so I am used to it," she said.

Once they arrived at the door, Caleb unlocked it via the keypad and they went inside. Over the next few minutes, they shed their outdoor clothing and put away their gear. "So, do you want to keep that sjambok in your room with you?" he asked her. "Yes, if that is okay," she responded. "I like having it with me." "No worries," Caleb replied and headed to the living room. Angeline came out of her room and joined him in the living room. He had been a bit of an audiophile back in the day and had a Pioneer stereo system with a decent set of speakers spread around the room. He showed her how to work that as well as the entertainment center so she could play video games, watch movies, or listen to music. "Sorry, but no internet anymore; I am sure you know that." "Not having Instagram or TikTok was hard to get used to," she admitted. "I think all the chaos we were going through helped me forget about it." Caleb – "Well, then I guess the chaos was good for something," he quipped. After getting her acquainted with the features of the living room, he made his way to the kitchen and dinner preparations. After eating, they hung out in the living room for the rest of the evening before making their way to bed. Tomorrow was going to be an interesting day.

CHAPTER THIRTEEN

JACKPOT

Mitch and the team headed further south. Their next stop was at a baking supplies warehouse they had learned about. As they approached the destination, they slowed down and pulled to a stop a half block away. Mitch exited his truck, as did Evan and Kyle with theirs. Ryan put out the kickstand on his bike and pulled his helmet off. The building they were looking at was a mustard yellow-colored warehouse. It was sitting between two other similarly sized buildings. All three buildings were nondescript and uninteresting-looking. The faded sign over the entry was still legible. The door and windows were all in one piece, and the parking lot was empty. Mitch took these as good signs.

"Let's walk around to the back and take a look," he suggested. The men hefted their firearms and headed in that direction. Mitch estimated it to be a 30,000 square foot warehouse. On the smaller size for a warehouse. This lesser size and innocuous location might have worked in their favor. Making their way to the back of the building, they could see four box vans much like their own parked in a row. The company logo was on the side of the delivery trucks, and three of the four were backed into the loading docks. There was a small set of metal stairs leading to the rear entry door, which was currently closed. Taking the four stairs up, Mitch reached out and gave the handle a tug. Locked. "Check if that overhead door at the end is locked down," Mitch said to the guys. Kyle and Evan walked around the parked vehicles. Once they got to the door, they worked together to try to push it up. Nothing. Definitely secured from the inside. The two men shouted their findings to Mitch. He took a closer look at the door he was facing, a metal door with a stout-looking metal frame. "We are going to need some tools to get past this door. Why don't you guys bring the vehicles around back here, and we can get to work on cracking this nut open." The guys voiced their agreement and left for the parked vehicles. Mitch tossed the keys for the Tacoma to

Evan so he could bring the pickup around as well. Mitch noticed the men were deferring to him more and more and the decisions he was making. Being more of a loner by nature, Mitch found his new role as leader a bit unusual. He was less uncomfortable than expected.

The sound of the approaching vehicles brought him back to the present situation. The box van backed into the vacant loading dock. The motorcycle and pickup parked near the small set of metal stairs. Kyle brought a small sledgehammer and a larger gooseneck pry bar with him from the vehicle. Evan had a straight pry bar and a couple of metal wedges. Mitch knew the majority of warehouse doors had push-bar exiting mechanisms. A horizontal bar which, when pushed from the inside, depressed the latch allowing exit. Mitch decided they would attack the door frame at the latch and try to pry it open. "Here, Evan, put the tip of the bar here," he said, pointing to the approximate position he thought the latch would be. Evan inserted the bar, and Kyle got his sledgehammer going on it. After several heavy whacks, the door frame was getting pushed aside. Mitch could see the latching mechanism. Mitch took the gooseneck and inserted the straight end in after Evan pulled his bar out. The space was too small for the pry bar to fit in. "Do we have a blade screwdriver?" Ryan answered, "There's one in the truck. I'll go grab it." A minute later, he was back with a hefty blade-tipped screwdriver. Mitch took it and inserted it into the space. It easily fit, and with a little toggling, he was able to push the latching mechanism into the door. Then, using his other hand, he pulled the warehouse door open. "Success!"

When the door opened, they could see inside. It was dark as the lights were out, but there was enough daylight streaming in; they could make out the racking. Racking which looked full of goods! Mitch turned and looked at the other guys, "Pay dirt!" They all broke into grins. All three men dug out their headlamps and put them on. Carrying their tools with them, they entered the warehouse. Mitch shone his flashlight up and down the aisles and was surprised by what he saw. The racking was full of cooking oils, baking powder, many types of flours, honey, and a wide variety of other baking goods. The place was a virtual bonanza of foodstuffs. The men walked through the facility looking at all the available items. "This is more than we can fit inside the van. More than we could fit in a freight truck, as a matter of fact," said Kyle. They got to the last loading dock where their own vehicle was backed in. Mitch grabbed the hanging chain to raise the overhead door. It had been padlocked shut. "I'm going to go back to the pickup and get my bolt cutters for this lock," he told the other three and headed back outside. The men muttered their approvals. They were more fascinated by examining all the pallets of flour and edible items. "Look, a whole pallet of sunflower seeds!" called out one of the guys. "I haven't had sunflower seeds for well over a year now!"

Mitch opened the passenger side door of his pickup, removing the bolt cutters from the floor. Bolt cutters were highly prized and highly useful items in the new world they existed in. He had done more break-and-enter type activity in the last year than he had done in his whole life prior to this. Strange how things shake out, he thought to himself. Looking overhead, he could see seagulls flying by. Weird how they live this far from the sea or ocean, he thought to himself. The usual spot you saw them in pre-collapse days was in McDonald's parking lots begging for French fries. No more McDonald's in the new paradigm. I wonder what they eat now? he wondered.

Closing the pickup door, he went back in and headed straight to the overhead door. Ten seconds or less of cutting with the bolt cutters, and the chain was free to be used. Evan pulled down on the chain and released it from the hooking mechanism that held it in place. He began raising the door hand over hand, by pulling on the chain. Mitch swept the warehouse with his flashlight. There was a lot of material higher up in the racks. The chances of one of the two forklifts he could see having any charge in their batteries were effectively zero. He did see a couple of manual pump jacks lying about. This would enable them to move pallets into the back of their box van. "Hey boss. The dock leveler is electric – how are we going to get the pallets in the back of the van?" Mitch walked over and had a look. "See that ring attached to that chain there?" he said, pointing to the center of the dock leveler. "If you pull on that, you can open it manually, and we are good to go. You need to open up the roll-up door in the back of the box van first, of course." Kyle nodded his understanding of the directions given. He unlatched the roll-up door of the van and elevated it. Whoever had backed in had done a good job. The rear of the vehicle was flush with the bumpers on either side of the loading dock. This meant the dock leveler could be deployed without issue.

Mitch looked at Kyle. "Give a pull, sir!" Kyle bent over and grasped the metal ring and pulled up and back. The dock leveler came up out of its resting place and the beavertail on the end flipped open. Kyle walked forward on the elevated leveler and, with his weight, lowered it into the bed of the van. "That was easy!" he announced. Mitch then led the men into the rows where the food rested on pallets. "I think we should bring back a variety – not just flour or just salt or whatever. We might come back here and find the place emptied out. We made a lot of noise hammering the pry bars into the doorframe and who knows who is on their way here now." All three of the men acknowledged his suggestion. Ryan said, "I say we choose the biggest pallet of each type of item and wheel it onto the truck." Mitch considered the suggestion for a moment and countered, "How about we check the tare of the vehicle and not overload it? We don't need broken suspension on our way back." All three stared at him expectantly. "Tare? What the heck is a tare?" one of them asked. Mitch explained, "G.V.W. is gross vehicle weight. The tare is the portion of that you

can load on a vehicle bringing it up to full G.V.W. Get it?"
The men all nodded. "How do we figure that out?" Evan
asked. "The GVW and the tare are usually painted on the
side of the vehicle for easy access. Why don't you head
outside and have a look at ours and see what it says?" Evan
agreed and took off. Mitch looked at the two remaining men.
"When he gets back, we will know how much we can take
and do some tabletop math with what's here. It shouldn't be
too hard to determine how much we can carry and go from
there."

Evan trundled back in a minute. "It says 7,500 kg tare
on the side," he reported. "That's about 15,000 pounds."
Mitch continued, "Okay, so we know what we can handle.
Let's stage all of the pallets of the items we want and then do
a count and some math. Don't forget the pallets themselves
have weight. I see a variety of grocery pallets and plastic
pallets under this stuff. Each weigh something different. We
will err on the side of being lighter than heavier and not risk
damaging our equipment. The men fanned out and began
calling out the items they found. Sadly, the sunflower seeds
were on a skid in the second level of the racking. Not
accessible with a manual pump jack. Ryan was interested in

getting some and went hunting for a ladder of some sort. Five minutes later, a happy shout from the far end of the warehouse revealed success in his ladder hunt. He came back with a big smile carrying his prize. "Good job," commented Mitch. Ryan placed his ladder against the racking and started scaling up. Mitch hustled over and held the base of the ladder. "We don't need any mishaps," he said to the rest of the crew. Ryan climbed into the racking and pulled out his pocket folder. He started hacking the stretch film holding the large sacks of sunflower seeds in place. A minute later, he had managed to pry one free. "I will lower it down to you, Mitch," he said as he pulled on the large plastic sack. It must have weighed at least forty pounds. Balancing himself carefully, Ryan handed off the clear plastic sack to Mitch. Mitch took it and lowered it to the ground. "While you are up there, why don't you lower a few more and we can collect them on subsequent trips?" he suggested. "Great idea!" came back to him from Ryan. Minutes later, they had a half dozen of the big sacks on the floor near the base of the ladder. Ryan then descended back down.

Another hour of dragging and pushing, and the team of men had assembled a load in front of the overhead door leading inside the box van. Mitch had found a clipboard on a desk on the inside wall between the dock doors and a pen inside one of the drawers. "All right, guys – phase two. Give me a count of each pallet and call out what the sacks or buckets weigh each." The men each picked a pallet and began moving things around as they performed counts. Evan had the lead pallet of enriched white flour. "Sixty on this one, Mitch," he called out. "Forty-eight," from Kyle. The men worked their way through the pallets until everything had been counted and the weights tallied. Mitch did the math on his liberated clipboard. "Okay, as suspected, we are overweight. Let's peel ten of those flour sacks off, a full layer off of the buckets of honey, and a layer of baking powder." He named each of the pallets in sequence, designating how much to remove to get to the right weight. The men began the removal process and, in a matter of minutes, were finished. "That should do it, fellas. If my math is right, we are good to go." Evan pushed a pump jack under the first pallet and began enthusiastically elevating the pallet. "Give him a hand, guys. Those pallets can pick up a bit of speed rolling in, and we don't want to punch holes in the interior of the van." One by one, the men rolled the pallets inside the vehicle without incident. "Leave the pump jack inside the last pallet and turn the handle," Mitch advised. "We can use it to unload on the other end. As a matter of fact – load the other pump jack in on the other side, and we'll take both with us. Maybe that might slow down anyone else who has the same idea as us and wants to empty this place out." Kyle ran the other pump jack in and pulled the overhead door of the box van down and latched it closed.

"That went smoother than expected and we got a lot more than the last place," remarked Mitch. "I think we have enough daylight left to head back and spend the night in our own beds. What do you say to that?" All three of the men made their agreement loudly known. Ten minutes later, they were back in their vehicles getting ready to leave. They had closed the door and placed a large stone they had found in the parking lot against the outside of the door so it did not swing open for any reason. The fact no one had found this place or that any animal had made its way inside to eat what was so well stored was a minor miracle at least. Mitch wished he had a hasp and some self-tapping screws to put a padlock on the outside of the door. This could keep others out, but he knew how effective those things really were. Padlocks kept honest people out, and that was about it. Getting past a padlock was a two-minute job if you were serious and would only stop the most casual of passersby.

The team pulled out onto the road and began the journey back to where they had begun their day. Mitch could see pink in the sky as the day came to a close. 'Pink at night – sailors' delight,' he said to himself, remembering the saying. This meant the setting sun was sending its light through a high concentration of dust particles. Normally, this indicated high pressure and stable air coming in from the west. This usually meant there was going to be good weather coming tomorrow. Good weather means a good time to come back again, he thought. This warehouse had been overlooked, but there was no guarantee it would continue to be overlooked. Depending on how late they got back tonight and when they got unloaded, Mitch was sure additional trips back were going to be necessary. He thought it highly unlikely the group would run into a food bonanza like this one again, and they needed to make maximum use of the opportunity.

After a few turns, they were back on Barlow Trail heading north again. Kyle was ranging forward on his motorcycle, checking out the road ahead. Mitch was pulling up the rear with his Tacoma this time while following the heavily laden box van. Mitch could see it was riding low with the amount of weight it was carrying. He did not want to be stuck on the side of the road with all this food treasure on board — overnight in the dark. That would be a bad scenario all the way around, he thought to himself.

A half hour of steady driving passed when he saw the van slowing down and then stopping. Pulling alongside, he hit the power window on the passenger side of the pickup and asked Evan what was up. "I don't see Kyle and he isn't answering the radio," Evan replied. "You weren't answering your radio either." Mitch picked up his radio and realized he had turned the volume way down. Damn. Stupid move. They should have done a radio check before leaving. All the excitement about the big food haul had knocked them out of their regular SOPs. "Sorry about that. Had my radio turned off by accident. Did Kyle say anything before disappearing?" Evan responded with a shrug. "I didn't hear a thing. Maybe he has his radio off like you did?" "God damn it, I don't like this. Stay put with the van and I am going to range forward a bit and see what I can see. Keep your eyes peeled." "Check that," came the response. Mitch did a weapons check on his firearm and then pulled ahead. "Mitch for Kyle. Mitch for Kyle – please respond." Radio silence was all he got in return. He drove slowly forward. After about five minutes, Mitch spotted the BMW. It was lying on its side on the road. Mitch stopped short and scanned the area. There was no sign of Kyle. Thumbing his mic, he called the men behind him in the van, "stay put. I spotted the bike but Kyle is not visible. Weapons free." Mitch clipped his radio back in place and opened his door. He slid out of his vehicle and brought his weapon to bear. Checking all around himself, he advanced to the motorcycle. As he approached, he could hear the engine still running. Squatting down, he reached out and switched the keys to the off position. There were abandoned vehicles ahead and behind him on both sides of the road. These afforded many hiding spots for potential adversaries. As he searched with his eyes, he spotted Kyle's helmet lying on the road next to a minivan which looked long abandoned. Standing back up, he swept the area with the muzzle of his rifle looking for any sign of movement. Walking slowly, he arrived where the helmet lay and picked it up. The visor was smashed and the front of the helmet looked like it had been hit with a baseball bat or something similar. He noticed the chin strap had been severed by something sharp. Setting the helmet back on the ground, he keyed his mic again. "Definite foul play here, guys. Be ready to make haste at any moment. I found Kyle's helmet and it's been cut off of him. The front is smashed in so someone hit him with something. No sign of Kyle anywhere."

Retreating with his rifle covering the area he just left, he headed back to his vehicle and drove back to where his colleagues were waiting. "What's going on?" Evan asked. "I don't know. I think Kyle was ambushed. There is no sign of him, but with the amount of damage his helmet sustained, I don't think he was even conscious when he hit the ground." "So, what are we going to do?" Ryan asked. Mitch replied, "Don't know yet. I'm thinking. If we can't find him immediately, he has likely been taken away from here. We have no idea of direction or distance. There are only three of us, and we can easily lose this van full of food we just got." Evan interrupted, "It sounds like you want to abandon Kyle! We can't do that. He's counting on us!" Mitch continued, "Listen, I don't like the sound of that either, but what's the better choice? There could be another ambush waiting for us, or a team could be approaching us right now. This food can keep the whole group at the acreage eating for months, and

Kyle is one guy. What is the better choice?" The two men stared at him and looked glum. Ryan tried next, "Would you want us to abandon you if the roles were reversed? He can't be far away. We should go look for him." Mitch stared at the sky for a moment and then looked back at the anxious faces in front of him. "If it were me, I would understand the bigger imperative at play here. I wouldn't be happy, but I would understand." "Easy for you to say now!" Evan shot back. "You're not in that position, and all you are thinking about is saving your own ass and high-tailing it out of here!" Mitch sighed loudly. "Guys, I hear you, but he could be miles away by now. I am guessing he was knocked out by the impact of whatever hit him, which means there are probably at least two of them in order to pick him up and carry him away. Probably to a vehicle waiting nearby. We don't know their intentions, and we are standing around talking when they could be getting ready to hit us. We need to get a move on and come back in greater force and more heavily armed. I think that is the best answer given the situation. This expedition was assigned to me by Kate, so I am going to take responsibility for the decision. We are leaving – now!"

The men grumbled a bit more but got back in their vehicle. Mitch overheard one of them comment, "This is such bullshit," but they started the box van up and made ready to leave. Mitch got back in his Tacoma, started it up, and moved the stick into drive. Accelerating, he thumbed the mic of his radio again, "Let's drive faster now. If they're going to try and hit us, they're going to have to deal with a speedier set of targets. Stay frosty." He punched the accelerator and sped ahead. Moments later, he was passing the BMW on its side and still saw no sign of Kyle. Looking at both sides of the road as he drove, Mitch did not see any sign of a moving vehicle or group of people on foot. The box van followed behind him and gradually picked up speed to stay with the pickup Mitch was driving.

Luckily, the rest of the trip back to the acreage was uneventful. The vehicles slowed and accelerated as conditions allowed. They continuously wove among abandoned vehicles. There were no more signs of life on the trip back. As the sun set, it became progressively darker until the vehicle operators had to put their headlights on. Arriving at the gate, Mitch honked the horn of his truck repeatedly. Lights turned on in the house, and shortly thereafter, Kate and a couple of other men headed out to meet them.

"You're back early!" Kate called out. Mitch got out of his vehicle. Kate could tell immediately from the look on his face that something was wrong. "What's wrong?" she asked him. "Kyle is missing." "Missing? How can he be missing?" she asked him. "He was ambushed on our way back. He was scouting out in front of us and then he was gone. His bike was on the side of the road and we found his helmet with the visor smashed in." "Did you look for him?" she asked. "Briefly, but there was no sign of him. We have a van loaded with food and there are only three of us. I decided to hurry back here so you could unload the food and we can form a team to go back and look for him." Kate scowled. "He could be anywhere by now! How are we going to find him?" Mitch felt his temperature starting to rise. Stay calm, he reminded himself; hot tempers were not going to help Kyle. "I made a decision based on the information I had at the time. I was worried about Kyle but also worried about getting this load back here. Lots of people are depending on what we found, plus there is a lot more there to go and get." Kate considered his answer and seemed to calm down a bit. If anything, she responded with a logical reply despite what her internal feelings were telling her to do.

"Let's get you unloaded and make plans from there." She turned to the two men who had come to the gate with her and pointed to them one by one. "You follow these men to the unload point and you go inside and round up some additional help." The men nodded and swung the gates fully open to enable the vehicles to pull in. Once that was accomplished, they carried out the duties she had delegated. Evan drove the box van to the unload point with Ryan, and Mitch drove his pickup in and parked it in the usual spot. Kate followed him on foot and approached him as he stepped out of the truck. "Sorry if I came at you a bit hard there; I was in shock from what you told us. Thinking it through, I would have probably come to the same decision as you did." Mitch appreciated her support and said as much. Kate asked him to provide more details as they walked to the house and made their way to the dining room.

In the time it took to make their way to the dining room, Mitch gave a high-level overview of his and the team's activities and findings. Kate made appropriate noises at different points in the debrief and seemed excited by the big find of food at the non-descript warehouse. Kate pulled out a chair and sat down. It was late, and no one else was roaming around the house at this hour. "I have some more news for you," Kate said to Mitch. "News which could impact us strongly, but I don't know if it will be in a positive or negative way." This got Mitch's attention. "This afternoon, a blue Ford F150 pulled up outside of the exterior gate. They hit their horn a couple of times and waited for us to show up. "What did they want?" Mitch asked. "Seems they are members of another group like ours. They wouldn't share exactly where they are from, but they want to establish a connection for mutual defense and possibly some trading." "So, they just 'showed up'? Doesn't that seem a bit odd? Maybe they have been watching us for a while, trying to learn our routines and group numbers," Mitch remarked. Kate replied, "I don't know. At this point, it is what it is. We can try to determine their intentions, but it will all be speculation at this point. They want to have a meeting at a neutral spot, and I want you to represent us." "Me? Why me?" asked Mitch. Kate paused and seemed to gather herself, "With the death of Frank, we have been somewhat in a state of flux. We ran with a committee for a while, but that seems to have failed. I asked the members to reach out to everyone within the group for some sort of consensus, but no one seems to be doing anything at all about that. The reality is – everyone is now deferring to me and my decisions. I am not trying to assert myself, but it just seems to be going that way. Frank was clearly an alpha male, and leadership came easily to him. With his absence, we are in a bit of a leadership crisis. This could hurt us more than an outside force attacking us. So, as much as I don't really want to be in charge, I guess I am going to have to be." Mitch said, "I always believed those who really want power are usually the worst people to be allowed to have it. The fact that you are not craving it actually makes me feel better." Kate smiled, "I guess I am a 'reluctant' leader, but without leadership, we are going to fail. I am going to make a concerted effort to stay level-headed and not get an inflated ego. If we happen to find the right person to lead down the road, I will happily surrender the title, but between now and then, we need to get things done."

Mitch looked at her, "You have not answered my question – why me?" Kate explained, "I see you coming out of your shell. You hang around with Rick but don't have any strong alliances with anyone else and are largely independent. The single female members of the group seem interested, but I have seen nothing reciprocal out of you, so I see you as being a sigma." Mitch stared at her, "Sigma – what the hell is that?" Kate spread her hands, "It is a bit of a long explanation, which we don't really have time for right now, but it is a way of understanding the hierarchy of men. Most men are deltas, guys who are good at their jobs and take pride in that, but there are some other types who reveal themselves with their behaviors. Generally, people know what an 'alpha male' is, but there are further gradations. It's a topic for another day, but it has been a useful way to understand the dynamic between men and other men, as well as men with women. I think the nature of your character would make you a good person to negotiate with an outside group for us." Mitch looked at the ground for a long minute, "So, my 'nature' indicates I will be a good person for this. Is that the case, or are you trying to create pillars of support under your leadership for the time when push comes to shove?" Kate smiled, "I see you are a bit savvier than you have let on. Not many of the other men around here would have come to that conclusion on their own and seen things for what they are versus what they want them to be. I am going to be honest with you and say yes, that is part of my motivation. I may not crave power, but I have to be realistic about the nature of it."

Mitch looked at the mountains on the horizon and then back at her again. "Okay, for now you have my support and yes, I will go to this parley and see what they want. I need to discuss our position and what we are willing to agree to/not agree to before leaving. What about the rescue mission for Kyle? As we stand here talking, who knows what is happening to him? Every minute we delay is another minute he is in the clutches of someone else." Kate responded quickly, "Let me organize the Kyle rescue mission. Renaldo was a member of the committee and is stronger than he lets on and is calm under pressure. I will task him with going after Kyle and add a half dozen men to that team." Evan and Ryan can go as well as part of that team and guide Renaldo and the rest to where he went missing and see if they can find him. The food can sit in that warehouse for another day or two while we prioritize finding our friend and group member." Mitch shrugged his shoulders. "Okay, boss lady. I presume I am leaving in the morning for the parley. Am I supposed to be going alone or am I going to have some armed men going with me?" Kate said, "We will send two or three with you. We have too many away from the acreage at the same time, which makes our ability to defend ourselves constrained. This parley could be a ploy to get some of us off-site when a raid hits. We don't have a radio channel to talk to them with, so we can't delay a day or two. If you get there and it seems the least bit 'off,' high-tail it out of there and get back." "Understood," responded Mitch.

"Let's meet in the morning and go over broad strategy and discuss what we want to achieve with this meeting. What we can reveal and what we need to hold back," Kate suggested. "Agreed," replied Mitch, who was now thinking quite seriously about hitting the sack as the fatigue from the long day caught up with him.

CHAPTER FOURTEEN

SOLO SCOUT

Caleb lay in bed for a while after waking. The Hudson's Bay wool blanket was now on his bed after being washed. There was a sheet between it and him as wool tended to be itchy, but it provided excellent warmth. His other blanket was fine, but he had an affection for the much-storied blanket. Its multicolored stripes of green, red, yellow, and indigo were the iconic colors of the company that gave its name to the wool blanket. Indigenous peoples received them as a trade good across the country when explorers and later settlers arrived.

Shifting his attention away from the warm blanket, he reviewed his plan for the day and what he was going to show

Angeline before he left. He realized he couldn't just take off but needed to show her a number of things in case he didn't come back. This had never been a consideration for him before, as he had always been alone. He had presumed if something happened to him, someone, at some point, would find his place and either take it over or simply pillage it. The thought of having someone go through his belongings and steal whatever they wanted annoyed him. He realized this was a useless thought as he would, in all likelihood, be dead. With that happy thought, he swung his feet onto the floor and got up. Another day, another dollar, he said to himself with a laugh. It was funny how quickly he had become accustomed to not going to work in the morning. His new job was staying alive, and the only pay for that job was continued breathing. Caleb pulled his clothes on and headed to the kitchen for his morning coffee. There were no signs of stirring coming from Angeline's room, so he let her sleep for now.

Ten minutes later, he was sitting at the kitchen table, sipping a hot brew. Coffee was a morning ritual for him. Caleb had put away considerable freeze-dried coffee in his stores, as he did not know how long it was going to be before the beans would be imported again... if ever. If coffee production and importation didn't get organized within a few years, he was going to run out of stored coffee. He would have to figure out something different to start his day with. Putting that thought out of his mind for now, there were more immediate pressing concerns to deal with. These riders he was going to investigate concerned him. Caleb knew there were other groups around, but thus far none had entered "his territory." He smiled at that thought. When did it become 'his territory?' As he finished that concept, the door to Angeline's room audibly opened. Walking out and rubbing her eyes, a sleepy-looking Angeline plopped down in a chair opposite him. "Hot chocolate?" he inquired. She gave a sleepy nod. Putting the kettle on, he asked, "How did you sleep?" "Deep, real deep," she answered. "I didn't even hear you get up. How long have you been up?" "Not long," Caleb replied. "Just enough time to get some coffee in me." She nodded and rubbed her eyes some more. "You still going to track those riders we saw?" she asked. "How long do you think you are going to be gone?" Caleb nodded. "I am planning on being gone all day, as I have no idea how far I am going to have to go and where the trail is going to take me. It's going to be slow, as I am trying to remain out of sight. I don't want to stumble into an encampment of theirs by accident, as that would be bad. Capital B bad!" "It's going to be a boring day for me," Angeline commented. Caleb looked at her. "Are you a Lord of the Rings fan?" Angeline replied, "I don't know what that is." Caleb smiled a big smile. "Then you are in for a treat. I have the extended version of the set, which runs 11 hours and twenty-two minutes. If you like it, you will barely notice the hours going by – it is a mesmerizing story. One of my favorites." Angeline looked hopeful with his suggested plan.

Coffee finished, Caleb stood up and put his mug in the sink. "I need to saddle up and get going. It's going to be a long day. You can finish your hot chocolate and rustle up some breakfast if you like. We can go over some of my procedures for this place after you eat and before I go. I am going downstairs to select gear for the day. I will be back up in ten or fifteen, maybe twenty." Angeline acknowledged the suggestion and made her way to the refrigerator. Caleb headed to the staircase. As he was going to be going cross-country on foot most of the day, he opted for lightweight gear and a low noise profile. He also wanted to emphasize camouflaging himself to avoid getting spotted. That factored into his clothing and gear choices. He liked his Olympia Arms heavy-barreled AR15 for its accuracy, but the heavy barrel added unnecessary weight. He opted for a Daniel Defense M4A1 RIII built around a 14.5-inch cold hammer-forged barrel with an attached flash suppressor, an ergonomic buttstock, and pistol grip. It came in at 6.39 pounds before adding the optic and sling. He had hand-painted the camo pattern on it himself. The red dot optic had flip-up caps on each end to eliminate reflection off the lens until he actually needed to use the sight. His jacket and pants were German army flecktarn pattern issue items he had picked up. Deciding on what camo had been a real dilemma for him when he was making his original purchases. He liked some of the newer patterns the western military had, but they hadn't hit the surplus market at that time. He also did not want to be mistaken for a military service member in the jurisdictions he was going to be operating in. The German pattern was a popular type in the Bundeswehr and had been around for a while.

He had a daypack in the same pattern, which helped it blend in with his outer apparel. A matching boonie hat completed his kit in terms of clothing. He decided on a pocket folder instead of a large fixed blade like he usually carried. A clinch pick knife was added to his belt in case of any close encounters. He liked the clinch pick due to its ease of draw and usefulness in grappling range. The daypack would have a few extra items, including energy bars and some beef jerky for sustenance. His CamelBak contained 'snake juice.' That name always made him laugh. He had picked up the recipe from a guy on YouTube. It was a mixture of sodium, potassium, and magnesium in ratios that didn't give you the runs. When you bought the components in bulk and made your own, it was way cheaper than Gatorade. When you were traveling cross-country and sweating a good amount, water by itself was not enough. To avoid painful cramps and fatigue, snake juice was a good thing to have.

He brought his gear to the front door and went to find Angeline. She had finished eating the breakfast she made for herself. She had changed out of her bedclothes and into a pair of her new jeans and a pullover. Her hair was in a ponytail and her face looked freshly scrubbed. "Let me show you a few things," he said, leading her to the room where he maintained his camera surveillance of the exterior and his solar array. He showed her the basics of it at a level a ten-year-old would understand. "If for some reason you need to go outside… and I recommend against it, but if it is essential, please take the time to survey the surrounding areas via these cameras. At the very least, it will give you a glimpse of what is out there waiting for you." He then went through a number of other procedures he had in place for the day-to-day operation of the place. He had devised a couple of emergency shutdown standard operating procedures he shared. She appeared to understand them. He made her repeat them back to him in her own words so he had a sense of confidence in her level of understanding. With those basics covered, they headed for the front door. He wanted to tell her more but knew she was getting information overload. Additional sharing was pointless at that time.

He looked at her intently. "Be careful. Stay inside if at all possible. Keep yourself busy with movies and snacks. Go check the cameras every couple of hours when you go to the washroom. Don't open the doors for anyone except me. Remember all of the other instructions as best you can. Maybe tomorrow I will begin the task of writing them all out in point form for you so you don't have to operate solely on memory. I never did that before because I figured I was going to be the only one here." Angeline surprised him by giving him a hug. "Be careful, Caleb," she said in a small voice, followed by a smile. Caleb hugged her back and then picked up his rifle. "See you later."

Locking the door behind him, he did a chamber check and took a good look around. The wind was coming in from the west, and over the mountains in the same direction, low clouds obscured the peaks. The temperature was getting noticeably cooler as summer wound down and autumn made its timely arrival. Looking at some of the deciduous trees, he could see the leaves beginning to change. Fall was his favorite season, as he loved all the colors that came with it. Overhead, he saw Canada geese on their way south from points north of here. He doubted the local flocks would move yet, but the weather was further along in the north. Their honking was a familiar sound to anyone living in this part of the world. Caleb was not fond of them. They left enormous amounts of feces on beaches near local lakes, which stank a lot and ruined the area for recreational purposes. He also saw a red-tailed hawk making its way by. He had much more affection for that species, as it kept rodent populations down. Looking at his watch, a Tough Solar Casio, a brand he liked for its ruggedness. In this case, it was solar powered, which removed the need for battery changes. He calculated the remaining hours of daylight. In his daypack, he had tossed a military-grade rain poncho, which could serve as a shelter if need be, in case he ended up being stuck out overnight. It weighed next to nothing, and with some of the twine he had included, it could give him a place to sleep with ease should he need it.

Setting a brisk pace, he headed west towards the place he had seen the riders. After about an hour of trekking with occasional stops to glass the area around him, he arrived at the hoof tracks left by the horsemen. Looking down, he could see the horses were shod, or in other words – fitted with horseshoes. Caleb knew there were farriers still in business prior to the collapse but wondered how many there were now. He estimated ninety percent of the population had not survived the downfall of modern society. The chances of farriers being part of that percentage seemed slim. In all likelihood, most of the professions had suffered a terminal decline, and many of the old-world skills were going to have to be rediscovered. Back to looking at the tracks, he could count ten distinct sets of tracks. His time spent at the tracking school was time well spent, and he suspected it would serve him well many times in the future. While hiking over to this point, he had already decided to go down the back trail of this group. There were no signs of their having come back this way. There was a fifty-fifty chance he was going to get it wrong, but a better chance of encountering them if he followed in their tracks. At least that was how he thought of it to himself.

Scanning east and west, he followed the tracks north. Once in a while checking his six, he headed along the tracks towards where this group of riders had come from. After a solid hour of walking, he stopped and sat on a downed tree close to the trail. Taking a long pull from his CamelBak, he dug out some beef jerky and rolled it around in his mouth to make it soft. The trail had continued veering in a roughly north by northwest direction. He was crossing rolling prairie, which made for relatively easy travel. Standing back up, he carried on. The wind from the west had picked up a little bit, but so far there was no sign of rain. Another hour passed and then another. At the end of the last hour, he could see a town in the distance. It was too far to see any signs of life, but that would change, presumably, as he got closer. Continuing on, he followed the horse tracks in the ground. A couple of times, the party had stopped and milled around for some unknown reason, but there had definitely been pauses. At one of the pauses, he could see boot prints in men's sizes in the dirt, as they had dismounted for one reason or another, perhaps to relieve themselves. After another thirty or so minutes had passed, he could see a wooden fence with a gate. The tracks headed straight to the gate, and even though he couldn't see yet, they presumably went inside that entry point. Caleb could see the fence went on for some distance east and west of where he was. Due to the large stands of trees on the inside of the fence, he could not tell what was there.

Walking some more, he headed to a small copse of trees and went inside. Finding a stump, he sat, had a short rest, and took a large drink from the tube clipped next to his neck. He sat for five minutes and ruminated upon the situation. Getting up, he went to the edge of the copse, got his monocular out, and began scoping the area inside the fence. From his new vantage point, he could see the back of a building. He could definitely hear sounds coming from the distance. He thought they might be voices, and he heard the clink of metal on metal a couple of times. Outside of that, there was nothing of note. The stands of trees inside obscured the buildings on the far side. He imagined the people or community inside had sentries of some sort posted – it was crazy not to in the world they inhabited. He looked again with his monocular for an LP/OP (listening post/observation post), but to no avail. Caleb decided to circumnavigate the property while remaining under cover as best he could to get a better look at what he was facing. The next stand of trees was one hundred meters to the east of where he was, and a completely open field separated the two points. He decided he would take short dashes and go to ground, covering territory in a leapfrog fashion. This was a faster way of traversing the ground between trees than doing a long leopard crawl on his belly. If he spotted any kind of static surveillance, he would change his tactics.

Caleb moved to the edge of the tree cover and looked around. No one was in sight, so he took off at a lope and covered a third of the distance to the next bunch of trees. Going to a knee, he stopped and froze in position. Looking and listening for a couple of minutes, he used that time to slow his breathing. He took a quick sip from his CamelBak, and when there appeared to be no reaction to his motion, he stood and did it again. He followed the same routine again and was soon safely back inside a stand of trees under concealment. He reminded himself trees were concealment and not cover, as they offered little ballistic protection. He knew people often got the two confused, especially when cover could provide both, which confused some people. He moved within the stand of trees as quietly as he could and got close to the outer edge. From here, he observed the area past the fence again. With this new angle, he could see considerably more than before. There was a group of buildings visible. All were painted a forest green color with white trim. As he watched, he saw a man walk across the gap between buildings. Caleb could see a handgun of some sort on his hip, although at this range it was impossible to determine what sort of firearm it was. At this distance, the man's features were not visible, so Caleb figured it was around 200 meters. Caleb watched for a few more minutes but saw no further movement. Deciding to continue on his course of action, he looked for his next observation point. The gap between this stand of trees and the next was double the distance and closer to the fence.

"In for a penny, in for a pound," he said to himself and began the next stage of movement. This time, when he finished a third of the gap, he went right to the ground, deciding taking a knee wasn't sufficient. Same routine... he used his monocular to sweep the area past the fence, looking for any information of use and any movement of people. Catching his breath and not overheating. This pattern of movement and surveillance continued for the next hour. By the end of the hour, Caleb knew a lot more than when he had first arrived. From his various angles of study, he could see this was a ranch of some sort. He had seen upwards of a dozen people moving about. All of the men were armed and none of the women were. He hadn't seen any children in any of his observations. There were close to twenty buildings, all painted the same green and white motif, even the barns. Barns were traditionally painted red in this part of the world. There were a number of corrals that held about forty head of horses of various breeds. Smoke came out of the chimneys of a couple of the buildings. It was not cold enough to need heat yet, so Caleb figured they were emitting smoke from cook stoves inside the buildings.

Caleb didn't see any motor vehicles, which was a bit curious. There wasn't any more fuel production going on, at least nowhere he was aware of, but he expected there would be cars and trucks parked here and there. Relics left over from the days when gas and diesel were plentiful. Another thing that he observed that was out of the ordinary was the sheer number of crosses present in different places. One of the buildings had an obvious church look to it, and the large cross mounted on the front removed all doubt about that. In addition to the church, several of the buildings also supported crosses. Caleb suspected this was some sort of religious-based community. They possibly eschewed motor vehicles and perhaps some other aspects of modernity as a reaction to the massive change in the world. Maybe they were simply early adopters of the new way of life forced upon society as a whole. As he sat and watched, he began to hear the sounds of mounted men coming towards the compound. Looking westward from where he had come, he could see a plume of dust rising as riders approached on horseback. This group numbered nine or ten and was approaching at a canter. As they arrived at the gate, one of the riders dismounted and swung the gate open. Caleb noticed it did not appear to be locked, nor did anyone approach the gate from inside as the group arrived. This suggested several things to Caleb. One – they were not particularly concerned with security. Perhaps they felt so confident in their dominion over this area they were not worried about external threats. Two – security might be a nighttime issue for them, and they only locked up at sunset or something similar. Three – the possibility that they had radio communication with those inside. Everyone would know what was going on, and there was no need to approach the gate. All of this was, of course, speculation, and Caleb knew as much. There could be other reasons for this behavior with motivations he could not even begin to ascertain.

Looking at his watch, Calen knew he was going to have to make a decision soon. He had not learned a lot about these people, but if he stayed any longer, he risked having to travel in the dark, which he was reluctant to do. Nighttime travel, even with night vision gear, was far riskier, even if he was only considering trip hazards on the trail as he made his way back. Stepping in a gopher hole could break his ankle and leave him stranded on the prairie for days. With that small amount of reflection, he decided against staying any longer and made ready to head back. He opened his pack, wolfed down a pair of energy bars, and drank some water. Looking around prior to moving, he stood and began his retreat from the ranch. The group of horsemen who had just arrived had ridden to one of the large barn-like structures and dismounted. He had seen a couple of teenage boys come out and help unsaddle the horses and lead them inside the building. Well, they did have some young men in their group at least, he thought to himself, but the lack of children concerned him. Did they have a school for the kids who were inside at this time of day? Questions formed, but there wasn't time to dwell on them as he had hours of walking ahead of him. He would have liked to stay longer or even overnight. Concerned Angeline would become frightened and perhaps do something foolish if he didn't return tonight, he decided to leave. Caleb did decide he was going to come back. Perhaps build himself an observation post inside one of the stands of trees and watch this place for a couple of days. What he had seen thus far created more questions than answers, and he was both curious and concerned about this group located to the north of him.

Careful in his retreat, Caleb didn't encounter anyone from the ranch as he moved progressively further away. The sky had become completely overcast, and the sun was hiding somewhere behind the clouds. Looking at his watch, he figured he had time to make it back before complete darkness, but just barely. Focusing on hiking at a quick pace, he began knocking off the miles. After a couple of hours of walking, he heard a 'huff' noise from a pile of logs to his right. He froze in place and did a quick chamber check of his rifle. He then heard some movement noises in the vicinity of the sound he had just heard. Undecided, he stood his ground, and at that moment, saw what was making the noise. A mid-sized grizzly bear was deliberately walking towards him and definitely had Caleb in its view. Caleb turned his head from left to right as training kicked in. Not wanting tunnel vision from this immediate threat, he broke visual contact for a second and checked his flanks. The bear was almost fifty meters away, but that distance was shortening with every stride it took. Indecision overtook Caleb for a moment as he was unsure what to do. He was carrying a .223 caliber rifle designed for two-legged predators, not large game in excess of six hundred pounds. He knew he could kill it with what he had, but he was reluctant to. The bear was reacting to

Caleb's surprise arrival while busy looking for insects inside logs or mice under the wood or whatever. He didn't need to die because Caleb had happened upon it. Making a decision, Caleb stood as tall as he could and let out a loud yell and fired a couple of rounds into the ground ahead of the bear. The bear stopped and stood up. Caleb knew bears had good senses of smell but poor vision. Despite what movies out of Hollywood depicted, a bear standing was no more dangerous than one on all fours.

Caleb fired off a couple more rounds overhead the bear. The grizzly dropped back down to all fours and made a short retreat. Caleb stood still with his finger on the trigger. The bear was deciding whether to charge or retreat, and Caleb knew it could go either way and was ready. The big bear swung its head from side to side and let out a couple more huffs. Then, thinking better of it, it turned and ambled away. Grizzlies were not afraid of anything, but many of them had encountered men with rifles before and were smart enough to know what that meant. His success in driving Caleb back seemed to satisfy it, and the grizzly went back to the log pile to continue doing whatever it had been doing. Caleb let out a long breath, realizing he had been holding his breath. In all of his expeditions out of the retreat, he had never come face to face with a bear, let alone a grizzly! He knew they tended to stay closer to the mountains west of here and rarely were in the open prairie. Perhaps the lack of armed men over the past year had emboldened this particular one. It was ranging further in its hunt for food prior to the upcoming hibernation season. Regardless, Caleb was happy he didn't have to shoot it. He didn't want to kill it unnecessarily, and he was not certain his small-caliber rifle could have stopped it before the bear killed or maimed him.

Turning Caleb resumed his hike. A couple of minutes, he had a case of the shakes overcome him as the adrenaline wore off. A wave of nausea rolled over him but he was able to avoid puking out his guts. Caleb had come down from adrenaline several times in the past year due to various encounters, and each time he hoped it was going to be the last. Approaching death or dismemberment had a way of overcoming your intellectual defenses against it. A couple of minutes passed, and he felt better again, although he was still a bit weak in the knees.

Heading south, his steady pace ate up the distance. Fatigue was growing from both from the hiking and the constant state of vigilance he maintained. Having taught Angeline about the color codes of awareness, he knew he was in orange since the bear encounter. This was more exhausting than the relaxed yellow state in which he should have been. Easy to say - hard to do, he thought. Half an hour later, he spotted the trees hiding his solar array, and knew he was home. Twilight now, he was mere minutes away from actual nightfall. He approached the house and observed for a while. He didn't see or hear anything coming from inside, which was a good thing. The blackout blinds were still in place, and no light seepage came out of the windows. Near as he could tell, the place was vacant and empty, exactly what he wanted to portray to the world.

Walking to the front door, he stood in front of where he knew a camera would reveal him. He did not know when the last time Angeline checked the cameras was, but he hoped to give her a heads-up so she wasn't scared. Then he realized it was dark out and he was a lone figure standing still outside, which to her ten-year-old mind would be scary and creepy. Chuckling to himself, he walked to the front door, keyed the code in the touchpad, and let himself in. It was after ten p.m., and she might have fallen asleep.

Entering without a noise, he took off his boots and shed his pack and set them on the floor in the mudroom. Going into the house, he could hear the monitor making movie sounds in the living room as he approached. On the big screen, the final scenes from Return of the King were playing. Getting closer, he could see her curled up on the couch, an empty box of Ritz crackers on the floor in front of her soundly sleeping form. Looking back into the kitchen, he could see a plate and cutlery still sitting there, as well as a glass. He was going to have to speak to her about kitchen protocols at some point. He reached down, picked up the remote for the monitor, and shut it off. She could back up the movie later and watch the parts she had missed. "Hey, you're back," came the sleepy response from her as she awoke from her slumber. Caleb figured the lack of noise had woken her. "Yes, I am back. You should get yourself to bed, young lady. We can talk in the morning, and I will bring you up to date." He reached out and took her hand to help her up from the couch and then led her to her room. Tucking her in, he was tempted to give her a fatherly kiss on the forehead but held back. He wrinkled his brow, wondering where that impulse had come from. "Tomorrow," he thought to himself and headed to his room. Five minutes later, he was undressed and under his own covers. Tomorrow would take care of itself.

CHAPTER FIFTEEN
NEGOTIATION

Mitch got himself a coffee and went to sit in the dining room. Kate was already there looking at paperwork and working on her own cup of coffee. "Good morning," he greeted her as he sat across the table from her. Kate stopped reviewing what she was looking at and turned her attention to Mitch. "How did you sleep?" she asked. "Like the dead," Mitch answered with a smile. Kate gave him a brief smile. "So, well rested I presume?" "Yeah, rested enough," he replied and took a sip of his coffee. "Let's talk about the meet today," she suggested. Mitch nodded. "As I am sure you are aware, this meet is both an opportunity and a risk. We know next to nothing about these people, and they may know more about us than we think. This could be a diversionary tactic to reduce our headcount here on the property. If I send enough men out to demonstrate a show of strength, we might be sufficiently reduced here to make a play for the acreage worth their while. What they don't know is we have a team out looking for Kyle." "You have?" asked Mitch. "Yes, last night while you were sleeping, I organized a new team to go after Kyle. Renaldo is leading the team. He is taking Evan with him and four other men. They are well armed and all have their plate carriers on. We are operating under the presumption they are going into a confrontation of some sort to retrieve him. I have another team of the same size on backup to reinforce them if need be. I sent a truck with a radio as a repeater station to park at the halfway point so we can stay in constant radio contact." "Why didn't you just send the whole team to look for him then?" Mitch asked. "Because I want to keep the second team here in case, we need them here." "Oh, duh! That should have been obvious," Mitch said. "Sorry for the dumb question."

Kate smiled, "Let's talk specifics. The point of the meet today is to learn as much about them as we can while sharing as little as we can about ourselves." Mitch nodded. Kate continued, "Since they set the location of the meet, I am presuming it is territory they are familiar with. If it looks like an ambush, just barrel out of there and come back as I am presuming, they would be hitting us when you are there. If everything seems relatively normal, establish relations but do not make any promises. I know it is hard going in blind, but they have us at a disadvantage. I wish we had done a better job scouting our immediate area and found them before they found us, but that is water under the bridge now and we are just going to have to deal with it." Kate took a breath and continued, "I am sure you would think to get a count of their numbers and the number of vehicles they brought. Look for uniformity of weapon types and calibers. If there is a lot of that, I am going to presume they did a lot of pre-planning and pre-purchasing prior to the collapse. If every one of them is carrying something different, it tells me they are a little more ragtag than we are."

Kate stopped and took a sip of her drink. "Any questions so far?" Mitch shook his head. "Pretty straightforward to me." "Good. I will carry on. Do not assume whoever is doing the talking is the actual leader. A smart leader might let an underling do the talking for him and simply observe the goings-on." "Like me," suggested Mitch with a wry grin. "Well, technically yes, you have me there," agreed Kate with a smile. "You are going to be the local leadership at this meet." Mitch noted he was now "leadership," which was the first time he had heard that term in reference to his name and the group at large. He had led expeditions before but never a negotiation like this one. Kate kept going, "see if they have any type of identifying clothing or tattoos or anything else that signifies membership to their group. We know they are a group because they are together but maybe they have a way of identifying to each other in different circumstances and if we can learn that it may be an advantage to us. If you can figure out where they are located, that would also be helpful but that is an obvious thing to not discuss in a first meeting. They have been watching us for some time; I have no idea how long, and they want something; otherwise, there is no reason for this meeting."

Mitch looked at the grain of the wood in the large table he sat at. Made from red oak, it had some reddish streaks in it, and more than a couple of rings from coffee cups stained the surface. He looked up at Kate, "Is there any chance they just want to get to know us and maybe cooperate in some way? All of the things you are mentioning seem like you are quite suspicious of their intentions." Kate sat back in her chair, "I understand how you could see it that way. Sadly, the price for failure is so high we have to take things almost to the point of paranoia. If I'm wrong about their intent and everything is rainbows and unicorns, then great, but if it is not – we need to be ready to react and defend ourselves. I firmly believe only three types of people have survived this far into the collapse: the prepared, the extremely lucky, and the ruthless. I don't know which one this group is." Mitch nodded his understanding again. "I know a lot of this is pretty basic stuff, and you might have already thought of this. I just want to cover all the basics so we don't miss anything. This is our first meeting with an organized outside group, and I would like it to go well," Kate shared. Mitch continued for her, "I agree we need it to go well. There is a lot at stake. They may have skills or supplies we lack, and at some point, we need to begin rebuilding society so we can get back on our collective feet." Kate played with her cup, rolling it in her hands as she thought. Looking at it, she realized it was a pattern called 'Old Country Roses,' and before all the hoopla of the past year, it would have been worth quite a bit; now it was just a cup to drink from. She looked at Mitch again, "You do realize we are not going to make it long-term if we don't expand beyond our current layout?" Mitch looked back at her quizzically, "What do you mean?" Kate looked back down at the cup she was holding, "What I mean is – despite your find at that warehouse in the south, which we absolutely need to return to and empty out – I have been looking at the numbers, and they are not good. We are grinding through our resource's day after day, and I don't think anywhere here other than Ian gets it. Everyone wants to eat every single day – strange! Currently, we don't have any large-scale farming capabilities, and more importantly, we do not have the fuel to power the equipment if we had it. Sure, I can send you into the city to find a tractor dealership; maybe, just maybe, there is enough diesel inside the tank to drive it back here, but what then? We have no ability to make gasoline or diesel." Mitch interrupted her, "What about horse-drawn equipment? That doesn't need diesel to work." Kate smiled at Mitch, "How many head of horses do we have?" she asked as kindly as she could muster. Mitch frowned, realizing he had made another stupid comment. "We could get horses; maybe these people have horses, and we could trade for them," he said hopefully. Kate looked out the window this time, "Mitch, if

they had horses and were even willing to give them up —
what could we possibly offer them for such a priceless and
useful item of their property? If somehow by miracle they
were willing and we had something they wanted — how
would we feed it? You need to have significant quantities of
hay to feed them over the winter. You need to shoe them,
which means a farrier and a blacksmith to make horseshoes.
You need tack to saddle them and harnesses if you want
them to pull a plow. We don't have any plows or horse-
drawn wagons and about ten other things we are lacking."

Mitch stood and started pacing. The concern was
obvious on his face. He mumbled to himself with this
newfound information. Kate sat patiently and let Mitch
process the information she had shared. Finishing pacing, he
turned and looked at her anew. "What about greenhouses?
We could grow a lot of food inside of greenhouses, and it
would extend the growing season!" Kate replied, "I think
you are on the right path. We certainly could grow a lot, but
what type of food generally gets grown in greenhouses?" she
asked him. "Fruit and vegetables," he announced somewhat
triumphantly. "Correct," she replied. "And what type of
foods do you eat when you want to lose weight?" she asked.

"Fruits and vegetables," replied Mitch with a somewhat downcast tone of voice. He could see where this was going. "Right, low-calorie foods which put you in a negative calorie balance, and you take off the excess weight." "And eventually starve to death," Mitch finished for her. Kate resumed, "We can and will grow fruits and vegetables in greenhouses. That is a good idea, but we need a high-calorie staple to generate enough food energy to keep us going. Luckily there is one that grows in this country and is relatively easy to grow." She had Mitch's full attention now. "Potatoes," she replied. "Ireland built a whole culture on the cultivation of potatoes and so can we. We understand where the potato blight came from and so we can avoid it. There is just one problem." "What is that?" asked Mitch. "We don't have any seed potatoes," Kate answered.

"I can see how that would be a problem," offered Mitch. "Yes. We put away a lot of powdered restaurant-grade potatoes, but powdered potatoes cannot be planted as seed. We need seed potatoes, and we need a lot. It is extremely unlikely there are any sitting in a warehouse in the city that haven't rotted by now. So, we need to find some and trade for them. I am hoping this group has some, and if we can't get a lot, if we get even a single sack full, we could plant them in the spring and then harvest that first crop for seed and plant them the following year for a much larger crop. With what you found in that warehouse and with what is hopefully still there, we might just make it. In the meantime, we build greenhouses out of whatever we can find to survive this." "So, are you starting to see why this meeting is so important?" Mitch nodded his acknowledgment.

"When is the meeting scheduled for?" he asked her. "Four p.m. this afternoon," she replied. "I want you to take Ben and Will with you. They are there for back-up and nothing more. They are not to engage in discussion with these people at all. I have spoken to them so they know what to do. Go armed but not over the top. We want to dissuade any bad ideas but not come across as intimidating. Any questions?" Mitch asked, "Do you want us to go in separate vehicles or just one?" Kate thought for a moment. "Take the Forerunner. It's a 4x4 and has pretty heavy-duty off-road tires which may come in handy if you have to travel cross-country for some reason. Maybe you need to get around stalled cars or something." Mitch nodded. Kate said, "Last thing. Take notes right after you have left and ensure your two colleagues do the same. Details are quickly forgotten and I don't want to miss a thing. It may appear small or unimportant now but could be highly useful later. You can take turns driving back and write down everything you can remember. Take note of their vehicles, weapons, and everything else you can remember as well as what they say."

Kate went back to her paperwork she had been reading, so Mitch figured out the meeting was over. Getting up, he took his coffee cup with him and headed back to the kitchen. Mitch was detecting changes in Kate's behavior already in the short time she had been 'in charge.' He wondered how much she would change over the upcoming months. He mentally filed that under 'future Mitch problem' and forgot about it for now. Heading out into the yard, he began looking for Will and Ben. Walking towards the Quonset hut where they parked the majority of the vehicles, he could hear Will's voice from inside. Will was usually in good spirits and liked to laugh. His sense of humor made him popular among the members of the group, as he was enjoyable to have around. As Mitch rounded the corner, he heard Ben replying to Will. Ben was more of an introvert than Will and kept to himself somewhat. He liked to read, and when not working on some delegated project, he could be found with his nose in a book. He was a good source of information on many topics, and his curiosity about the world meant he was always accumulating more information. "Hey guys," Mitch said to the two of them as he approached. "Oh, oh, Kate's guy is here – straighten up!" Will said, coming to attention. "Knock it off, Will. I am not 'her guy.' I am just a working stiff like the two of you." Will rolled his eyes. "Sure, you're not. We see the handwriting on the wall around here, buddy."

Mitch ignored the last comment and changed topics – "Are you preparing for the trip?" Ben turned and pointed at the Forerunner. "We topped it up with gas, checked the air pressures, oil level, and all the other fluids as well. The spare tire has air in it, and we put an additional spare on top of the roof rack." He pointed up as he spoke. "Although it is a relatively short trip, we also topped up some jerry cans and put them up top as well. Just in case we get diverted or something." Mitch smiled in appreciation. "What about weaponry?" Will spoke up this time. "We were thinking semi-auto 12 gauges with double 00 buckshot for firepower and some slugs in the bandoliers for reaching out further.

Handguns all around for us and a scoped .308 Ruger Scout rifle for a little more reach in case we need it." Mitch thought about their choices and could not see a flaw in their thinking. Few things could wreak as much damage and as fast in a close encounter as a semi-auto 12 gauge in trained hands. Anyone seeing that would have to take them seriously. "Sounds good, guys. What about food and water?" Ben spoke this time. "We just figured some day trip snacks as we should not be gone that long. Some 2-liter bottles of well water with a little low-calorie flavoring to make it less boring. Strawberry banana okay with you?" Mitch gave his approval and chuckled. "Low-calorie flavoring" – like weight loss was a thing in this new environment they inhabited. Everyone was thin to the point of being skinny due to the constraints on food. If only they could go back to the world of plenty before the collapse when almost everyone was overweight. If nothing else, the collapse had been good for everyone's waistlines.

"Ok guys. I'm going to take care of some small errands I need to do. I will meet you at 1 pm to open the armory and check out the items you have suggested. An hour or so later we can depart." Ben and Will voiced their agreement and returned to what they were doing. The Forerunner was a nice shade of blue. Heritage blue is what I think they called it, Mitch thought. Every car manufacturer seemed to come up with unique names for their colors. Blue was blue in Mitch's mind – all of these variations seemed to be semantics. Heading back to the house, he headed for where he might run into Abigail. He hadn't seen her since the day they had arrived together, and he wondered how she was fitting in. Asking Bonnie, the brunette who worked in the kitchen, he got directions to Abigail's whereabouts. Today she was helping with the laundry, so he headed there. "Hey Abigail – how is it going?" Abigail looked up from the laundry she was folding and saw Mitch. A big smile spread across her face. "Hey Mitch! It's great to see you! How are you?" Mitch couldn't help but smile back as her smile was infectious. "I am good. Trying to stay out of trouble but not succeeding." Abigail smiled again. "I heard about the big cache of food you guys found. That's really great news! Sorry to hear about Kyle. Do you think we are going to get him back?" Mitch scowled. With the business of the morning, he had forgotten about him. This was irritating for Mitch as he knew a team member was out there, alone and not knowing if anyone was even looking for him. "Did I say something wrong?" Abigail asked, seeing his swift change in demeanor. "No, it's not you. I am worried about Kyle and wish I was one of the people looking for him." Abigail looked concerned. "I hope he is ok." She went silent, not knowing what to say or how deep the connection between Mitch and Kyle was.

Mitch changed the topic. "How are you fitting in? How are the kids doing?" The smile returned to Abigail's face. "It is so much better here! The people have been really welcoming and make us feel like we belong. I am so happy you brought us here. I feel like we really have a chance for the long haul." Mitch smiled back at her as his mind returned to the conversation he had earlier with Kate and their long-term prospects. He decided to keep that information to himself. "I'm glad you are liking it. There really are a lot of good people here. Frank did a good job vetting who was invited to join. He was smart and knew people. I think he chose people more for their compatibility than their skill sets in some cases." Abigail carried on. "The kids are adapting well. I think kids are more resilient than adults in many ways. I don't know what the long-term effects on them are going to be having lived through this, but there is nothing I can do about that right now, so I am focused on their basic needs." Mitch replied, "I'm glad to hear the kids are adapting. We aren't really set up for school or anything like that yet, but at some point, that will have to be addressed. I think once winter hits and we are not so overwhelmed with things 'to do,' we could look at some basic sort of education program for them. Nevertheless, I just dropped by to check in on you and see how you are settling. I am going off-site on another mission today, so I am going to run for now. Talk to you later." "Later," she replied with a particularly warm smile. Mitch thought to himself — she seems overly friendly. I wonder if there is more there or she is just grateful for the help I have given. I will have to see.

Mitch went back to his quarters for a shower and some hygiene matters. It had been a few days since his last shower, and he was sure people were beginning to smell him before they saw him. His teeth also needed a good scrub. Clean clothes were also on the list.

A few hours passed, and Mitch had taken care of his personal tasks and talked to different folks. People were curious about Kyle and what was happening. Mitch passed them on to Kate for the most part, as he was intent on readying himself for this afternoon's interaction. After meeting with the guys and Ian with his keys at the armory he went to his quarters to grab his sunglasses which he had forgotten. He then made his way to the assembly point where his teammates were waiting. "Who's driving?" asked Will upon his arrival. Mitch looked at Ben, "Are you cool with playing chauffeur?" Ben nodded. "Let's get this show on the road," Mitch said to the two other men and opened the passenger door of the SUV. Will got in the back seat of the four-door vehicle and settled in. Ben drove the vehicle to the first of the two gates and stopped. Mitch got out to open the first one and close it behind the SUV. As he did that, Will opened the outside gate and stood aside as Ben pulled through the second gate. Once everything was closed and locked up again, the trio headed south for a short distance and then turned west on the road and headed towards the sun. Mitch had thought about bringing a map, but the distance was so short it didn't seem worth it. They knew where they were headed – the Fairfield Inn parking lot on the northeast side of town. After about ten minutes of driving, they could see the structure. The sign was still up, and the building looked intact.

As they closed the distance, they could see three pickup trucks in the parking lot. They were parked in a row facing east. Ben drove off the road slowly and into the parking lot, stopping thirty feet back from the line of trucks. Standing in front of the vehicles were a dozen men of varying sizes and shapes. None of them appeared to be carrying long arms, but from what Mitch could see, they all had sidearms of some sort on their hips or in leg holsters. They were all dressed in what he would consider ordinary working attire. There was no camouflage clothing or uniforms present, just everyday working man clothes. Mitch opened his door and stepped out. Ben and Will did the same. The group across from them shifted a little but mostly stayed in place. Mitch immediately felt outnumbered and nervous. If violence did break out, with their twelve to three ratio, it would not go well for him and his team. He and his two companions left their long arms in their vehicle, mirroring what the men across the parking lot had done. Ben did leave the engine running, though. The sun was in the west but not so low on the horizon that Mitch was staring into it. He walked towards the group of men and, at the halfway point, stopped. "Greetings," he said to no one in particular. The men across from him broke into smiles. Greetings, Mitch thought to himself – who the hell says greetings? Feeling stupid. Based on the smiles he was getting; Mitch guessed the group of men was thinking the exact same thought.

From behind a knot of men directly across from him came a voice, "Greetings indeed, Mitch," and stepping into view was Frank. Mitch felt his jaw drop open. Frank! What the hell! Frank was dead! Mitch looked at his colleagues and saw their mouths were hanging open as well. "What is going on, Mitch?" yelled Will, who was visibly shaken. Mitch stared back at Frank, but it wasn't Frank. This version was three or four years older somehow. Maybe a little shorter than Frank's 6'4." The Frank who wasn't Frank spoke again, "I can see you are a little confused, Mitch. How can I be standing here when, as far as you know, I am dead? Is that right?" All Mitch could do was nod like a fool. Frank not Frank smiled again, "Although I was often mistaken for my little brother, I am not him. I know he is dead, and I know you are Mitch based on things he told me about you. I do not know your two companions. My name's Ray, and I am Frank's older brother." Mitch felt his mouth finally close as the shock wore off. He had heard Frank talk about his brother Ray, and in not the most endearing of terms. Ray had taken a different path in life, an opportunist who lived off of other people's naivete and innocence. Ray and Frank had not spoken for some years, and yet here he stood, large as life and seemingly in charge of a large host of men. Looking across the group, Mitch realized the smiles were not friendly but condescending and haughty. Mitch definitely did not like the feel he was getting from this group. Ray smiled again and gestured at the hotel they were parked in front of. "Why don't you join me inside so we can sit down and talk? Your men and mine can wait outside here for a bit while we parley."

The hotel had large glass doors and a well-windowed restaurant in front which was visible from the parking lot. Mitch didn't like the idea of being separated from the guys but felt if he refused, he would appear weak. Nodding his acceptance, he started walking towards the structure. Arriving at the door first, he held it open for Ray who entered ahead of him. Now that he was up close, Mitch could tell this was not his dead friend. There were more telltale differences which were not apparent at a distance. Ray definitely had more gray in his hair and wore it shorter than Frank had worn his. Ray pushed open the inner door and walked to a booth in front of one of the large windows. It was relatively dim inside but the late afternoon sunlight provided sufficient illumination that the interior of the defunct restaurant was not unreasonably dark. Mitch took up a seat across from Ray and placed his hands on the table where they could be seen. Ray did the same and had a small smirk indicating Ray knew Mitch was keeping his weapon hand visible. Ray cocked his head to the side and queried, "Are we that worried? Have you felt some sort of threat you feel concerned about?" Again, he gave the disingenuous-looking smile. Mitch squirmed a little in the knowledge Ray had read him so easily. Ray looked out the window and spoke, "Why don't we just lay our cards on the table? I mean I have a pretty good idea of what you and your people are up to on that compound you have built and I know what resources I have at my command." He looked back at Mitch and seemed to be looking through him. "That lady you have running the place — and I do mean lady — whew, she is quite the looker, isn't she?" Mitch didn't like the familiarity Ray was giving himself to Kate. Ray focused on Mitch again, "Did Kate and Frank ever have a thing? You know?" Mitch felt irritated and uncomfortable with the question. "I have no idea. Frank never said anything like that and Kate certainly has never said such a thing." Ray smiled broadly, "So she's available then?" Mitch rather too quickly replied, "No. I mean, I don't know." Ray leered at him, "Oh, saving her for yourself then?" Again, Mitch answered too quickly, getting flustered, "No. I am not saving her for myself. She doesn't see me that way." Ray chuckled, "But you do see her that way?" Mitch could feel his temperature rising. This was not the direction this discussion was supposed to be taking. He felt manipulated and out of control.

"We came here to talk trade and cooperation, not who is dating whom," Mitch blurted somewhat hastily. Ray smiled and said nothing. His eyes appeared to be weighing and measuring him as Mitch sat across from him. Ray exuded a sense of superiority that bothered Mitch. He had met men like this before, and it was a personality type that rubbed him the wrong way. Ray spoke again, "What I came here for was a proposition for the lovely Kate and her band of merry makers. As she deigned not to come here herself and sent an errand boy in her place, I guess I am going to have to extend the offer to you. We would be willing to absorb you into our greater group and make you branch members. You would have limited autonomy in exchange for a certain amount of monthly tribute, and in exchange, we would provide protection from the larger forces that roam the land." Mitch really did not like the sounds of this. This was a shakedown, not a collaboration proposal. He reminded himself of Kate's words and stayed calm and did not offer up any information. "I can certainly take your 'offer' back to Kate, although I doubt, she is going to like it," Mitch retorted. Mitch started to stand up, signaling the meeting was coming to an end. "What's the rush? We barely got to know each other?" Ray said with another one of his smiles. Mitch took a step and replied, "I think I have learned what I need to know. I will pass your message on to Kate and let her decide what she is going to do with it. For now, I am done. My guys and I are heading out." Mitch turned and walked outside. He could see his two guys engaged in conversation with some of the other men. Mitch signaled to them that they were leaving and headed to the vehicle.

Ben and Will got back inside and closed their doors. Ben had turned off the vehicle while Mitch was inside but started it up again. "How did it go?" he asked Mitch. Mitch just waved him onward and looked out the window at the receding group of men who were now standing across from

Ray. Mitch had a bad feeling after this meeting, and a sense of unease settled upon him. The Forerunner picked up speed as it headed back towards the acreage and the group. "What did the two of you find out?" he asked the other two men. Will spoke up, "Not much other than they call themselves 'the Outfit.' It was mostly just small talk, and they were not revealing much at all." "What about you? What did you learn?" Mitch turned and looked at them, "It wasn't good. Not good at all."

www.ingramcontent.com/pod-product-compliance
Lightning Source LLC
Chambersburg PA
CBHW051132300726
48978CB00011B/250